David had yanked me and Kitty back inside when the p
came, and whispered for all of us to be real quiet so they
didn't bust down the door. My mom came home after all
the shit was through and started packing our shit that very
night. She said she wasn't going to let her kids get lynched by
some damn Ku Klux Klan, we was getting our asses back to
Harlem.

If it were any other family, that might have been the end
of it. But nope, not the Quinoneses. See, my father may have
been this nice, sweet, genius crazy person, but the rest of his
family was a bunch of raving lunatics. He had two brothers,
three sisters, and an aunt who had come up from Puerto Rico
at the same time as my grandfather, and married and had a
bunch of kids. Those were the Osarios. The Quinoneses
and Osarios ran a moving company—Las Mudanzas—out of
116th Street, but they had a reputation for being some real
crazy muthafuckas. When my Aunt Pat and her twin brother,
Uncle Pete, found out what happened, they rallied up every
soul they could find and the next afternoon Harlem paid the
Bronx a visit.

My cousin Belinda led the charge.

**The novels of Karen E. Quinones Miller are
"hot-blooded in every way"
(*The Philadelphia Inquirer*)!**

Also by Karen E. Quinones Miller:

Passin'

Satin Nights

Uptown Dreams

Using What You Got

Satin Doll

Harlem Godfather with Mayme Hatcher Johnson
(nonfiction)

An Angry-Ass Black Woman

Karen E. Quinones Miller

GALLERY BOOKS / KAREN HUNTER PUBLISHING
New York London Toronto Sydney New Delhi

Gallery Books
A Division of Simon & Schuster, Inc.
1230 Avenue of the Americas
New York, NY 10020

Karen Hunter Publishing
A Division of Suitt-Hunter Enterprises, LLC
P.O. Box 692
South Orange, NJ 07079

First Karen Hunter Publishing/Gallery Books trade paperback edition October 2012

GALLERY BOOKS and colophon are registered trademarks of Simon & Schuster, Inc.

For information about special discounts for bulk purchases, please contact Simon & Schuster Special Sales at 1-866-506-1949 or business@simonandschuster.com.

The Simon & Schuster Speakers Bureau can bring authors to your live event. For more information or to book an event contact the Simon & Schuster Speakers Bureau at 1-866-248-3049 or visit our website at www.simonspeakers.com.

Manufactured in the United States of America

10 9 8 7 6 5 4 3 2

Library of Congress Cataloging-in-Publication Data

Miller, Karen E. Quinones.
  An angry-ass black woman / Karen E. Quinones Miller.—1st Karen Hunter Publishing/
  Gallery Books trade paperback ed.
    p. cm.
  1. Miller, Karen E. Quinones. 2. African American authors. 3. African American families—
  New York (State)—New York. 4. Coma—Patients. 5. Harlem (New York, N.Y.). I. Title.
PS3563.I41335Z46 2012
813'.54—dc23

                                                                        2011047077

ISBN 978-1-4516-0782-6
ISBN 978-1-4516-0899-1 (ebook)

Maferefun Olofi
Maferefun Oshun
Maferefun gbogbo Orisha
Maferefun gbogbo Egun

This book is dedicated to
all Angry-Ass men and women
of the world.

prologue

I ain't scared of death.

In fact, death can kiss my black ass.

And I ain't one of those people talking about they ain't scared of death when they mean they don't care if they die. Those muthafuckas are pussy-ass wimps. They's just accepting what they consider fate.

Ain't nobody deciding my fate but me. And when I say I ain't scared'a death, I mean when that bitch comes my way I'ma kick her ass from here to Mars.

Yeah, let that bitch come tugging on my fucking sleeve. She'll learn better than to fuck with An Angry-Ass Black Woman.

Wait. Let me take a breath. Just, please, hold on just a moment while I try to get myself together. Where the hell am I? Oh God. That's right. Oh God.

Okay. I'm alright now. Please excuse my language and my tone. I'm usually a reserved and considerate woman. Well, maybe not usually, but at least quite often. It's just that life—my life—has made me retreat into my Angry-Ass Black Woman mode so often that it sometimes seems to take over me. And whenever I'm in a crisis, the Angry-Ass Woman comes out full force.

So yeah, right now I'm in serious crisis mode. And like I said, when I'm in crisis, the Angry-Ass Black Woman in me comes out in full fucking force.

You don't like me cursing? Well, fuck it, and fuck you! I ain't apologizing for shit.

I've lived as a black woman on this earth for forty-seven years, and every punch I've taken, every insult that's been hurled at me, every *security guard who followed me in a store, every boss who's treated me like I was a slave, every caseworker who looked at me like I was shit, every man who was raping me while I thought he was making love to me, every fucking second I've lived in a racist-ass country that keeps telling me racism is all in my mind . . . all this shit has made me An Angry-Ass Black Woman, and An Angry-Ass Black Woman has earned the right to fucking curse anytime she wants, because of all that shit she's had to live through, and all the shit she's had to swallow just to live. So fuck it!*

Oh yeah, and let me get something else straight. If you think 'cause I curse like a sailor and I ain't speaking grammatically and politically correct that I'm ignorant and uneducated, then you're stupider than you think I am.

'Cause see . . . although I dropped out of school in the eighth grade, I went on to graduate magna cum laude from a major university. And I've worked as a reporter for one of the top newspapers in the country. And I'm now a college professor, and I've written seven books and been on the bestsellers list five times.

But no matter how high a station in life a black woman has attained, or was born into, once she puts on a T-shirt and a pair of jeans, and steps outside of the community in which she's known, she's subject to being treated as if she's a thieving, scheming crack 'ho looking to murder someone so she can score her next hit.

And goddamnit, when that happens she becomes—even if for only a few minutes—An Angry-Ass Black Woman ready to tell the whole fucking world to kiss her ass. To suck the dick she ain't got. And then they better move the fuck out the way before she stomps the shit outta them on her way out the door.

Naw, I ain't just saying all this because I'm in a bad mood. I'm in a bad way, okay? What's fucked up is that at the moment, I can't remember why. I gotta try and think back, and maybe I can figure it all out. Maybe by telling my story I can remember.

$\mathcal{M}$e and my twin sister, Kitty, were born in Harlem in 1958, and we lived in the basement of an apartment building on the corner of 117th Street and Seventh. Just for the record, Kitty's name is Kathleen, but my parents nicknamed her Kitty. My name is Karen, but they nicknamed me Ke-Ke. That's pronounced kay-kay, not kee-kee. I hate when people call me Kee-Kee.

Actually, we was born in Flower Fifth Avenue Hospital—I think that was on Fifth Avenue near 100th Street. It ain't there anymore, but that's where we was born. Mom took us home to the basement when we was five days old, then had to take me back to the hospital when I was a month old because I caught pneumonia. I was lucky. A kid from another family that lived in the same basement before us had two fingers bit off by rats.

The basement we lived in had cold concrete walls, and even colder concrete floors—so cold that even when you were wearing shoes it felt like you were walking barefoot in the snow. We didn't have money for rugs, so my mother used to put sheets and blankets down on the floor to give us some protection, but it didn't help much. The basement was freezing. I guess because the rats had fur coats they ain't care.

I was almost a year old when we graduated from the basement to a second-floor, two-bedroom apartment in the same building. We didn't live with rats anymore, but damn if we ain't have mice, and of course, roaches. Hell, everyone in

Harlem seemed to have roaches. No matter how clean you kept your house, you had roaches. It was one of the things you got so used to you didn't even notice after awhile.

My mom was collecting welfare, and also working as a bookkeeper off the books at a dinky real estate office on 116th Street. It wasn't that she was trying to get over on the government, but she had four kids to feed—my older brother, David; me and Kitty; and my younger brother, Joseph, who we called Joe T.—and welfare ain't give nobody enough money to survive in those days.

God knows my dad wasn't much help. Joe-Joe was a sweet guy and a fucking wimp. He was a ninth-grade dropout with an I.Q. of 215, and he became a raving lunatic because of it. He was Puerto Rican, from a poor family who lived in Spanish Harlem when Spanish Harlem was still Spanish Harlem. Fifth Avenue was the boundary back then between black and Spanish. Joe-Joe lived on 116th between Fifth and Madison (the Spanish Harlem side of Fifth) and my mom lived on 115th between Fifth and Lenox (the Black Harlem side of Fifth). Somehow they hooked up and he got my moms pregnant when he was twenty-five, and in those days, you got someone pregnant you'd better get married. Especially since Grandma had a shotgun she wasn't afraid to use.

Soon my dad was twenty-nine years old with four children, and couldn't get a job but as a window washer. That 215 I.Q. musta eaten him up when he was hanging outside high-rise windows with nothing but a belt holding him up. He never complained, though, and he loved us kids and loved taking care of us. He became a big doper, using whatever kind of drugs he could find. The big joke was when my dad came to your house you couldn't let him use the bathroom because he'd clean out your medicine cabinet. Joe-Joe would swipe the cold medicine, the aspirin, and even the mouthwash, poor guy. Yeah, they might call it self-medicating these days, but back then it was just called doping like a muthafucka.

Joe-Joe wasn't a real big guy, only about five foot eight, but he was really muscular, so muscular he didn't have to walk around in a T-shirt for people to notice. But there was nothing intimidating about him because he always had this real dreamy smile on his face, even when he wasn't high. And he was the sweetest and most caring man in the world. He was the type of person who would walk down the street and say hi to everyone he passed. And if he saw someone who looked a little down he'd stop and talk to them, even if they were total strangers, to make sure they was okay.

Everyone in the neighborhood loved Joe-Joe. Everyone who ever met him did. But he was just crazy. Sometimes he'd be sitting on the stoop reading a newspaper and all of a sudden he'd get up, walk to the middle of the traffic-filled street, and start reading the funnies out loud to the cars zooming by. "Beetle Bailey" seemed to be his favorite, because he could never get through it without doubling over with laughter. Then he'd get all serious again when he read "Rex Morgan." It was so weird for me to see him standing there on the yellow line reading from the newspaper, me being too young to cross the street to persuade him to come in the house. After he read the funnies, then he'd start reading the editorials and then the local and national news. If we'd lived back in the 1700s when the city had a town crier who walked around ringing a bell and letting people know what was going on in the world, Joe-Joe would have a guaranteed job. But it was the early 1960s, and people had radio and television, so they ain't need to get their news from the neighborhood nut.

Most of the cops in the neighborhood knew him and pretty

much left him alone, and some were even nice enough to direct traffic so that none of the cars passed too close to him. But every now and then there'd be a new cop on the beat and all hell would bust loose. Joe-Joe would ignore the new cops when they came up and told him to get out the street, and when they tried to take his arm and lead him back to the sidewalk Joe-Joe would simply walk away. But if they kept tugging, or got rough, Joe-Joe would fold the newspaper into quarters or eighths, stick it into his belt, and punch the cop in the chest. Then they'd be rolling around in the street. Inevitably, Joe-Joe would wind up hauled off to jail, and then off to the nut house.

Anyway, he was in and out of the loony bin since I was five. So while he sat around in a nice, clean hospital, getting three square meals and sleeping in a warm bed while telling people how bad he felt, my mom was left to raise four children on her own.

Yeah, I come from a long line of Angry-Ass Black Women.

Being the enterprising woman that all Angry-Ass Black Women with children are, Mom did make the best of the situation. In those days, nut houses like Bellevue had this thing where if you brought a crazy person in off the street they'd give you five bucks. And back in the early sixties you could buy a family of five almost a week's worth of dinners for five dollars. I mean, shit, a quart of milk only cost twenty-five cents back then, a pound of potatoes was, like, eight cents, and a pound of ground beef was only fifty-nine cents. So whenever we got real broke, my moms would call my father at the hospital and tell him to break out so she could turn him back in and get five dollars.

Growing up in Harlem was the shit. It really was. The early sixties was after the white folks stopped coming around because of the riots, and before the black folks started talking about black power. But I gotta tell you, all the bullshit I hear about people being poor when they was kids but not knowing it, is just that. Bullshit. Hell yeah, we knew we were poor, and everyone else in the neighborhood knew they were poor, too.

Like I said, I lived on 117th Street, between Lenox and Seventh Avenues. They call them Marcus Garvey and Adam Clayton Powell, Jr. Boulevards now, but for old-time New Yorkers like me, it's always gonna be Lenox and Seventh.

I lived on the same side of the street as Graham Court, that grand old building on Seventh Avenue that took up part of 116th and 117th Streets. All the rich folks lived at Graham Court. And there was a big old fence around it, which I just knew was there to keep us poor folks out. Didn't matter. We knew how to scale fences. We'd climb the fence all the time to play hide-and-seek. See, Graham Court was a big old-ass complex, and actually had four buildings inside that fence. I bet in the real old days they had doormen at each building, but by the time I was up and playing over there, there weren't no doormen. They had intercoms, though, and you could just keep ringing bells until someone let you in. So when someone became "it" and had to count to a hundred, all of us other kids would scale the fence and start ringing bells to get in one of the buildings. Inside was just beautiful. They had real brass doorknobs and door trimmings and there was even a chandelier in the lobby. The stairs were made of marble, and they had the old-fashioned elevators where you had to open the door and then open a gate to get inside. Oh man, Graham Court was the shit. When I used to dream of being rich I would think about having an apartment at Graham Court. But it seemed like an impossible dream. Especially when hide-and-seek was over and we'd have to go back to our homes filled with mice and roaches. I don't care how clean your mom kept the apartment you had mice and roaches, and like I said, when we lived in the basement we had out and out rats. I remember my mom bought a cat 'cause she thought it would scare the rats, but one day we woke up and the cat was dead—a rat had bitten the shit out of it.

Most of the buildings on the block were five-story walk-ups, but there were also a couple of brownstones. They were built, like, in the 1900s to be townhouses for white folks, but after blacks took over Harlem most of them were turned into rooming houses. Everybody was finding a way to make ends meet.

I remember there was one kid who moved on the block when I was about five years old. A real uppity kid who believed his parents when they told him he was too good to be playing with us. I think his father used to be a butler or something for some rich old white man in Long Island, and when the rich old man died his grown-up kids swept in and swept the old faithful butler out on his ass, and down to Harlem without a job.

Anyway, we used to call the uppity kid Poindexter, because his nose was always stuck in a book, and his head stuck up his ass. Don't get me wrong, we ain't hold the fact that he liked to read against him. At least, I didn't. Maybe because both my mom and Joe-Joe were such prolific readers, I started reading real early myself. I had moved past the illustrated fairy tales long before I was five and attending kindergarten, and was already tackling books on the fourth-grade level like *Snowbound with Betsey* and *The Black Stallion*. Yeah, I loved to read, so Poindexter's nose in the book didn't bother me, but the fact that if one of the kids tried to talk to him he'd look at us as if we were dirt and scurry off without saying anything back did bother the shit out of me. Bothered the shit out of all the kids on 117th Street. I mean, Poindexter actually believed the crap his parents were telling him about him being too good to associate with riff-raff like us. And on top of that, he was scared of us kids although he tried to hide it at first. But see, kids in Harlem can smell fear like a shark can smell blood. Brucie, who lived up on the fourth floor of my building, was the first one to corner the fool.

It was in the summer, and all us kids were in the street. Nobody had air conditioners in those days, least not anybody on 117th Street, so from sunup to sundown the kids were out in the street. On this particular day, just like any other day, the boys were playing skelzies—a chalk game drawn on the black pavement and played with soda tops—and the girls were jumping double-dutch. The older men on the block had cordoned off both ends of the street with trash cans so no cars could disturb us. But none of them was around to save Poindexter, and probably wouldn't have if they were. They ain't like his folks just like we ain't like him.

So Poindexter was coming out the building, trying to guide a big two-wheeler bike down the front stoop. An English Racer. Just like we used to see on the TV commercials. I don't know if they even make them anymore, but they were the shit back in 1963. It was the last gift the rich, old white man bought for Poindexter before he dropped dead. Brucie looked up and saw Poindexter, and saw that bike, and it was on.

He got up from the skelzies game and walked over to Poindexter.

"I heard you called my little cousin a bitch," Brucie said.

Poindexter held the bike's handlebars, and looked around, his eyes getting all big like.

"I haven't called anyone out of their names. I don't even know your cousin."

"You'se a liar!" Brucie looked around quickly to see who was available to play his make-believe cousin. "That's her right there," he said, pointing to me.

I sucked my teeth because I was next in line for a jump, but walked over to play my part. Brucie had a good pick, because I was the best actress on the block. I had plenty of experience because my big brother David was one of the baddest kids on the block, and he was always getting me involved in his little get-over schemes.

"Yes, you did call me a bitch," I said, putting my hands on my hips and wiggling my little butt and shoulders. "You said it yesterday when I was coming outta Mr. Tom's store on the corner. And you hit me on the shoulder, too!"

"And I saw him do it!" another girl said as she came up behind me. All the kids had gathered around by now.

"Why you hit my cousin, huh?" Brucie stepped up and pushed Poindexter on the shoulders with both hands. An "oooh" went up from the crowd.

Brucie was six, a full two years younger and three inches shorter than Poindexter, but he had a big, mean pit bull head and a two-inch scar on his left cheek from when he got cut with a jagged bottle six months before. Brucie looked really tough, and was even tougher. And scaredy-cat Poindexter didn't want no part of him.

He tried to run back in the building, and mighta made it, too, if he ain't try to bring the bike with him. Before he could get the bike up the front steps, Brucie was on him. He punched Poindexter in the nose, then grabbed him by the throat and threw him on the ground and just started wailing on him. Punch after punch landed on the screaming

Poindexter's bloody face, until Brucie got tired of swinging and started banging the boy's head on the pavement. We were all crowded around, jumping up and down and cheering Brucie on. I was right in the front, elbowing anyone who tried to get in front of me, and screaming for Brucie to kill him.

He probably woulda, too, but all of a sudden Miss Hattie, who lived on the first floor of my building, pushed her way through the crowd and grabbed Brucie by the scruff of his neck and pulled him off of Poindexter. Brucie was still swinging and almost hit Miss Hattie, but he pulled his punch just in time. Ain't nobody fuck with Miss Hattie 'cause that woman was *really* crazy. She was a big fat woman with a real cute face, and always had her hair done up real nice, and wore a big smile on her face so you could see the gold cap on one of her front teeth. She was always calling us kids "Sugar," and "Honey," but we all knew there was another side to Miss Hattie. We were in the street that time she threw lye on some woman who was messing around with her husband, and we saw when she pistol-whipped that husband when he came home later that night. Naw, Miss Hattie wasn't the one to be fucking with.

She shook Brucie a few times, then shoved him to the sidewalk and walked over and tried to help Poindexter up off the ground.

"You okay, sugar?" she asked, dusting off his clothes.

"Look." I pointed at Poindexter. "He peed his pants."

Everyone started laughing, and Poindexter got embarrassed and started crying even louder and tried to run into the building, but Miss Hattie grabbed him. "Don't pay them no mind, honey. You okay? Or you want me to take you to the hospital?"

Now you know that stupid-ass Poindexter, who was too

scared to fight Brucie, decided to take a swing at Miss Hattie? I guess he thought he could take his frustrations out on her and she wouldn't do nothing to him 'cause she was a grown-up. That goes to show you he ain't know Miss Hattie. His fist landed on her chest. She grabbed her big boobs, and she let out this little "Eek." Then she hauled off and slapped the shit outta him. Poor Poindexter was on the ground again, and this time he was out cold.

It was the first time I had seen anyone unconscious, and I stepped closer to take a good look, but unfortunately he was only out a couple of seconds. When he woke up, Miss Hattie was holding him in her arms and cursing us out for beating the poor baby.

We pretty much lost interest after that. But one good thing came out of that beating Poindexter got.

My big brother had popped up on the scene while Brucie was beating up Poindexter. David never really cared about brawls he wasn't in, so while we were all crowded around watching the fight, he had made off with Poindexter's bike. David was a slick little con man even then, and he realized that if he kept the bike at our place, the cops might come looking for it. So he started renting the bike out for a dime a day, so the bike was never in anyone's apartment long enough for them to get caught. Everyone on 117th Street learned how to ride a two-wheeler that summer.

Believe it or not, Poindexter grew up to be a city council-man, but he never lost his fear of the 117th Street kids. As we got older, whenever one of us got in trouble, someone from the block would go pay Poindexter a visit. He got more people outta jail than any other politician in New York. We were all hoping he'd become president someday so we can have our own punk in at the White House. But wouldn't you know it? The little weasel got caught taking kickbacks from some contractor.

I never felt sorry for Poindexter, and looking back, I still don't. But it was really his parents' fault we hated him like we did. They ain't had no business moving on our block and acting like they was the shit when they were just poor as us. It was bad enough that everybody else in the world treated us like we were trash, we didn't need anyone on our block treating us the same way.

★　★　★

Damn! I'm not a control freak. I mean, I don't give a shit about controlling other people, but I do like being able to be in control of myself. And I never knew just how much it would bug me to not be in control until just now as I realize I can't move a fucking muscle! I mean, I'm lying here—I know I'm lying down—on some kind of bed or something but I can't open my eyes. I can hear the humming and beeping of machines so maybe I'm in . . . oh yeah, that's right. I'm in the hospital. But damn if I remember why. Did I have a heart attack or something? Maybe I'm dead.

No, no, that can't be right. If I was dead I'd probably be in a better fucking mood.

Shit!

two

*H*old up, hold up! I bet you're wondering why I'm telling you about my childhood, huh? Keep your pants on. How you gonna understand how I got to be An Angry-Ass Black Woman if you don't know the child that became the woman?

Now let's see . . . where was I? Oh right.

We moved around a lot when I was young. That's because we were poor, and poor people had to move around a lot. Soon as the landlord got us evicted because we ain't pay the rent we'd get another apartment and live there until the new landlord did the same thing. That was in the days before computers and instant credit checks. You can't pull off shit like that anymore.

Maybe I should define "poor" for you assholes who think I'm just throwing around the word for the hell of it.

Poor ain't wearing hand-me-downs from one child to another. Poor is you wear your clothes till they're rags, and they ain't fit to be handed down to a younger sister or brother. Poor is putting cardboard in your shoes to keep the rain out, even though those shoes were already so tight they be putting corns on your toes. Poor was going over to Daitch Shopwell on 116th Street and bagging groceries for tips to bring home to give your mother so she could buy dinner. And even when you were too young to do that, you went over to Sloan's Supermarket on 115th Street because they ain't had those automatic swinging doors, and held the door open for people hoping they'd put a penny or nickel in your hand so you can contribute, too. Poor was going over to the butcher shop on 118th and Lenox and waiting around until closing time so you could beg for bones to flavor the pinto beans you got from welfare. Poor is when you ask your mother what's for dinner and she says pork roll and grits, and you know that means she's telling you to poke (pork) out your mouth, roll your eyes, and grit your teeth.

I gots big-time money now. I done wrote seven bestselling books, been on television, and been interviewed by a whole buncha big-time magazines and newspapers, but looking back, I still ain't gonna lie and say there was a good side to being poor. Not having money sucks big time.

Anyways, like I said, we moved around a lot, but 117th Street seemed to be our ground zero. We moved to 115th Street, 116th Street, 118th Street, and 119th Street. Once, my mom actually moved us to the Bronx. I'll never forget the address: 525 Rosedale Avenue. It was in an integrated housing project, the Bronx River Projects. First time we'd ever lived around white kids. We weren't there for long, though.

Me and Kitty was six then, and David was seven. Me, him, and Kitty all used to take the school bus to P.S. 100 every morning and back every afternoon. There was this little white girl in David's class who used to ride the bus, too. Dorothy had long, wavy blond hair and big blue eyes. She was tall for her age like David, and so pretty that everybody went around talking about how pretty she was and that she should go into acting and become a movie star. She was really that pretty. My guess is she grew up and changed her name to Kim Basinger.

But this one day on the bus, all the kids were singing that stupid "Doo Wah Diddy Diddy" song by Manfred Mann when someone noticed that Dorothy and David were holding hands while they sang. This skinny white boy, Alvin, pointed at Dorothy and said, "You letting that nigger touch you?"

Well, black people on 117th Street called each other "nigger" all the time, but even at seven you knew better than to let a white boy say that shit. David punched him in the eye, and that white kid went flying back over the seat. And then, oh boy, it was really on.

There were probably as many black kids on the bus as white, but not one jumped in when all them white kids jumped on my brother. Me and Kitty was in it at once. We both grabbed one of the kids on the top and lit into him. Turned out we both picked the same kid, leaving David to thug it out with the other ten, but boy, me and Kitty really whaled on the boy we got. And man, David was holding his own with them other ten. I mean after all, he got his training on 117th Street, ya know? And he was representing like a muthafucka.

The school bus driver finally stopped the bus and put the instigators of the fight out on the street, meaning me, Kitty, and David. We were bruised and mad as hell, and we ain't say shit to each other as we walked the eight blocks home. My mom was still at work, so we let ourselves in, and Kitty went and got two-year-old Joe T. from the woman next door, and we fixed ourselves something to eat. I finally said to David what was on my mind the whole way home.

"How come your stupid girlfriend ain't jump in to help you out?" I screamed on him.

David looked at me, dropped his spiced ham sandwich, walked over, and punched me in the mouth. "She ain't my girlfriend," he said as he walked back and picked up his sandwich and started eating again.

Well, if he ain't never told the truth in his life, he sure told it then. 'Cause I ain't never seen a girlfriend turn on her man quick as that little white bitch turned on David.

My mom didn't usually get home until, like, seven or eight, and we were all watching *My Favorite Martian* on our beat-up old TV so I guess it was, like, six o'clock when we heard a banging at the door. Us kids looked at each other, because we'd only been in the projects, like, a month, and ain't nobody had it like that with us where they could be banging on the door like it was all right.

David walked over and stood on a chair so he could see through the peephole. He must not have recognized whoever it was he saw, because then he shouted out, "Who is it?"

"Open the door," a man's voice rang out. It wasn't a voice we recognized, so we all gathered around the door.

"Who is it?" David shouted again.

"Is your mother in?" a woman's voice yelled back.

Me and Kitty froze because our mother had drilled into our heads that if we didn't give the right response the child welfare people would come in and take us all away because we weren't supposed to be home by ourselves. But David ain't hesitate before giving the answer we were all trained to say.

"She's 'sleep. What you want?"

"Wake her up," the woman's voice called out again.

"I can't. She told us not to," David answered.

All of a sudden there was this big bang on the steel door, and David almost fell backwards off the chair. Then there was another bang, and another, and all of a sudden there were so many bangs on the door it sounded like there was thunder trying to get in our apartment.

David ran over to me and Kitty. "They're hitting the door with baseball bats," he said in a loud whisper.

"Niggas! Open up this goddamned door," someone yelled out as the banging continued.

Like I said, I'd heard the word before, and even spat it out when we lived on 117th Street whenever another kid pissed me off. And, you know, the kid on the bus used it against David, which was how all this shit started. But I ain't never heard the word used with such hate. Oh yeah, those mutha-fuckas on the other side of the door was using the word in its purest sense. It didn't even make me mad, it just hurt and scared the shit outta me at the same time. And I mean, really scared me. Fucking chilled me to my six-year-old bones. I ain't never used the word after that, because that day I really learned what that word meant. I ain't like it then, and I don't like it now.

So anyway, they all started chanting some shit about "killing niggas," and how they got rope and shit, and still banging on the door and we were all scared to death. My whole body was shaking, and David's face turned almost white. Kitty started jumping up and down and crying, and that made Joe T. cry, too, as he lay on the living room couch, almost forgotten.

"What are we going to do?" I asked, grabbing David's arm. "And who are they?"

"I don't know," David answered me. "A whole bunch of white people. And Dorothy's out there, too!"

The baseball bats continued to thunder, and dents began to appear on our side of the steel door. So now David, Kitty, and I were huddled together in the foyer, shaking, and Joe T. was on the couch crying. Suddenly we heard the shrill voice of Miss Florence, the woman across the hall, rise above all the noise in the hallway.

"I called the cops on y'all. They gonna be here in a minute, and they's gonna lock the whole lot of y'all up," she yelled.

"That nigga boy in there tried to rape my daughter," a man's voice responded.

"That boy ain't but seven years old," Miss Florence said back. "Why you white folks always thinking colored boys ain't got nothing better to do than trying to get between some white girl's legs?"

There was quiet in the hallway for a minute, so I pushed David aside and climbed up on the chair to look through the peephole. I was just in time to see a big, mustached white man bring a baseball bat up over his shoulder and then swing it with all his might at Miss Florence's face.

I screamed and fell off the chair, and told David what happened, and he unlocked the door and swung it open, and jumped on the man's back. Me and Kitty were right in there with him, punching, biting, and scratching. Suddenly all the doors on the first floor opened, and white, black, and Puerto Rican families were all out there swinging. A lot of the time in the projects the Puerto Ricans couldn't seem to figure out whose side they were on, but that evening they were right there swinging with the blacks.

Police came, and damn if the only folks hauled off to the jail were the blacks and Puerto Ricans. Poor Miss Florence was still scrunched up in a corner, trying to put the bits of teeth back in her bloodied mouth. They grabbed her up and put her in the paddy wagon, too.

David had yanked me and Kitty back in the house when the police came, and even though they banged on the door and ordered us to open up, David whispered for all of us to be real quiet, so they didn't know for sure we were still in there, and they didn't bust down the door to find out. My mom came home after all the shit was through and when she found out what all had happened, she started packing our shit that very night. She said she wasn't going to let her kids get lynched by some damn Ku Klux Klan, we was getting our asses back to Harlem.

If it were any other family, that might have been the end of it. But nope, not the Quinoneses. See, my father may have been this nice, sweet, genius crazy person, but the rest of his family was a bunch of raving lunatics. My mother was an only child, so we didn't have any aunts or uncles from her side of the family, but my father had two brothers and three sisters. He also had an aunt who had come up from Puerto Rico at the same time as my grandfather, and married and had a bunch of kids. Those were the Osarios. The Quinoneses and Osarios ran a moving company—Las Mudanzas—out of 116th Street, but they had a reputation for being some real crazy muthafuckas. When my Aunt Pat and her twin brother, Uncle Pete, found out what happened, they rallied up every soul they could find and the next afternoon Harlem paid the Bronx a visit.

My cousin Belinda led the charge.

Belinda was, like, nine years old and the toughest person I'd ever known. She and her sister, whom we all just called "Sister" since that what Belinda called her, were our Aunt Bernice's only children. Belinda wasn't big for her age, or husky, and was actually kind of cute with those two thick braids hanging down her back. But she was all muscle, and could throw a mean-ass punch. She was only eight the first time she knocked a boy out. And he was a big boy, too—a known bully who made the mistake of feeling Belinda's butt one day after school. He stood there laughing with his friends, and Belinda—cool as all hell—dropped her red plaid book bag on the sidewalk, brought her shoulder back so far it almost touched the ground, then came up and caught the boy on his jaw. *Bang!* She knocked him out cold with just one punch! She picked up her book bag and walked home like nothing had happened. My cuz was bad!

So anyway, Belinda rode up to the Bronx in the backseat of a car my Aunt Pat had borrowed. My other cousin, eight-year-old Georgie, and me and David and Kitty were all in the backseat, too, but we was all squeezed to one side to give Belinda all the room she wanted because she was already breathing hard, which meant she was mad. Belinda had asthma, and sometimes when she got upset she'd get an attack, but Belinda wasn't upset that day, she was on a mission.

Both Belinda and Georgie were wearing New York Mets ball caps and holding wooden baseball bats. When we got to the Bronx River Projects we kids piled out the car and ran to the park where all the kids was playing since it was Saturday. Me and Kitty and David pointed out a group of kids, and Georgie and Belinda went to work. They was swinging and cursing and all hell was breaking loose. There was some parents standing outside the park, and others looking out their apartment windows, and they all hauled ass over to save the kids, but see, Uncle Pete had pulled up by then. He was a long-distance mover by trade, and he was driving this long-ass moving van. He walked to the back and opened the trailer and there musta been fifty Harlem homies up in that mug, and they ran out screaming and swinging their own baseball bats. Everything that was white was turning red with blood. I had to run over and save Blanca, who was a Puerto Rican girl but looked white. And wouldn't you know stupid-ass David saved that bitch Dorothy? The most important thing, though, is we all got the hell outta there before the cops arrived on the scene.

That was the last time we lived in the Bronx. After that it was Harlem all the way.

★ ★ ★

Wait a minute. I can hear voices.

"Oh my God! She looks horrible!"

"Aunt Kitty, don't say that. She can hear you."

That's Camille! My baby's here. And that's Kitty acting all hysterical, isn't it?

"Camille, I just want you to know even though your mama's gone you can depend on me, child. I'll take care of you like you was my own."

"Aunt Kitty, please! My mother's not gone, and she's not going anywhere. And please stop saying things like that. Mommy's going to pull through. And I already told you she can hear you."

Camille is using such a stern voice talking to her aunt that I have to smile. Inwardly, anyway, since I can't get my face muscles—or any muscles in my body—to move at the moment.

"Camille! I got here soon as I could. What's going on? Is she gonna be okay?"

I know that voice, and the wheezing that punctuates every other word. My cousin Belinda is in the room. Hooray! If anyone can shut Kitty up it's Belinda. Except it seems like she's on the verge of another one of her asthma attacks.

"She's going to be fine. She's just asleep. She's probably going to wake up any minute now."

"Asleep? What do you mean asleep? The nurse told me she's in a coma."

"Aunt Kitty, would you please just shut up? Coma, sleep, whatever. She's going to wake up any minute now. And like I said, she can hear you. So please stop trying to convince my mother she's going to die. She's not."

Now how does she know I can hear her? Camille is something else. But that's my baby. Always looking out for her mother just like I've always looked after her. All these twenty-two years since she's been born it's been me and her against the world. And we've always won. And I'll be damned if I'm going to let her down now.

three

We moved back into the same building we used to live in on 117th Street. The landlord had sold the building and he didn't tell the new owner, Mr. Goldberg, about the deadbeat Quinones family—but he soon found out the hard way. We'd only been there six months before we were four months behind in the rent.

We'd just gotten kicked off of welfare because they found out my mother had opened up a savings account and had managed to stash $125 in it. Welfare wouldn't allow you to have more than a hundred dollars in the bank, so they shut down my mother's case. Yeah, if you was poor enough to get on welfare, you was supposed to stay poor. Ain't that some shit? And if you tried to do something to better yourself they'd shut you down like a muthafucka. You couldn't even own whole life insurance, the kind where you'd get premiums after a couple of years. They find out you had that shit they'd cut you off, too. Naw, man, you was supposed to stay poor through life *and* death.

Oh, they used to throw you off of welfare for all kinds of shit. Once we got cut off because the caseworker came and heard the telephone. See, you wasn't allowed to have a telephone if you was poor and needed assistance. Ain't that some shit? My mom beat my ass for that one, 'cause it was my job to hide the telephone whenever the caseworker came over. I hid it under the pillow like I was supposed to, but I forgot to take the receiver off the hook, and the fucking thing rang while that bitch was there. We got cut off for two months behind that shit.

When we was on welfare we used to go to the welfare food distribution center to get cans of peanut butter, blocks of butter and cheese, and bags of beans, flour, and cornmeal and bring it back to the apartment in our beat-up shopping cart. We also used to get some old nasty canned meat, kinda like Spam, but worse. We hated that stinky shit and used to stick it in the back of the cabinet. Good thing we did, because when the welfare cut us off we had, like, fifteen cans of that meat stockpiled, and soon we was eating it for breakfast, lunch, and dinner. We fried it, stewed it, baked it, and smothered it with ketchup and barbecue sauce. No matter what we did with it, though, it always tasted and smelled the same.

But anyway, like I was saying, they had just kicked us off of welfare again, and the people at the real estate office cut my mother's hours, so money was really tight. We was going to get kicked out of the apartment for sure. None of us kids wanted to get kicked out, but we decided if we did, we'd have to manage to find another pad on 117th Street. Yeah, we decided 117th was home, no matter where we moved, so we might as well keep moving there.

People on 117th Street was tight. Everybody knew each other and hung together. The grown-ups would all go off to bars and clubs on Friday and Saturday nights and come back up all drunk and fighting each other. The kids would play hooky together, shoot marbles together, pitch pennies together, and fight together. There was a lotta fighting on 117th Street, but there was a lot of making up, too. And a whole lotta love, I realize now. We looked out for each other on 117th Street. We could fuck each other up, but don't nobody outside the block better come up looking for somebody to pick a fight.

There was mostly big five-story apartment buildings on 117th Street, but there were a few brownstones on the north side of the street. Weren't no rich folks on 117th Street, though. Even the people who owned brownstones had to rent out rooms in order to pay their mortgage. Whether they worked or were on welfare, almost everybody had their little side shit that they did to earn money so they could make ends meet.

A few buildings down from ours, there was one old guy, Mr. Fred, who used to sell socks. And Mr. Ray would go over to 116th Street and sell the gloves and scarves that his wife knitted. Across the street, Miss Roberta, who used to tell us she had a bit part in *Gone With the Wind,* used to give voice lessons. *Gone With the Wind* didn't used to come on television back then, you know, and VCRs weren't invented yet, so I didn't get to watch it until 1970-something. By then Miss Roberta was dead, so she couldn't point out which slave she was. There was a couple of men on the block who were numbers runners. And Miss Jenny lived on the first floor of the corner building, and she'd freeze Kool-Aid in Dixie cups and sell them to the kids for two cents each. Everybody on 117th Street had some kind of hustle.

We lived on the second floor of 146. Brucie still lived on the fourth floor with his parents and five brothers—Junior, Booby, Koo-Koo, Digga, and Pooga. Yeah, they had some stupid-ass names, but nobody teased them about it because those Bennett kids were crazy. Well, we did tease Pooga sometimes behind his back, not because of his nickname, but because of the name his mother gave him. Who in the hell would actually name their kid Dick? What? If she had a daughter would she name her Pussy?

We lived at 146 W. 117th Street. Elaine lived at 148. That was one bad chick. Not bad like Belinda bad. Bad like always starting some shit. Shit that someone else had to finish.

See, Elaine was one of them "light, bright, and damn near white" girls, with long, jet-black hair. That was before black was beautiful, so you know the boys were falling all over her. Come to think of it, they still fall all over themselves for that type to this day, but now they at least try and cover it by saying the girl got brains or some shit. Yeah. I'm sure it was Vanessa Williams's PhD in aeronautical science that got her to be the first black Miss America. But at least Vanessa's pretty. Elaine wasn't pretty, she was just light. And that's enough for most of these stupid-ass black men out here.

Where was I?

Oh yeah.

Elaine looked just like her mother. Her sister, Maxine, took after her father. So she was skinny, black as charcoal, and had hair that was almost too short to braid. Truth is Maxine made Elaine look all that much better to the boys on 117th Street. And did I mention that Elaine was wicked as all shit? She never mentioned her looks, so I can't say she was conceited. But she would start shit, and then twirl her hair around her finger until someone bailed her out. And boy, she could start some evil shit. Like the time she got the idea that we should stick up our landlord, Mr. Goldberg.

Back in those days the landlord would come around in person on the first of the month to collect the rent. A three-bedroom apartment was only a hundred dollars a month, but there were four apartments on every floor, and five floors in the building. Let's see, that comes to, yeah, two thousand dollars. That was a fortune back in 1964. Think about it. Most black men in Harlem weren't making but, like, sixty dollars a week.

So Elaine twirled her hair and got Brucie to agree to do the dirty work. And then David had to get involved, because Brucie was tough, but he was stupid as all hell so David was the brain of every operation that went down on 117th Street. And if David was involved, then I had to be involved, and Kitty did everything I did. We didn't talk about it, but I knew David and Kitty was thinking the same thing I was—we could pay the back rent with the rent we stole from Mr. Goldberg, and then we wouldn't get kicked out the building. Didn't even feel like stealing when you looked at it like that, because even though we was robbing him of his money we'd be giving it right back when we paid the rent. Made a whole lotta sense at the time.

So it was Elaine, who was seven; Maxine, who was eight; Brucie, who was seven; David, who was also seven; and me and Kitty, who were six. Yeah. We was gonna pull off this two-thousand-dollar heist. We was all excited about pulling off this real grown-up robbery, and started calling ourselves The Magnificent Seven, like the Yul Brynner movie we all liked, even though there wasn't really but six of us. So whenever we saw each other we'd start humming the tune from the Marlboro cigarette commercial since it came from the movie. We was all feeling like we was the shit.

Elaine had come up with this brilliant idea on the twenty-seventh, so we had, like, four days to get our shit together since Mr. Goldberg collected the rent on the first of the month.

Mr. Goldberg started his rent collections on the first floor and worked his way up to the fifth, so our plan was to be on the roof waiting for him, then sneak down just after he collected the rent from the last tenant. Brucie was gonna bop him on the head with a baseball bat, and then we'd grab the envelope stuffed with money that Mr. Goldberg always stuck in his suit pocket and run. We agreed that we'd all wear disguises, so Mr. Goldberg couldn't identify us to the police. My disguise was an old Halloween fairy princess mask, Kitty's was a Cinderella mask, David wore a Batman mask, and Brucie just had a bunch of white shoe polish all over his face that made him look like a zombie. Elaine and Maxine had a whole bunch of their mother's makeup on, and hats pulled low over their hair.

My job was to stand by the roof door and peek into the building so I could let the crew know when Mr. Goldberg collected the last rent. So I stood there, with my blonde fairy princess Halloween mask on, waiting.

It took about an hour but finally I saw Mr. Goldberg come trudging up the steps to the fifth floor. He was a short, middle-aged man who wore a long black coat that was a little too big for him, and a black brimmed hat that was a little too small. I signaled to the crew that he was coming. I watched him as he took a fancy handkerchief from his suit pocket and wiped the perspiration from his forehead. He was probably sweating from all them stairs. I was sweating, too, and not because of my fairy princess mask, but because I was nervous as shit. Brucie and David and them crowded all up behind me, almost pushing me through the door, but I signaled them to keep it quiet as Mr. Goldberg starting knocking on doors. His first three attempts at collecting money was successful. The tenants knew what day and time he was coming and they had their money ready. Mr. Goldberg took the money, marked it in his ledger book, and then wrote out a receipt and moved to the next apartment. But Miss Lovie Mae lived in that last apartment, and she wasn't planning on giving it up like that.

"Mrs. Jenkins, I know you're in there," Mr. Goldberg shouted at the door after his repeated knocking went unanswered. "I can hear you moving around."

"That's these big-ass rats you got in this slum-ass building you hear moving around," Miss Lovie Mae shouted back.

"Mrs. Jenkins, I'm here to collect the rent." Mr. Goldberg stepped closer to the door.

"Well, you ain't getting shit today, Jew man. My check is late."

"Mrs. Jenkins, you're two months behind."

"You don't have to tell me. I know how much I owe. You think I'm stupid?"

"Mrs. Jenkins, why don't you open the door so we can talk like civilized people?"

"I ain't opening shit. Go away. I'll mail you your rent when I get my damn check."

"Mrs. Jenkins, I'm a reasonable man. I'll tell you what. Why don't you give me, say, five dollars on the rent just to show your good faith?"

"I'm a Christian woman, and if I wanted to give somebody money to show my faith I'd be giving it to my pastor."

"*Oy vey,*" Mr. Goldberg said, shaking his head.

"Don't you be cursing at me in Jewish!" Miss Lovie Mae screamed through the closed door.

"I didn't curse, all I said was . . ."

"I heard what you said! I told you I'm a Christian woman. Don't be standing outside my door talking no heathen language!"

"Mrs. Jenkins, I'll see you next month." Mr. Goldberg

snapped his ledger book shut. "I hope you have a pleasant day."

He stood there for a moment, as if he were waiting for a response, but finally shrugged his shoulders and started walking back toward the stairs.

"Now!" I said in a loud whisper and stepped aside. Brucie, David, and Maxine all rushed out the door and down the stairs. Elaine and Kitty held back, but I waved them forward, saying, "Come on!"

In his rush, Brucie had forgotten his bat on the roof, but by the time we ran down the stairs, he had already jumped on Mr. Goldberg's back and David was punching the man in the stomach.

Mr. Goldberg musta been in shock, because he didn't start yelling right away. When he did, Maxine tackled his legs and he fell backwards to the floor. Well, actually he went down, but since Brucie was still on his back, Brucie was the one that actually hit the floor.

"Get him off of me!" Brucie started yelling.

"Get the envelope out his coat," David shouted at me as he started kicking Mr. Goldberg, who was still yelling and trying to get up.

I ran over to comply, but by now all the doors on the fifth floor had opened up, and people started pouring out, so I froze.

"What the hell is going on? Y'all kids stop playing with Mr. Goldberg," one woman shouted at us.

Kitty, who had been doing nothing but leaning on the wall watching us, suddenly piped up. Wouldn't you know my stupid-ass sister said, "We ain't playing with Mr. Goldberg. We's robbing him."

"Y'all are what?" Miss Lovie Mae had finally opened her

damn door and stood in the hallway in a raggedy, pink flannel robe holding a broom. "Lord, help us," she said and started to laugh. "A bunch of elementary school kids trying to be crooks."

Then she started swatting us with her broom. "Get off that man. Get off him right now."

We immediately put our escape plan into action, running back up the stairs and onto the roof.

You know what roof hopping is? Well, the apartment buildings in Harlem were so close together the roofs were only a foot or so apart. Normally I didn't like hopping from one roof to the other because I'm scared of heights, but I was one roof-hopping muthafucka that day. We all was. We hopped roofs from Seventh Avenue to Lenox, then ran down the stairs of the last building and hauled ass over to Mount Morris Park, which was, like, four blocks away. I think they call it Marcus Garvey Park these days.

Anyway, the plan was we was supposed to meet over by the bell tower. Me and Kitty was the last ones there. We all collapsed on the ground, gasping to catch our breath. David didn't even wait until he caught his before turning to me and asking, "You got the money?"

I shook my head. "I tried, but I couldn't get it. And then Miss Lovie Mae and all them came out and I ain't wanna get caught."

Elaine jumped up. "Why you gotta be so stupid?" She kicked my arm. Hard. "We did all this and you ain't even get the money?"

I started rubbing my arm. "Don't kick me," I warned her.

"I'll kick you if I want to, stupid." Elaine kicked me again. This time in the head.

The thing is, Elaine was really the stupid one, 'cause if she had just waited a couple of seconds David woulda started kicking my ass himself about not getting the money. But see, David wasn't gonna let nobody hit his little sister. Not even Elaine, as much as he liked it when she let him feel her bootie.

"Don't you be kicking my sister," he said, walking up on her.

"I'll kick her if I feel like it," she said defiantly. "What you gonna do about it?"

"Do it again and see."

I was standing up by this time, but Elaine kicked me in the leg anyway, so David punched her in the shoulder. Not real hard, but hard enough to let her know she'd better not fuck around or she'd get real hurt.

"Don't be hitting Elaine." Brucie jumped up and punched David in the back of the head, and they started fighting. So then I hit Elaine for making my brother fight, and we started fighting. Then Maxine tried to jump in to help her sister, and Kitty grabbed her by the collar and swung her around, and then they started fighting.

All that fighting only lasted a few minutes because we was all so tired already from all the running and roof hopping. When we broke it off we started walking home, me and David and Kitty walking on one side of the street, and Brucie, Elaine, and Maxine on the other. We shouted insults at each other the whole way home. But hell really broke loose when we reached our block. Soon as we turned the corner, Herman, one of the older teenage bullies, grabbed David in a headlock and started pounding on him.

"Gimme the money," he said, punching David on the head. "Gimme the fucking money you took from Goldberg."

"I ain't got no money," David yelled while trying to break free.

"Yes you do! And you better give it to me or I'm gonna kill you right now in the street," Herman said, as he continued his blows.

Me and Kitty started pulling David by his waist to get him loose from Herman, when all of a sudden we heard this Tarzan yell and we looked up and saw Brucie flying across the street toward David and Herman, a crazy look on his face.

Herman musta been twice the size of Brucie, but he wasn't stupid. He let go of David and stepped back and put his fists up to face Brucie, but Brucie ignored those fists and went headfirst into Herman's stomach. Herman fell back against the building, the wind knocked outta him. Before he could get his breath, we was all on him. Elaine and Maxine jumped in, too, and we was all punching and biting Herman. We might not have pulled off a successful robbery that morning, but we sure beat the shit out of Herman that afternoon. We beat him so bad he never showed up on 117th Street again. After all, how could a sixteen-year-old bully show his face on a street when a bunch of elementary school kids beat him up?

Yeah, we was congratulating each other all the way back to our buildings and humming the Marlboro cigarette song real loud 'cause we felt like The Magnificent Seven again, but when we got home it was our turn to get our asses beat. Turned out that Halloween masks mighta shielded our identity from Mr. Goldberg, but they ain't fool the fifth-floor tenants. They ain't tell Mr. Goldberg who we was, but they hadn't wasted no time telling our parents. My mother beat me and David and Kitty until she was tired, then rested up and beat us some more. And we could hear Brucie upstairs getting his ass beat, too, and we could tell by his screams that his mother had broke out the extension cord.

But would you believe Elaine and Maxine managed to

convince their mother that the neighbors were lying and they didn't do nothing?

The next day me and David, Kitty, and Brucie got together and decided that it didn't matter if Elaine twirled her hair until she was bald, we was never going along with any more of her crazy-ass schemes.

* * *

I can hear voices again. I don't know whose yet. Oh good, Camille's still here. But then I knew she would be. Who else's voice is that? Nah. It can't be.

David?

"I'm sorry, y'all. I wasn't trying to make no scene, but I had to put Kitty's ass out. Talking all that doom shit, when Camille kept telling her to stop."

"That's okay, Uncle David. You did the right thing. Mommy needs to be around people who love her, but she doesn't need them stressing her out."

"David, I swear to God I told her to get the hell out. I woulda put her out myself but I'm still kind of winded."

"You sure you don't need your asthma inhaler, Cousin Belinda? Or do you want me to call a nurse or maybe one of Mommy's doctors to look at you?"

"Child, please. I'm going to be okay. We just need to concentrate on your mother. David, how'd you hear about what happened? I'd been trying to get in touch with you for days."

"I ran into Maxine, from around the way, and she told me you was looking for me, and why. But shit, I didn't know she was in such a bad way until I got here just now. You think she's gonna be okay, Belinda?"

"Yeah, Dave. I think so. We all pulling for her. But you know your sister. She's gonna pull through."

"Well, the news is spreading around Harlem fast. I bet it's gonna be on the news, even. Would be real interesting if it weren't my sister they're talking about."

"Yeah, I already got, like, two telephone calls from reporters from The Amsterdam News *asking me to confirm Mommy's condition. I was nice, but I told them I didn't have any comment for now, and we'd appreciate them respecting our privacy, Uncle David. But I know they're going to have something in the paper."*

Damn. I'm gonna be in the newspaper? I hope they don't use the picture my publisher made me take last year. Way too much fucking makeup. I shoulda insisted on them having a black makeup artist, but I had given them so much hell already about taking the picture I didn't want to make too much more of a fuss. But I wound up looking like an Asian kewpie doll on the back cover of my last book.

"Uncle David, come on now. Please don't cry. Mommy's going to be okay. I promise you."

David crying? I can't hear him. But then he never did make any noise when he cried, even when he was a kid. And God knows he had enough to cry about.

four

Black men got it hard in this world, or at least in the United States. They really do. Shit. I'd feel a lot more sorry for them if they ain't feel like they're supposed to take all their fucking frustrations out on black women, but I do feel sorry for them. I don't buy into that stereotype that all black men are criminals or dope fiends, but I can definitely see why some of them get caught out there like that. They be going through some real fucked-up shit.

You know what? I really liked my brother David. Sure he used to beat my ass all the time, but he sure wouldn't let anyone else fuck with me or Kitty. And boy, could he fight. The only person that could take him sometimes was Brucie, and that was only sometimes. See, David could box. My father used to box, and was always hanging out at Gleason's Gym when he wasn't in the nut house, and he taught David how to fight. And David was good. He was like a little Cassius Clay. He'd dance around, give you a punch, then dance out the way before you could hit him. The fucked-up thing was that boxing wasn't the only thing my father taught my brother. The first time David shot up dope it was with my father.

Brucie ain't had no real skills when it came to boxing but he was strong as shit, and if he managed to get through your punches and bull his way inside, he'd beat the shit outta you. Him and David used to fight all the time when they was, like, in kindergarten, and their shit used to last for days. They'd fight until they got tired, go upstairs and go to bed, and get up the next morning and pick up where they left off. But they stopped by the time they got to the first grade and became best friends.

I think I mentioned before that Brucie was stupid as shit, but David was a natural-born conniver. And he was really handsome, even when we was kids. It was cool having him as a brother. I'ma tell you something that I sometimes wish I had told David—he was my hero.

Being real poor was hard on all of us kids, but David really seemed to take it hardest. I put a lotta the blame on my mom, 'cause she used to tell him all the time that since Joe-Joe wasn't really around, that he was the man of the family.

Here's a warning to all single mothers: Don't do that shit to your son!

He ain't the man of the family, he's a fucking kid. It's your job to look after him.

Don't try to put that burden on him, okay? It fucks them up. It sure as hell fucked David up.

He used to be torn up when the marshals would come to evict us when our mother couldn't pay the rent. He'd go downstairs and sit on a car looking mean, and beat up anyone who laughed when our furniture got thrown out on the sidewalk.

I don't know if they do that shit anymore, but back in them days, they sure as hell would move all your shit on the street, and if you didn't have anyone to pick it up for you, the city would send a truck out to pick it up and put it in storage. The fucked-up thing, though, was they immediately started charging you a daily fee for the storage. So if you just got thrown outta your apartment, and was trying to scramble for money to find somewhere else to live, how the fuck are you going to afford all them storage fees? So then the city would sell all your shit at auction, by the lot. Someone could come up and pay your back storage fees and a little surcharge, and walk away with your whole house full of furniture and clothes. So when you did finally find an apartment you'd have to buy your shit all over again, piece by piece.

Me and Kitty was used to it since it happened so often, so we didn't really sweat it all that much, and neither did Joe T. when he got older, but David really used to get really fucked up about it. The deal was our family would help out as best they could, so Aunt Bernice would take in David, our paternal grandmother used to take in me and Kitty, and my Aunt Pat would take in my mother and Joe T. Every morning David would get up real early and come get me and Kitty and walk us to school. Then he'd play hooky and steal stuff he could sell and make some money to give my mother. Then when school was out he'd come get me and Kitty and we'd all look for bottles in trash cans and vacant lots that we could take to the store for refunds. About five o'clock we'd cash in all the bottles, then David would take us over to the real estate office where my mother worked and we'd all sit out on the sidewalk until she quit work. He never let us go in because once her boss said something about not wanting kids in his office, and David was afraid if we came in my mom would get fired, and then we'd really be up the creek. So rain, snow, or shine, we'd be sitting outside waiting for Mom to get off work. David would give us each ten cents, so if it was hot outside me and Kitty would get a soda, and if it was cold we'd get a hot chocolate. David always saved his ten cents to buy a Marvel comic book.

When my mom came out she'd give us a kiss then get on us about not going straight home to wherever it was we'd be staying. Then David would make a big deal of giving her the money we'd scraped up so we could hurry up and get another apartment. She'd give him a big hug, and say what a big man he was to be helping the family out like that. David would just swell up with pride, and that just seemed to make him more determined to figure out a way to give my mom even more money.

As we got older he graduated from stealing from little grocery stores to going downtown and robbing people on the streets. He went downtown because he figured that was where people had money to spare. Folks in Harlem sure as shit ain't seem to have no money. Also, since he was doing it downtown my mother didn't know what he was doing. But you know, she had to know something was going on, because David started bringing in, like, twenty or thirty dollars at a time, and started buying himself sharkskin pants—they was the shit back then—and alpaca sweaters. Ain't no way someone was making that much money cashing in bottles. But see, my mother was into "don't ask, don't tell" long before Bill Clinton coined that shit. She was just glad to be able to pay the rent and the electric bill so we ain't had to run no extension cord from our place to a neighbor's apartment for us to have lights. And Mommy would buy us Breyers vanilla ice cream twice a week. Life seemed really good with David taking care of us.

David was, like, eleven, and he was looking sharp as shit and feeling good about himself for being such a good provider, so he wasn't even beating me and Kitty up so much. He used to beat me up more than Kitty 'cause he said I had a smart mouth. He never beat up Joe T., though. That was his little six-year-old darling. He'd buy Joe T. some really boss little clothes, sailor suits and shit, and take him to the park every weekend and read him Marvel comic books.

Everything was really cool until David got popped after he

robbed some white couple near Columbus Circle. He got hauled off to the Midtown North police precinct, and my mother had to go pick him up. She beat his ass when she got him home, and I mean bad. She told David she wasn't raising no damn thief, and that people worked too hard for their money to have some little bastard like him be stealing it. But as hard as she whipped on him, he never uttered a scream; he just kept looking at her as if to say, "I don't believe you're doing this to me."

I think she recognized the look, and that she deserved it, because she kept beating him like she just wanted him to cry instead of looking at her like that. He was wearing a white T-shirt, and me, Kitty, and Joe T. started crying our eyes out as we watched it become red with blood. She beat him till she got tired, then sat down on the couch and started crying. Through her sobs I could make out her saying over and over, "Oh my God. My little boy is a thief. How am I going to pay the rent? How can I be such a bad mother?"

David could barely move, so me and Kitty dragged him into the bedroom and tried to comfort him. Tears finally started streaming from his eyes and down his swollen face, but he still didn't sob or whimper. He just kept saying over and over, "She ain't say nothing when she was spending the money I gave her."

I knew what he meant. Even then I thought she was more mad about him getting caught and people knowing we was living off stolen money than the fact that he was robbing people. But just like that, David went from being the man of the family to a no-good little thief in my mother's eyes.

That beating ain't change nothing, because he didn't stop going downtown and robbing folks. He just didn't give her the money anymore.

Movies used to cost twenty-five cents back then, or at least the movies at the Regun Theater on 116th Street did. One Saturday Mommy went to get her change purse so she could give us some money to go to the movies, and she couldn't find it. She looked all over the apartment, then started cursing at David and accusing him of taking it 'cause he wasn't nothing but a no-good thief. When he said he ain't do it, she got even madder and started beating him, and said she wouldn't stop beating him till he gave her back the change purse. She beat him for two days, and only stopped because she had to go to work Monday morning. That's when she found out that she had left her change purse on her desk. She was devastated, and apologized all up and down to David, but things were never the same after that.

And I guess he really felt he had to prove her right about calling him a thief, because he did start stealing from the house, too. Nothing big, at first. Just like if she left a dollar on the dresser, he'd make off with it. He stole just enough to make sure she knew he was stealing. Then she'd beat his ass with an extension cord, and the next day he'd steal something again. I think they was both just too stubborn to break the cycle, and it lasted the rest of their lives.

David was really a different kid from that point on. He was staying out late and sniffing glue with his friends. That was the big thing back then, buying that cement glue from hobby shops and then sniffing it. I don't know why they don't really do it big-time anymore, but that was the get-high for kids back then. Drinking cough medicine was big back then, too, because you could get the stuff with codeine right at the drugstore, and David started doing that, too. Then he started smoking pot, and finally graduated to sniffing heroin.

When my father got a visit from the nut house and my

mother told him what was going on, he went out looking for David. He found him in a building on 116th and Fifth. David had just bought a packet of heroin. Instead of beating David up and sending him home, Joe-Joe's eyes got big at the idea of some dope. Instead of trying to teach his oldest son about the evils of drugs, my father convinced David to cook the heroin up so they could shoot it together instead of sniffing it, because mainstreaming—shooting the dope into your veins—gave you a better high. David was twelve at the time. I did mention my father was crazy, right? I swear, between my mother and father, I don't think David ever really stood a chance.

* * *

Someone's holding my hand. Stroking it. Whoever it is, they probably think it's soothing, but it's actually irritating as shit.

"Mom. I know you can hear me. Everything's going to be okay, alright? I'm right here with you and I'm not going to leave you. I'm right here."

Oh! It's Camille touching me. Now that I think about it, it's not irritating at all.

"Camille. I, uh, I gotta make a quick run, okay? I'ma be right back. Maybe in about an hour. I just gotta take care of some business real quick."

"Oh what? You gonna run out on your sister so you can shoot up real quick? Now ain't that some shit?"

"Will you shut the fuck up, Belinda? I just said I gotta make a run. I'll be right back."

"Will you shut the fuck up, who? Yo! Don't make me get up from this chair and whip your ass. 'Cause you know I will, you—"

"It's okay, Uncle David. Mommy knows you were here, and I'm

sure she understands if you have to leave for a little while. You are coming back, right? Because I know she's going to want to see you when she wakes up, aren't you, Mommy?"

I don't hear him answer, so I guess he just went ahead and split. That's okay. It's good just knowing he was here, just like Camille said. Kitty, David, and Belinda. Four of the five people I love most in the world. Joe T.'s out in Nigeria again, else I know he'd be here, too. It's kinda nice having all this love in the room, and being the center of attention. Damn shame it had to be because of this.

"That damn David makes me sick. Ain't nothing worse than a fifty-year-old dope addict. Camille, baby. Why don't you go home and take a little break? You've been here, for what, thirty-five, forty hours? I'll be right here and I'll call you on your cell if there's any change."

Forty hours? Three days? I've been laying here that long? Damn!

"No, that's okay, Cousin Belinda. My mother needs me right here, and right here is where I'll be. See, I know she's going to be okay. She's a fighter, and she's going to fight through this."

"Yeah, your mother's always been a fighter, but . . ."

"And she's going to fight through this. You watch. My mother is going to be okay. I know she is."

Oh God! Why didn't I notice before the anxiety in my baby's voice? I have my little girl all worried, and for what? A mother should be worrying about her daughter, not the other way around. What kind of mother am I?

five

*N*ow I'ma say some shit that's gonna piss a lot of people off, but I don't give a fuck. 'Cause it pisses me the fuck off when I see black women wearing dreadlocks when they ain't gotta clue what it means. It's supposed to be about pride in your nationality and spirituality, not a fucking fashion statement. And oh yeah, I really know they ain't got a fucking clue when they be dyeing their locks blonde. I mean, what the fuck? I remember when Black women started wearing afros it caused a fucking commotion, but the women who was wearing them used to walk down the street with their head so fucking high ain't no way they could have noticed the people sneering at them. My mom used to love the soul singer Millie Jackson till she did a monologue on one of her live albums wolfing on Black women wearing afros, talking about they needed to go home and put a hot comb through their nappy hair. Mom threw out all her Millie Jackson records, then went down to the barber shop and cut off all her long pretty hair and made an afro. It was a political and cultural statement she was making. That was cool with me. What wasn't cool with me was that she had me and Kitty sit in the barber's chair after her. I cried the whole time my thick black hair was falling from my head onto the tile floor. It was 1965 or '66, and I was, like, six or seven at the time. Shit, I bet even Angela Davis wasn't sportin' a 'fro back then, and I'm sure me and Kitty were the only kids in New York who were. It sure felt like we were, because we got teased all the time. My mom didn't care, but then she wasn't a kid and didn't have to fight everyone who said something to her about her hair like I felt I had to do. Yeah, I fought anyone who said anything about my hair, Kitty's hair, or my mom's hair. I was one fighting heifer in the mid-sixties.

My mother was always real race conscious. I remember when Crayola came out with the flesh-colored crayon my mother had a fit. Pink certainly wasn't the color of our flesh. She went down to the school and raised hell till they agreed not to provide the crayons to the kindergartners, and then wrote a letter to Crayola calling them bigots. She sent the letter to the *Amsterdam News,* the black newspaper in New York, and they printed the letter in the paper. How cool was that?

Back in the day they used to call a man who felt like my mother a "race man." You know, the kind who was black and proud before there was such a thing as black and proud. They weren't so much into integration as just wanting to kick any white man's ass who got in their way. In fact, my moms was like dead set against integration. Don't get your drawers up into a bunch; that don't mean she was prejudiced or some shit. She just felt that black folks would do better on their own. And she had a point!

Ever heard of a place called Lawnside in New Jersey? It's a small town in South Jersey, not far from Philadelphia, one of the first black towns incorporated in the United States. It used to be a stop on the Underground Railroad, and a whole lot of blacks settled there. And back in the fifties the place was the shit. They had their own black-owned banks, which meant that blacks could get mortgages, and so there was a whole lot of black homeowners. And the night life was really jumping! All the black acts from around the country stopped there: Redd Foxx, Nat King Cole, Billy Eckstine, Jackie

Wilson, and just about everybody. (Hey! Do you remember LaWanda Page? The woman who played old ugly Aunt Esther on *Sanford and Son*? Well, LaWanda Page was an exotic dancer back in the day, and she used to perform in Lawnside, too. I saw a picture of her from when she was in her twenties, and girlfriend's face maybe wasn't all that, but I bet when you was looking at her dance, you wasn't looking at her face. That chick had a body that would even make a heterosexual woman drool with lust and envy!) Eartha Kitt used to appear in Lawnside, too. And Sarah Vaughan and Billie Holiday. Since things were still segregated, even in the north, black folks from all over the east coast used to flock to places like Lawnside to party because they couldn't get into the high-class joints in Atlantic City. And Lawnside thrived because of all the money that was coming into the city.

Then in the late fifties and early sixties the white resort areas started letting blacks come, and you know what? They was so happy to be able to sit down and drink next to white folks, they stopped going to the black joints that had always welcomed them. Pretty soon the black clubs had to close, because there weren't enough folks going to them for them to have enough money to pay class acts anymore. And then blacks really started feeling integrated and started going to white banks to get their mortgages. So then the black banks had to close.

See, the thing is, *integration only goes one way*. If whites started going to black clubs like blacks were going to white clubs, then all the clubs coulda stayed open. And if whites started going to black banks like blacks were going to white banks, then black banks wouldn'ta had to close.

So then Lawnside's economy started going bust, because all the black people were taking the money elsewhere because they was so happy they could. And there wasn't as many homeowners as there was before, because even though the white banks would give out mortgages, they wasn't as understanding as the black banks were when someone was late with their mortgage payments. Yeah, Lawnside really got fucked in this one-way integration shit.

My mother was right. Integration sucks.

My moms was born in Harlem, just like my dad, but her parents were from Trinidad. She ain't tell us too much about how she grew up, but one thing she was real proud of was that her mother participated in the Silent March in Harlem organized by the NAACP in 1917. Mommy used to talk about it all the time for some reason. And when she heard about the March on Washington in 1963 she just went wild. She tried to save up enough money for all of us to go, but she couldn't swing it. So the morning of the march my mom got us dressed and marched us over to Seventh Avenue where she hailed a cab, and then convinced the driver that he should be ashamed of himself for not being in Washington supporting Dr. Martin Luther King, Jr. She shamed him so bad that he said he would go. Then my mother said since he was going anyway he should give us all a ride there and back. My mom was something else.

When Black Power came around, my mom was all up in it. When the Black Panthers started coming around the neighborhood wearing dashikis and wooden beads and talking about cops were pigs and we needed to seize the power, a lot of the older people on the block was leery of all that shit, but Mom was down. And when they started a breakfast program, she used to get up extra early to fix us kids oatmeal and toast, then haul all of us down to 116th Street to help serve eggs and pancakes to all the kids who ain't had no one at home fixing them something to eat before they went to school.

Then she started hauling us to the Black Panther meetings, and had us carrying signs and shit at protest rallies. It was cool, though. David was all into his own shit—he hardly ever went to school and he'd started selling weed—but me and Kitty and Joe T. were down with Black Power.

After awhile Mommy started letting various Black Power movement figures—and fugitives—crash at our home when they needed a place to stay. I can remember at least two times police coming to our door saying they'd been called by neighbors because our music was too loud, and trying to use that as a pretense to get in the house. How did we know it was a pretense? First off, because we were friendly with all of our neighbors and they would have just knocked on the door if they felt our music was too loud. Secondly, and most importantly, because we weren't playing music!

It got so that we could tell our mail was being opened because it was always a few days late, and sometimes you could see the glue adhesive had been tampered with; and we could hear clicking noises on the phone when were talking to people, letting us know our phones were being tapped. By whom? We didn't know. Our best guess was the FBI. Damn good guess, in retrospect. No one knew, back in the mid-1960s, that Edgar Hoover had started a program called Counter Intelligence Program (COINTELPRO) which was designed to keep an eye on, disrupt, and harass organizations and groups that posed a threat to "national security." Mommy was in good company—other individuals who were monitored included Malcolm X, Dr. Martin Luther King, Jr., and Ralph Bunche. I doubt that the FBI thought Mommy herself was dangerous, but I think they believed she had information about dangerous folks—or they wanted to know what the dangerous folk who were in and out of our apartment were talking about.

In 1967, we realized just how bad they wanted to know.

One Sunday, Mommy and all of us kids were sitting in her bedroom watching *The Ed Sullivan Show* when all of a sudden the telephone rang. Now, this wouldn't have been such an unusual occurrence, except for the fact that our telephone had been cut off for about three months because of non-payment. Well, when the telephone rang, we all got real quiet and just looked at it as if it was some kind of foreign object. Finally, on about the eighth ring, Mommy picked up the phone.

"Hello," she said tentatively into the receiver.

"Hello. Is this 348-6712?" a brusque male voice that sounded white said on the other end, loud enough for everyone in the room to hear.

"No, it's not," Mommy answered.

"Are you sure it's not 348-6712?" His voice rose even louder when dictating the telephone number.

"I'm sure," said Mommy.

"Listen. I dialed 348-6712," the voice insisted.

"Well, you have the wrong number," my mother insisted just as strongly.

With that the man hung up. Mommy placed the receiver back on the cradle and just stared at it. It wasn't even a full minute before the phone rang again, and this time Mommy picked up immediately.

"Hello, is this 348-6712?" the same male voice asked.

Mommy motioned for me to hand her a pen. "What number is that you're trying to reach?" she said into the receiver.

"Three-four-eight, six-seven-one-two," the man said slowly, and enunciating every word clearly.

"Okay, thanks," Mommy said after she'd written the number down, "but you have a wrong number." She hung up and picked up a dime from the nightstand near her bed and handed it to me, along with the number. "Ke-Ke, hurry up and run to the corner store and use the pay phone to see what happens when you call this number."

I went. I called. Mommy picked up. Yeah, we now had a working telephone. And not only could we receive calls we could make them, too. Not just local calls, but long-distance calls. International calls, too! I guess the FBI wanted to tap our phones so bad that they decided they'd go ahead and pay the damn bill themselves. We had free telephone service for more than a year. We let everyone know about it, and soon everyone was coming over to our house making free telephone calls. Back then the telephone company charged by the minute rather than having a set rate, so by coming over and calling on our free phone, everyone saved the charges on their own. We had people calling Jamaica, Trinidad, Cuba, Africa . . . all over the world. Mommy put a note over the telephone, though: "Enjoy your free calls, but don't say anything you don't want Uncle Sam and Cousin Edgar to hear." That phone stayed on for more than a full year, and everyone benefited.

Yeah, I know what I said earlier about how my mom fucked over David, and I guess I gave you the impression that she was a horrible mother and a horrible person. I didn't mean to give you that impression. I just wanted to run down some truths to you, dig? What happened, happened, and I wanted to tell you what happened, is all. Yeah, okay, my mom had some fucked-up shit about her, but even back then I knew she was doing her best. No matter how tired she was when she got home, she always cooked us dinner, went over our homework with us, and read us a bedtime story. And I don't mean no Dr. Seuss stuff. I can remember being, like, three years old and my mom reading chapters from *The Adventures of Robin Hood* or *Ivanhoe*. Then she'd get up early every morning and cook us breakfast. The only time we had cold cereal was when we stayed at someone else's house. In the summer we'd have something light like toast and sausage. David and Joe T. liked eggs, but me and Kitty didn't, so they would get scrambled eggs with their breakfast. In the winter we'd have oatmeal, or cornmeal, or Wheatena—but whatever hot cereal we'd have we'd add almost a whole can of evaporated milk. It used to crack my mother up, all the evaporated milk we dumped in our hot cereal. Actually, I think we got the habit from her. She didn't put a lot of evaporated milk in her cereal, but her cup of coffee was more than half made up of the stuff. She'd sip her coffee and we'd eat our cereal, and we'd just be in familial heaven.

And she made us read, and read, and read. Joe-Joe was the same way. They would have all kids at the kitchen table reading the newspaper together, and then we'd discuss what we'd read and how it made us feel. And when we had a television—which wasn't always—they'd let us watch our favorite shows on the condition that we also had to watch the news so we could know what was going on in the world. By the time I was in my teens no one ain't have to tell me to read newspapers or watch the news, because I was hooked. I wanted to know everything about everything that was going on in the world.

But as much as I loved learning I truly hated school.

When I was eight years old I got transferred from P.S. 184 on 116th Street in Harlem to P.S. 166 on 89th Street and Columbus—an almost all-white school in an almost all-white neighborhood—because I was designated an "intellectually gifted child," and there was no IGC program at P.S. 184. The school administrators made a big deal about my pending transfer, but my mother was leery of it; but then, my mother was leery of the New York City school system period. She thought it was a bad influence on children, and really ain't do shit for black children. But she finally okayed it for me to be transferred to P.S. 166. This may sound corny, but I think she was finally swayed because she found out that J. D. Salinger, the guy who wrote *Catcher in the Rye,* went to the school, and he was one of her favorite authors.

My mother might have been sold, but I still wasn't so sure. In fact, I probably wouldn't have gone if it wasn't for Mr. Johnson.

One of my mother's coworkers at the real estate office on 116th Street was a woman we called Madame. I never knew her real name, or if I did, I don't remember it now. In addition to being a real estate agent, she was also the local numbers runner. When she heard about me being selected for the IGC program, Madame, who had never said more than a quick hello to me before, reacted with such delight you would have thought I was her child. She said she wanted to reward me for doing so well in school by letting me hang out with her once in awhile. The very next morning Madame picked me up in her black Cadillac—she was the only woman I knew in Harlem who had her own Caddy—and drove me around for an hour, making stops all over the neighborhood, without ever saying a word to me until we stopped and got out at Graham Court—that huge apartment complex on Seventh Avenue. Oh God, I was so impressed! I was already feeling well rewarded for my academic achievements.

After we were buzzed into the building on the southeast

corner of the courtyard, Madame leaned down, told me to mind my manners, then smacked me across the forehead to drive her point home before knocking at the door of a first-floor apartment. A giant of a man with a tiny hat perched on the side of his head grunted us in. Madame left me sitting in an overstuffed chair in a room full of strangers—mostly men—all waiting around, some playing cards, while she went into a back room. I didn't care for the first half hour or so, I was busy taking in the apartment. The ceilings were so high I knew even my tall cousin Wesley wouldn't be able to reach it even if he were standing on one of our kitchen chairs. There was a chandelier, the first one I had ever seen, with hundreds of tiny bulbs. I wished that it was evening instead of in the middle of the afternoon so I could see the chandelier shimmer, or perhaps feel the warm glow of light that I just knew would come from the marble fireplace. I was so impressed with the apartment itself, I took no notice of the furniture. I just knew the person who lived in this grand residence had to be a millionaire. I wondered who it was. Certainly not one of the men who were in the room with me. They were big, rough-looking men, not the kind of men who could be the master of this magnificent home.

I wondered if instead it was one of the people in the other room who were speaking with Madame. I couldn't make out what was being said among the raised voices, save for Madame, attempting to "explain" something. Fifteen minutes later, a distressed-looking Madame walked back into the living room along with three men. One of them was Mr. Johnson.

He was dark-skinned, with hair so short he looked bald, and was dressed in an elegant, dark blue suit. When he entered the living room, everyone stood up. He paid them little attention; he looked angry, and was walking, fast, toward the front door when he noticed tiny me in the large overstuffed chair.

"Well, hello there," he said, his face breaking out into a crinkly nosed smile.

"Ke-Ke, sweetheart, say hello to Mr. Johnson," Madame said, suddenly all sugar. "Mr. Johnson, I'll have you know that my little Ke-Ke is the smartest little girl in her third-grade class."

Even as young as I was, I suddenly realized that Madame had brought me to the apartment because she knew Mr. Johnson would be angry with her about something, and that she also knew that Mr. Johnson couldn't stay angry around children. Especially smart children who liked to read Langston Hughes, I soon found out. He actually knew Langston Hughes, he told me at that first meeting. I was impressed. The one question I had, I blurted out immediately.

"Is he nice?"

"Real nice," Mr. Johnson answered with a laugh. "Go get this smart young lady some ice cream." As if by magic, there was suddenly two bowls of vanilla ice cream on the large, mahogany dining room table.

"What's wrong?" Mr. Johnson asked as I slowly picked up my spoon.

"Um, I like chocolate."

"Don't be rude, Ke-Ke!" Madame said sharply.

"Go out and buy Miss Ke-Ke some chocolate ice cream," Mr. Johnson said, his smiling eyes never leaving my face. "I like young ladies who aren't afraid to say what they want."

Our relationship was cemented over ice cream, vanilla for him, chocolate for me.

It was the first of many visits that summer. Each visit

would begin with a sometimes heated discussion between Madame and Mr. Johnson, and end with Mr. Johnson and me sitting at the table eating ice cream while he told me stories about Langston Hughes, Claude McKay, Countee Cullen, and other literary figures of the Harlem Renaissance, most of whom I didn't know. But his friendships weren't just limited to writers. Mr. Johnson said that he was good friends with the famous boxer Joe Louis, and that he had been best pals with Bill "Bojangles" Robinson, the man who tap-danced the steps with Shirley Temple. I was in total awe. I always hated when our visits ended, and would pout when Madame said it was time to go, but Mr. Johnson would smile and pat me on the head, saying, "You know you're going to be seeing me again, Miss Ke-Ke."

It was toward the end of the summer when Mr. Johnson sat me down and gave me a good talking to after he found out that I had been selected to go to a white school downtown because I was an intellectually gifted child, but didn't want to go.

"Miss Ke-Ke," he said, puzzled over my hesitation. "This is the opportunity of a lifetime."

"I don't care," I insisted as I gulped down the bowl of chocolate ice cream he always kept on hand for my visits. "I don't want to go to school with a bunch of white kids."

"Why not?" he insisted.

"Because."

"Because what?"

"Just because," I said, giving him my pat eight-year-old answer to all unanswerable questions.

But Mr. Johnson had a way with children, and it didn't take long before I was confiding in him that I thought the children at P.S. 166 on 84th Street and Columbus would laugh at me because I wore hand-me-down clothes that my mother didn't always have time to properly mend. Even the children at P.S. 184 laughed at me, and their clothes weren't much better.

"Miss Ke-Ke, you don't go to school to show off clothes, you go to learn," Mr. Johnson told me with a quiet smile. "But I know just how you feel. The kids in my school used to laugh at my clothes, too."

I looked at him incredulously. First of all, I never considered that Mr. Johnson could ever have been a child. I wasn't good at guessing ages, but I figured he must have been as old as my grandfather would have been if he was still alive. Secondly, I couldn't even imagine anyone teasing Mr. Johnson about his clothes. He was always dressed so nicely, always in a suit and tie, and even at eight, I could see that his suits and ties were very, very expensive. And of course, he must have been a millionaire—after all, he lived at Graham Court.

"Kids laughed at you because of your clothes?" I asked suspiciously.

"Yes, they did, Miss Ke-Ke."

"And what did you do?" I asked him.

"I beat them up."

There was a bunch of men in the apartment—Mr. Johnson always had at least two or three really big, burly men with him—and they hollered with laughter at his answer until he gave them a silencing glare.

"Now, I don't want you to go around beating people up, Miss Ke-Ke," he said, returning his attention to me, "because you're a smart young lady, and smart young ladies should fight with their brains. But you have to go to school to learn how to do that. And you have a chance to go to a really good school. Don't let the thought of people laughing at your clothes keep you from learning."

I was pretty much convinced. Clothes or no clothes, I was going to that white school and get as smart as Mr. Johnson, and maybe I would get to meet people like Langston Hughes and Bojangles, and live in a grand apartment, too.

Soon after, Madame stopped coming around my mother's house to pick me up, and the rumor on the street was that she had been sent to prison for something or the other, so my visits to Mr. Johnson's house stopped. But two weeks before school started there was a knock on our apartment door. My mother answered it, and a man gave her a white envelope that was marked, "From Mr. Johnson." Inside were five twenty-dollar bills, which in 1967 was enough to buy really nice school clothes for me and my twin sister and two brothers.

It wasn't until years later that I found out that Mr. Johnson was actually Ellsworth "Bumpy" Johnson, the Harlem gang-ster who fought the Jewish mobster Dutch Schultz in a gang war in the 1930s, and was still running Harlem in the 1960s. Movies were later made about him that depicted him as vio-lent and somewhat ruthless—and I'm sure he was all of those things. But I do wish more was told about the love he had for children.

So because of Bumpy Johnson I had school clothes, and I mean some nice school clothes, to attend P.S. 166. But, man, I hated that fucking school!

The white kids didn't beat me up, but they teased the shit outta me. They teased me about the way I dressed, the way I talked, and boy, did they tease me about my hair.

And some of the teachers weren't much better. There was this one teacher who took every opportunity to read us books that knocked black people. I used to love Mark Twain until she had us reading *Huckleberry Finn* and made a big deal about not reading the word "nigger," because she didn't want to offend the colored kids in class. So whenever she came to the word, she would cup her hand around her mouth and say it in a loud whisper. I know! How stupid, right?

Of course I was the only colored kid in the class, so all the other students in class started pointing at me and snickering whenever she said it. I told my mother and she was pissed, and I thought she was going to yank me out of 166, but for some reason she didn't. Then one day while I was pouring more evaporated milk in my oatmeal, I started softly singing, "I wish I were in the land of cotton. Old times there are not forgotten." My mother almost dropped her coffee. She asked where I learned the song and I told her my teacher taught us the words to "Dixieland" so that we could perform it in a class assembly. Well, that was the end of that. My mother went up there and raised all kinds of hell, banging her fist on the assistant principal's desk, and pointing her finger in the principal's face, talking about no teacher better be trying to brainwash one of her children that they should wish slavery was still around. Do you know the principal had the nerve to tell her if she didn't want her child singled out as a negro, that perhaps she shouldn't be sending me to school looking like a pickaninny? Said that he didn't know a lot about such things, but he knew that some negro mothers put some kind of hot comb in their children's hair before they went to school so they would look a little normal. Okay, so then my mom really went off on him, calling him a racist, a bigot, a . . . well, a whole bunch of other things. They had to call the cops to get her to leave. My mom left, all right. But that night she told David what happened, knowing that he would have a fit and want to do something about it. She reverted right back to that old "You're the man of the house" shit, even though she never said the words. And true to form, David stepped into the role. Let's see, if I was nine, David had to be ten, so it wasn't like he was going to go over there and talk to the principal man-to-man. So what did he do? Well, he got a bunch of his hooligan friends and went over to my school, kicked in the principal's door, and beat the crap out of him and all the administrators in the office. They had a mini-riot in there, and by mid-morning the place was swarming with police—but by then David had gotten away. The principal couldn't tell the police why he'd gotten jumped on, because David never said a word, but I think the principal kinda knew the deal.

I never set another foot in that school. But my mother still wanted me to be in the IGC program, so she told the school board that I was living with an aunt in the Bronx so I could go to one of the IGC schools there. Then when I was in the eighth grade my teacher, Mr. Levy, was talking about the English monarchy. Someone in the class was doing some kind of report or something, and referred to the current Queen of England as Queen Elizabeth the First. Mr. Levy corrected her and said she should have said Queen Elizabeth the Second, but added that the current queen was a direct descendant of Elizabeth I. Now, I know I was wrong because I didn't raise my hand, but I kinda blurted out, "Maybe a descendant, but not a direct descendant." Mr. Levy chuckled and said, "No. She's a direct descendant. She's her great-great-great-granddaughter. Give or take a great or two." So then I was like, "No. Queen Elizabeth the First was the virgin queen. She never had kids." Mr. Levy took up a real patronizing tone and said, "No. Queen Victoria was the virgin queen." Then he smirked and added, "Nice try, though."

So now I got pissed, because even if I was incorrect he didn't have to say it like I didn't know what I was talking about, you know? So I said I'd bet him a buck he was wrong. He walked over and patted me on the head and said he wouldn't take my money, and then smiled at the class—the kind of smile that says you want people to laugh—so the class started laughing. So now I was pissed as hell but I ain't say anything else.

But at lunchtime instead of going to the lunchroom I snuck to the library and got out a book on Queen Elizabeth I. Yep, I was right!

She was the daughter of King Henry VIII, the dude who had six wives and had two of them killed. The first one killed was his second wife, Ann Boleyn. That was Queen Elizabeth I's mother. Can you blame her for not wanting to get married? Not with all the shit her father did to his fucking wives! Huh! So anyway, they called her the Virgin Queen because she ain't never get hitched. I don't know about her being no virgin, though. I bet she was screwing around, but good for her!

And you know how I originally learned this information? Back in, like, 1966 or '67 there was a British group named Herman's Hermits who had a song out called "I'm Henry the VIII, I Am" about some dude named Henry who married a widow who had formerly married seven men—all named Henry.

I'm her eighth old man, I'm Henry
Henry the Eighth I am.

It was a really silly song, but I loved the way they pronounced "Henry"; they dropped the "H" and made it three syllables: "En-er-ry." Cracked me up! I used to love to sing the song, and one day Joe-Joe asked me if I knew who King Henry VIII was. I was only, like, eight or nine years old so I ain't know, so he took me to the library on 115th and St. Nicholas. I became fascinated by the guy and to this day I can still remember the names of all his wives, where they came from, and their ultimate fates. And I knew about his three children by three different wives. Elizabeth was the last of his children to sit on the throne. Since she had no children the crown passed to her third or fourth cousin, James. He was already King of Scotland, because Elizabeth had his mother—Mary, Queen of Scots—killed. Elizabeth was the last Tudor on the British throne. There was no way Elizabeth II was a direct descendant.

So, after us kids came back from lunch, I raised my hand and told Mr. Levy that I had books with me that proved he was wrong and I was right, and I could show him where if he wanted.

All the kids started going "Oooh," and Mr. Levy's face turned red. He started yelling at me, saying that I thought I was such a smart kid when I really wasn't, and he wasn't going to argue with me anymore because he had kids in the class who really wanted to learn.

I was stunned! I guess I didn't understand how important it was for him that he be right, because I was so concerned in proving that I was right. I didn't say anything else, but after class I went up to him to apologize, because I really didn't want him to think that I didn't want to learn, and I told him so. And you know what he told me? He very nicely said that I should understand something that I obviously didn't know—that he was Jewish.

He must have known from the stupefied look on my face that I ain't know what the hell he was getting at. He got that patronizing tone again and said that he understood that a lot of black people, and black kids, hate white people and didn't believe them when they said stuff because we hated them. But Jewish people weren't like other white people because they had suffered, too. So we could trust them and shouldn't try to embarrass them because they was only trying to look out for us. He ain't even address who was right or wrong, just that I couldn't correct him 'cause he was Jewish and Jewish people was friends to blacks. I stood there and just nodded my head because I ain't know what the fuck to say. I mean, first of all, I didn't hate white people. Yeah, I sometimes wore T-shirts with the slogan "Black Is Beautiful," but that didn't mean I thought white was ugly. Just like wanting Black Power didn't mean I was hoping or striving for white weakness. So, I ain't know where he got that "I hate white people" shit from.

And, secondly, what did white, black, or Jewish have to do with Queen Elizabeth I and Queen Elizabeth II?

Thirdly, and most importantly, I wondered why I had to pretend someone was right when I knew they really weren't. Or was I not only supposed to pretend they were right, was I supposed to actually think they really were right? Mommy and Joe-Joe had always drilled into us that just because someone was older than us that didn't mean they knew everything, and we shouldn't think we was smarter than them just because we knew something they didn't, or that they were smarter than us just because they knew something we didn't. Nobody knew everything, and that was okay!

I went home and told my mother. She just laughed and shook her head. Then I told her I ain't wanna go back to school anymore. And you know what? She ain't have a problem with it. And I never went back to school. Just like that. Know something else? The school board never sent a truant officer or a letter to my house to find out why I wasn't going to school. I think they was so sick of my mother going up there raising hell about racist shit that they was just glad to see me go.

Dig, I wasn't a high-school drop-out . . . I was a junior-high-school dropout. Remember, I wasn't but thirteen years old!

So I stayed home after that, and a couple of months later my sister Kitty said she ain't wanna go to school anymore, and my mother let her drop out, too. David played hooky so much that he may as well have been dropped out. Joe T., who was only nine, was the only one of my mom's kids going to school on the regular.

But my mom was still insistent that we learn shit, even if we weren't in school. So she gave me and Kitty a weekly reading list, and every Monday evening we'd all sit down and instead of reading newspapers together we'd talk about what we read and what it meant to us. She had us reading shit like *Animal Farm* by George Orwell, and *Native Son* by Richard Wright, and everything by Langston Hughes, and she also had us read every book Louisa May Alcott wrote, because that was her favorite author growing up. Then she had us go to the library and take out all these books by some historian named Will Durant. He wrote *The Story of Civilization,* and broke it up into eleven volumes. Took him fifty years to get them all done, and damn if we didn't read his first nine in a space of like two years. And, honest to God, some of those volumes had, like, a thousand pages!

Mommy also made us read *A Tree Grows in Brooklyn* by Betty Smith, but even though I realized I had some things in common with the girl in the book—we were both poor and lived in ghettos in New York—I really couldn't find myself getting into it. She always seemed so sweet and accepting of what was going on. I related more with the characters in *Manchild in the Promised Land* by Claude Brown, which was about a boy growing up in Harlem in the 1940s, and *Daddy Was a Number Runner* by Louise Meriwether, about a girl growing up in Harlem in the 1950s. They seemed more like me—poor, confused and frustrated and resentful as all hell, and distrustful because of all the people we saw doing shit to other people for absolutely no reason. And the kid in *A Tree Grows in Brooklyn* was a goody-goody. The kids in *Manchild* and *Daddy* was bad-ass kids like me and my friends—roof-hopping, penny-pitching, and shit-talking kinda kids. Joe-Joe wasn't really in our lives anymore, but he even pitched in and gave us a whole slew of *National Geographic* magazines. I know damn well we was the only kids on 117th reading that shit.

Meanwhile, while I was doing all this reading and learning, we was still getting evicted from one building and moving to another, and still getting kicked off welfare on the regular for one reason or the other. I was in my teens now, and my mother had developed diabetes and was always run-down and couldn't work at the real estate office no more. And whatever money Mommy could come up with David stole, so we was broke as ever. Like I said, Joe-Joe wasn't really in our lives anymore, but we still got some kind of disability checks from Social Security because he was too crazy to hold down a job. The check was for, like, $88.00. Even back then it wasn't enough to support a family with four kids for a month.

I had been outta school for almost a year but I had a part-time job babysitting for this actress, Beverly Todd, up on Riverside Drive. She later had roles in movies like *Lean on Me, Clara's Heart,* and *Crash.* I never liked kids, so I don't know how I got into babysitting. Oh yeah, that's right . . . I remember. I was doing a favor for my sister, Kitty, who had said she would babysit but had to find a replacement at the last minute. So I did her the favor, and I fucking fell in love with Beverly.

She wasn't a big-time star, but she had some good supporting roles in movies I had seen. I think I even had a crush on her. She was really gorgeous. She was tall, like five foot ten, and thin, with real pretty light-cocoa skin. She wasn't cute like Vanessa Williams or anything, but gorgeous anyway. She was the type of person as soon as you saw her you liked her and you didn't know why. She didn't seem threatening with her beauty. Just inviting. Yeah, I had a crush on her. Not like "I wanted to fuck her" kind of crush, but I wanted to be around her all the time. And I just adored her kid, Malik. He was the sweetest thing in the world, but spoiled as all hell, and he and I got along real good. I liked her husband, too. Kris Keiser. He was a movie director. Since they was into movies, Beverly and Kris had a whole bunch of big-shot, black Hollywood-type people coming to their house. I met Sidney Poitier, Harry Belafonte, Cleavon Little, and a whole bunch of soap opera stars, but I didn't really care about them because I didn't watch soap operas.

Now that I think about it, Kris and Beverly was responsible for me becoming a writer. I always got A's on my papers in school and everything, but that was kid stuff. And I had never tried my hand at nonfiction, just book reports and shit. But since Kris and Beverly were into movies they always had movie scripts laying around. I read the script for *Blazing Saddles* before the movie came out, and also the script for *The Mack* before that hit the big screen. Just so you know, the scripts were more exciting than the movies, even though the movies were damn good—especially *Blazing Saddles*. Remember the part in that movie when Madeline Khan (who was white) and Cleavon Little (who was black) was getting ready to get down, and the lights went dark but you hear her say, "Is it true what they say about black men?" and then a few seconds later she screams out, "It's true! It's true!" Funny, right? Well, in the script that I read, Cleavon Little then says, "Lady, why are you sucking on my elbow?" I fell out the chair laughing when I read that shit!

Well, one day I was pissed with Beverly and Kris because they kept going over and over the same instructions with me as if I didn't know what I was supposed to do after having babysat for them for months already. In retrospect I think they was both kinda high, but at the time I had a serious attitude with them, and couldn't wait for them to get out the house. Beverly noticed my 'tude and joked that I probably wanted them to get the hell out so I could read some more scripts. Then Kris said, out the blue, "Since you like reading scripts so much, why don't you write one?"

I shrugged and said, "Yeah, okay." Anything to get them to leave me the hell alone and get out the fucking house. So they finally left, and I pretty much forgot about what Kris said. I played with Malik and got him to bed on time, read him a bedtime story, and hung around his room until he was asleep. I was getting ready to find a script to read when Beverly called to check in. No big deal. But then she went over everything like she had a checklist that had to be marked off. I finally got her off the phone, and instead of reading a script like I intended, I started writing one. It was about a couple named Dirk Douglas and Betty Rodd (thinly veiled names for Kris Keiser and Beverly Todd) who were going to a fancy dinner party and were so excited that they kept saying the same thing over and over to their babysitter as they got ready to go. I don't remember all that was in the script, but I do remember it was funny as hell, and yeah, also biting. I gave Beverly the script when they got home, but I don't think she even read it, which was cool with me.

The next day, though, Kris called my house and said that he'd read the script and thought it was really good for someone who'd never written before, and especially someone my age. He also said that I should really consider writing as a career. I just said, "Yeah, yeah, okay." I didn't seriously think about writing again for something like twenty years.

Beverly and Kris used to have these small, fancy parties in their apartment, and she'd have me babysitting Malik while she was out there playing hostess. I loved it. I woulda loved it more if I coulda been out there mingling with the guests instead of stuck in the kid's room entertaining him, but I was thrilled just to be there with all those fancy movie people. I had never really thought about what I was going to do in my life, but I started thinking that being an actress wasn't too bad an idea.

Joe T. was, like, eight or nine then, and he was just as much into comic books as David used to be before he got all caught up in the streets. The *Incredible Hulk* was his favorite comic book, but he also dug the *Fantastic Four, Spider-Man,* and the *X-Men.* Joe T. was a real smart kid, but nobody ever knew it when we was growing up. I think he mighta been considered a doofus if he didn't have real cool siblings like me and David. Kitty didn't count because she was such a ditz, but me and David were considered real cool, so no one was going to be wolfing on our little brother.

Wanna hear something real funny? I remember when Joe T. was about seven years old he told us he and his friends had started a gang. I was like, wow! Joe T. in a gang? I ain't never liked gangs too much 'cause they was always starting shit with people, but I wasn't even mad when Joe T. told me. I was kinda, you know, amused. Then when I asked him what did he and his gang do, he told me, "Well, if one of us gets in trouble we help each other run." I was like, "What?" And he explained that when some bully would start picking on one of them they would all start running, and whoever was the slowest the others would yell over their shoulder, "Come on. Run faster." Well, I just fucking fell out laughing. Joe T. was funny like that. Real sincere, but weird as all hell. But wouldn't you know he grew up to be one of the smartest men I know, and made a mint in real estate? Go figure.

I always knew Joe T. was smart, though, even back then. I ignored him most of the time, but when he got to be around eight I started paying more attention to him. Not that I liked him any better, he still got on my damn nerves, but he needed someone to pay attention to him. He had been so used to David always taking him around, but then when David got hooked on dope the only time they talked was when David was beating him up to get his money. And Kitty, she used to try and act like she was his second mother, but then she turned teenager and was too busy giggling with her friends about boys. So every now and then I'd spend time with Joe T. Like I said, he was a cool little kid. Sometimes I'd let him read his comic books out loud to me, and then we'd start talking about how comic books kinda mirrored life.

Hey, do you remember when the Black Panther came out? He was a comic book hero who used to be in some of the other comic books, but Marvel finally gave him his own mag. Oh, man, that was such a big day for Joe T. A black comic book hero. Of course he bought the copy as soon as it hit the stands and read it on the walk home. I went and bought him another copy, and put it in one of those plastic bags and gave it to him for his birthday to keep it as a collector's item. We was kinda close, me and Joe T., but only kinda, because as far as I was concerned he was just a kid and after all, I was a teenager.

So anyway, I ain't tell nobody I wanted to be an actress, but I got Joe T. and told him that instead of him reading me comic books, me and him could act them out. We did the *Incredible Hulk* first. Joe T. played the roles of the Hulk, Bruce Banner, and General Talbot. I only played one role, Betty Ross, because I wanted to give my all to the part. We did one comic book, and Joe T. was so excited he ran in his room and got another and we did that one, too. I was excited too, because I was an actress, if only in my living room with my little brother. In fact, I was so excited I told Joe T. about my dream of being an actress. He went wild. Started jumping up and down and said if they ever made a movie outta the *Incredible Hulk* maybe I could play Betty Ross. Then when we started acting out another comic book, he kept interrupting the reading to tell me what a great actress I was, and how excited he was that he was going to be the brother of a famous star. That's the first time I really realized how supportive Joe T. could be. I mean he was a real trooper. I guess it was right about then that me and Joe T. became real tight, because I had a dream that I don't think I woulda ever chased, but Joe T. saw my dream and figured steps needed to be taken to make it a reality. Joe T. was real cool like that. Still is.

Even though I had sworn him to secrecy about my dream of being an actress, the next time Beverly came over to pick me up to go babysitting, Joe T. went right up to her and said, "My sister is an actress, too. You should put her in your next movie." I was so embarrassed I started blushing and punching Joe T. in the shoulder, but he kept saying, "What? She can help you, right?"

My mom was like, "You never told me you wanted to be an actress." And I started telling her that Joe T. didn't know what he was talking about. He ran in the room and got one of the Marvel comic books we had done. The *Sub-Mariner*. The one where his long-time girlfriend, Lady Dorma, dies.

"Here, read the Lady Dorma part like you did last time."

I glared at him and told him to get out my face, but my mom said, "Go ahead and read it, sweetie. Do it for me."

So I took the comic book and started reading Lady Dorma. At first I did it all in a dull monotone, but then I actually started getting it. Especially when Lady Dorma professes her love for the Sub-Mariner as she's dying in his arms. I did the hell out of a dying Lady Dorma. I really nailed it. And when I finished Beverly started clapping, and my mom was standing there with a weird look on her face.

"You're really good," she said real slow-like. "I guess we need to get you in some kind of acting class."

The look on her face, though, told me she was worried about how she was going to pay for it. I started feeling real guilty.

"Nah. I don't wanna be an actress. Me and Joe T. just be kidding around with this stuff." I threw the comic book on the couch and turned to Beverly. "You ready?" I asked as I started heading for the door.

"Wait a minute." Beverly placed her hand on my shoulder. "You really are good, you know. I think you should start acting classes." She musta seen the look on my face, because she then quickly added, "Kris will be teaching a class at the Negro Ensemble Company next month. I'm sure he can get you in the class for free."

My mother's mouth dropped open. "The Negro Ensemble Company? She can join the Negro Ensemble Company?"

She grabbed me by the shoulders. "Baby, the Negro Ensemble Company is famous. You're going to join the Negro Ensemble Company."

"Well," Beverly interrupted, "she wouldn't actually be a part of the company. She'd just be taking classes for now."

So then Joe T. started glaring at Beverly. "Why she gotta take acting classes? You just said she was already good."

Mom looked up from her hug. "Joe T. . . ." she began in a warning tone.

"No, Mom," Joe T. said, now really giving Beverly an evil-ass look, "she's just scared because she knows Ke-Ke is a better actress than her and she's going to steal all her parts."

Joe T. was never too good at social skills. But I knew even though he was talking like a little asshole he just thought he was looking out for his big sister. Thank God Beverly just ignored him.

And just like that I was taking classes at the famous Negro Ensemble Company. It was really cool. I mean, really. I was the only kid in my acting class. There was all these grown-ups, most of them downright breathtakingly beautiful, all getting together and just reveling in their creativity, and talking about how they was gonna be stars, 'cause the man could take almost everything away but he couldn't take away their creativity. They didn't say who the man was, but somehow I instinctively knew. And I started thinking, "Fuck the man." He couldn't keep me down, either.

Then, when I was about fifteen, I remember one day I was watching *Eyewitness News* on Channel 7 and they did a segment about this Vietnamese family who had opened up a grocery store after only being in the United States for, like, two years. The guy interviewing the family was making a big deal about how this was a real success story, and should be an inspiration for other people who didn't do anything with their lives because they used the excuse of not having anything to start with. I don't know how—I knew then but I don't remember now—but somehow I knew he was knocking black folks. He kept going on and on about here was this family who had just come to the United States two years ago with nothing but the shirts on their backs and were now proud business owners.

Then he stuck his microphone in the store owner's face and asked him how he did it. The guy was cheesing so hard all you could see was teeth, and then he said that he lived in an apartment with four other families who also came over from Vietnam. Each family had a welfare check coming in, and what they would do is live off one family's welfare check and save all the rest so they finally had three thousand dollars saved to use as a down payment on the store. Then he got up close to the camera and yelled, "God Bless America!"

The newsman then said something about other "groups" who have been on welfare for years, and use the excuse of being stuck in the system, but this family proved that with hard work and tenacity it was, indeed, possible to achieve the American Dream.

What the fuck?

They saved up three thousand dollars from welfare checks? But my mom got kicked off welfare because she had the nerve to save a lousy fucking $125 in the bank? I was so pissed off I threw my glass of strawberry Kool-Aid at the TV.

God Bless America my ass.

I wasn't quite An Angry-Ass Black Woman yet, but I sure as hell was a pissed-off, frustrated black kid.

* * *

The voices again. As much as I love hearing Camille and everyone, it's really a hassle listening to what's going on around me when I can't do a damn thing about it. I don't care about the fact that I can't move until I hear them. Why can't they just leave me to my thoughts? Hey! That's Joe T.! But I thought he was in Lagos. That's a seventeen-hour flight. How could he get here so fast? Oh yeah, that's right. Belinda did say something about Camille having been here forty hours.

"I just spoke to the doctors again. They just keep saying it's just a waiting game. Why didn't someone tell them until yesterday that she's a famous author?"

"I'm sorry, Uncle Joe. It didn't cross my mind, I mean, what difference does it make now?"

"It makes all the difference in the world. They needed to know from the start that your mother's a somebody, and a lot of people are going to be watching how they treat her. Don't you know anything?"

"I, um, I'm sorry. I just didn't think of it, Uncle Joe."

"No. Look. I'm sorry. I'm not trying to get on you, Camille. I'm just upset like everybody else, and I shouldn't be taking it out on you. Are you okay?"

"Yes, I'm fine. Just a little tired."

"I told her that she should go home and take a break but she wouldn't listen to me, Joe T. Maybe if you tell her."

"Are you insane, Belinda? Camille's not supposed to go anywhere. She's supposed to stay right where she is. This is her mother, and that means something. How can you tell her she should leave? That doesn't make any kind of sense."

"I was just saying that—"

"I know what you're saying, but this is her mother and she's not going anywhere."

I love the hell out of Joe T., but I wish he wasn't always so hard on everybody in the family. Funny thing is, he's the youngest and he has everybody so intimidated they walk on eggshells around him.

Not intimidated the way they are of Belinda, knowing if they say the wrong thing she's gonna haul off and slap the shit out of them, but intimidated that he's gonna look down on them more than he already does. And for some reason they fear that more than a slap in the face.

"How come Kitty isn't here?"

"She was but Uncle David put her out because she was talking so negative in front of Mommy even when we told her not to."

"David was here? What the hell was he doing here? I didn't think they even allowed scum like that in a hospital. I hope you had someone come in here and disinfect the place."

"Come on, Joe T. You shouldn't talk like that about your own brother."

"Belinda, you should stay out of it. This is family stuff I'm talking."

"Uncle Joe T., Cousin Belinda is family, too."

"I didn't say she wasn't. Let me sit in that chair for a minute so I can talk to my sister."

"Uncle Joe, why don't you grab another chair? I'm keeping this one because it's closest. She may be your sister, but she's my mother."

That's my girl. Joe T. might intimidate everybody else, but Camille and I have always been the ones to let him know that while we love him, he isn't the king of the world. And here's my baby keeping it real. Yeah, that's my girl. But I really wish they would all be quiet for a moment because they're distracting me. And I gotta keep my wits about me, because that damn bitch, Death, keeps hanging around, and I gotta keep beating her back. I mean, don't she know who I am? I'm An Angry-Ass Black Woman.

six

I was a fine, young, foxy filly when I was a teenager. And I mean I was really fine. I had a café-au-lait complexion with a light sprinkling of freckles across my face, and long, thick black hair that I'd inherited from my moms. It was 1972, so cornrows and braids weren't really the thing yet, but by then I had too much black pride to get a perm so I used to wear my hair in a big-ass afro, although sometimes I would let my Aunt Cora put a straightening comb through it so I could feel my hair hanging down around my shoulder blades.

And my shape. Oh man, I was shaped like a fucking brick house. I was only an A cup, but I was a fucking magnificent A cup, with a twenty-four-inch waist and wide hips, and an ass that jutted out so far someone could sit a cup on it. Five feet tall, 110 pounds, and 35-22-36, thank you very much. I was fucking fine.

In fact I was so fine that . . . oh well, you should get the picture by now. I was fucking fine.

And just thinking about how fine I was back then almost makes me want to go on a diet. But naw, that's the past. Even if I could get down to 110 again it wouldn't be the same. I was a sweet fourteen-year-old back then, and now I'm a cynical forty-seven-year-old mother fighting the worst fucking battle of my life. And you know what? I ain't fucking losing. Okay? Ain't no fucking way I'm losing this fucking battle. Got that?

Shit. I'm losing it again.

Okay, back to what I was saying.

Yeah. I was fine. And a virgin to boot! That was a big accomplishment in my neighborhood, where a lot of girls my age were pushing strollers. A lot of my girlfriends had been giving it up since they were, like, eleven or twelve. Some of them 'cause they was in love with a boy, but not all of them. For some it was a financial necessity.

Remember I told you about Mr. Fred, the sock man who lived near the corner of 117th and Lenox? I think I already mentioned him. He was an old guy, about sixty, which seemed really old to me at the time. Everybody knew he would pay a young girl five bucks if she let him eat her out, ten bucks if she'd suck his dick, and the price was negotiable if you let him stick it in.

The funny thing is I don't ever remember him ever trying to, you know, like, coerce anyone to get them in bed. Everybody knew he paid for his shit, and that was enough. He didn't have to really advertise, the word was out. I know one of my girlfriends gave it up to him like that. Sheila. She was a scrawny kid with a chicken neck and big pink blubber lips, and everyone thought she was pretty ugly. Okay. I admit I thought she was ugly, too. But I still liked her. I felt sorry for her, too, because she was the oldest of, like, eight kids, and she was always having to take care of them while her mother worked. She used to write short stories, and since I always loved to read, I'd read all her stuff. She was really good, too! So I was gonna be an actress, and she was gonna write all my movies. We just knew we was both gonna be rich and famous, and we'd be able to give our families a shitload of money so they didn't have to be poor anymore.

Then when she was thirteen her mother got married again, and she got a stepfather, and things really started getting fucked up for her then. She started spending the night at all her friends' houses because her stepfather kept trying to get fresh with her. Kept trying to feel her booty, or finding ways to brush up against her titties. And when she said anything about it to her mother she'd get a beating, because her mom said she was just an ungrateful little bitch who was trying to break up her marriage.

Ain't that some shit? I mean, how fucked up is that? Wanting to be with a man so much that you don't even care when your kid is saying he's pushing up on her? But as fucked up as it is, you know there's some pathetic-ass women like that, and Sheila's mother was one.

So finally, Sheila decided to confide in one of her teachers, you know, tell her what was going on so maybe she could do something like call the cops or at least tell her mother that she wasn't lying. But you know what the teacher did? She told Sheila that she shouldn't be broadcasting to people what was going on in her family. Told her she shouldn't be trying to air her dirty laundry in public. Ain't that some shit? I mean, I know that was before the school district started that policy about how teachers are supposed to report any problems they think their students are having at home, but still? I mean, damn. Ya know?

So anyway . . .

Sheila's family wasn't really too poor after the stepfather got on the scene, because he had a good job. A funeral director. He ain't own the funeral home, but he was the director, and he got paid good. But you wouldn't know it by the way Sheila looked. Her shit looked real raggedy because the stepfather kept telling her mother she ain't deserve no new clothes because she was such a snotty kid. "Snotty" meaning she wouldn't suck his dick. And she never had money to go to the movies or anything. It was hard for a kid of fifteen, you know?

So one day all us teenagers was lounging out on a stoop talking about going to the new Pam Grier movie, *Foxy Brown*, and Sheila was just sitting there looking pitiful, not saying shit. Then all of a sudden she got up and started walking home without saying anything. Like I said, me and Sheila was tight, so I ran and caught up with her.

"You okay?" I asked her.

"Yeah." She made like she was wiping her nose but I could see she was trying to wipe a tear that was coming out her eye. "I'm going to the show with you on Saturday, okay? Make sure you wait for me, 'cause I'm coming."

"You are?" I was real skeptical, 'cause I knew damn well her stepdad wasn't coming off the $2.50 it cost to get in the Loew's Theater on 125th Street.

"Yeah, I am. You watch."

"Okay, but, um, where you gonna get the money?" I was talking kinda timid like, 'cause I ain't never seen Sheila in such a funk, and I ain't know what to expect, but I wanted to know.

"Nunya business," she said real mean like.

"Come on, tell me," I urged.

"Nunya," she snapped.

"Well, okay, then." I stopped in my tracks and put my hands on my hips. "If you gonna act like that, I ain't waiting for you on Saturday then."

Now see, that was real mean of me. 'Cause I knew Sheila ain't had no friends but me and she wouldn't wanna piss me off 'cause then she wouldn'ta had nobody to hang with, so she'd have to act right if she wanted to stay tight with me. And acting right meant telling me something she ain't wanna tell me, and for truth wasn't none of my damn business.

And just like I knew she would, Sheila told me.

"I'ma go see Mr. Fred. And you better not tell nobody."

"Ooooh!" I started jumping up and down in the street like I was a five-year-old. "Ooooh, girl. You better not. You better not."

Sheila looked at me, and for a second I thought she was gonna yell at me, but then she just gave me the five-finger wave and started running toward her building. So I ran and caught up with her and grabbed her by the arm.

"I know you ain't gonna do nothing stupid like that," I said, all outta breath. "Why you gonna try and act like some kinda hussy?"

"Leave me alone and mind your business." She snatched her arm away from me, and that's when I noticed she was crying.

"No, I ain't leaving you alone. You better not do anything stupid like that, and I ain't playing." I felt bad about making Sheila cry, but I was holding my ground, 'cause I ain't want my girl going out like that.

"Ain't nunya," Sheila yelled at me.

"Yes, it is my business," I yelled back at her.

She got all up close to me. "Don't make me slap you."

Oh well, now see, why'd she have to say some shit like that? I learned early on from my cousin Belinda that if someone says they're gonna hit you, you should make sure you get in the first hit. So, me being me, and mad as shit at Sheila anyway, I hauled off and punched the shit outta her. So then it was on.

I beat the shit outta her, which both of us knew from the git-go I'd be able to do, and then when she was crying for real I told her I was sorry, and she said she was sorry, too. And then we just stood there for a while just being sorry as shit.

"Look," I said finally. "I just don't want you to, you know . . . I just don't want you to—"

"I'm not," Sheila cut me off. "I was just playing around."

"No you weren't." I was getting mad all over again now, because if she was just playing then she made me kick her ass for nothing. And that would make me wanna kick her ass all over again.

"Okay, I wasn't. But I ain't gonna do it, 'cause you're right." She wiped her eyes. "I just wanted to go to the movies so bad. But I ain't no slut, I ain't gonna do nothing with Mr. Fred."

I put my arm around her and walked her home.

Then late Saturday afternoon, when I was getting ready to go to the movies, Sheila shows up at my door.

"You ready?" she asked me.

I looked at her and I knew. And she looked at me and she knew I knew. And that was the end of that.

We met up with the rest of the gang and went and saw Pam Grier kick a whole buncha men's asses and I remember wishing it was me up on that screen, or Sheila up there kicking her stepfather's ass and Mr. Fred's ass, too.

Sheila had just enough money to get into the movies and buy a frankfurter and a bag of popcorn. Which meant she just let Mr. Fred eat her out. But as time went on Sheila started having more money, enough to treat me to the movies sometimes, and even started buying herself some nice clothes. That kinda let me know she went from getting head, to giving head, to getting fucked. I ain't say nothing, though. Sheila was right when she said in the beginning it weren't none of my business. And anyway, it wasn't like she was getting a reputation or anything. One thing I could say about old pervert Mr. Fred, he kept things on the downlow. He and Sheila worked out a system, so they would meet away from the neighborhood, and when he saw her in the street he would just nod at her real polite like he did all the other people on the block, so no one knew nothing was up. I knew what was up, but I wasn't saying shit. And I know her moms and stepfather musta known something was up since Sheila was wearing clothes they ain't bought her, but Sheila managed to play it off somehow.

But in the end she got messed up.

Sheila needed some money real bad to go enter some writing contest or the other. It cost, like, fifty dollars, and Sheila wanted to enter real bad because she had written this short story that she knew was going to win. And if she won, her story was going to get published in some magazine or the other, and maybe she'd get a fat contract from some publisher to write a book. That was her thinking, anyway. But see, the problem was Mr. Fred was on vacation in Jamaica, so she had no cash coming in.

Well, there was this old nasty-looking man, Mr. Bill, who had recently moved on the block. He had a truck he used to load up with watermelons every summer and he'd go around Harlem making money. I don't know if he propositioned Sheila, or if Sheila propositioned him. But I know me and Sheila was sitting on a car talking smack with some other kids on the block, when Mr. Bill walked over and felt her up right in front of everybody. Sheila jumped up and tried to slap him, but he danced out the way. So I had a bottle of Nehi grape soda, and I threw its contents on him. He started cursing, but me and Sheila was cursing him, too, and Brucie walked up to find out what was going on. See, after David got messed up, Brucie kinda adopted me as his little sister and would look out for me. Well, Mr. Bill hadn't been on the block long, but he lived there long enough to know that Brucie was gonna kick his ass if I gave him the go-ahead. So then he shouts at Sheila real loud: "Well, I don't know why you getting so uppity now when you ain't act all uppity when you was sucking my dick last night."

Man, everybody got real fucking quiet for a moment. Then I started yelling, "You a liar, and you know it." I turned to Sheila, who was standing with a face so red you woulda thought she was having a stroke, and I nudged her. One look at her and I knew Mr. Bill was telling the truth, and all the other kids knew it, too. They started yelling, "Ooh, Sheila," and pointing at her and laughing. Sheila still wasn't saying nothing, so I told Brucie to fuck Mr. Bill up, 'cause he was a liar. And you know that Brucie, who would kick somebody's ass for looking at him wrong, said no?

"To hell with that," he said. "If she's fucking him then she deserves to be called out. Fucking 'ho."

All of a sudden Sheila wasn't paralyzed no more. She turned around and started walking up the block to her building real fast, with her head down, but not saying nothing. I felt so bad that I walked over and kicked Mr. Bill in the shins. I know he wanted to say something to me but was afraid of Brucie. He just gave me a dirty look and limped away.

All the kids started talking about what a sleaze Sheila was and that she weren't nothing but a 'ho, and all this shit. I stuck around a little bit, but I couldn't take it anymore so I went over to Sheila's house. Her moms let me in and told me that Sheila was in her bedroom. I walked in and saw Sheila just sitting on the side of the bed, not crying, not even sniffling. Just a blank look on her face. I didn't know what to do, so I ain't say nothing, I just sat down next to her. I don't know how long we sat there, it felt like hours, but it might've only been twenty minutes. Finally Sheila sighed and lay back on the bed, staring at the ceiling.

"Here's the thing," she said to the ceiling. "Why should I

let my stepfather be the one to bust my cherry?" She said it just like that, no shit! If I ain't know what to say before I sure as shit ain't know what to say then. So I just kept quiet. Besides, I didn't even know for sure if she was talking to me, or if she even really knew I was in the room.

"'Cause it was just a matter of time before he actually raped me, you know. I ain't stupid, I know that. So why should I let him be the first man to fuck me?"

When she said it like that it almost made sense, but I still ain't say nothing 'cause I ain't know if I was supposed to. Sheila ain't say nothing else after that, so after about fifteen minutes I told her I had to leave. She ain't say nothing, and I ain't even sure she heard. So I just left.

When I got home I got started to thinking that Sheila was gonna do something stupid like kill herself. She did, in a way. She became the neighborhood 'ho, just giving it up to anyone who asked, and there was a lot of people asking. Sometimes she made them pay, sometimes she didn't. Then she started using speed and sniffing dope and getting drunk and sleeping in the street. By the time she was sixteen she looked like she was thirty. I still tried to be tight with her, but we ain't really had too much to say to each other anymore, 'cause our lives were so different. She did tell me that her stepfather was fucking her on the regular, though, and she was thinking about starting to make him pay. Personally, I thought she should make her stepfather and her mother pay, and I don't mean money. And she shoulda made Mr. Fred pay, and Mr. Bill, and all the grown-ups on the block who could see the girl needed help but instead'a helping, just humped her like a dog. Every time I saw Sheila, nodding out on heroin on the corner or going off with some man, I got real angry, and not at her. I got angry at the whole fucking world. I may have been a fine, young, foxy filly, but I was angry as shit.

* * *

Who's that doing all that crying? Oh, good. Kitty must be back. I never wanted her to go in the first place. Not that I was in any condition to sit up and protest.

"Kitty, you better stop all that noise, 'cause you know Joe T.'s going to throw you out again."

"No, I'm not going to do that, Belinda. She's supposed to be here. Just like you're supposed to be here. And I'm sorry if I was rude before."

"Oh, little boy, you know I'm not mad. Just like you said before, we're all a little upset, that's all."

Aw, isn't that sweet? Joe T.'s making nice. Camille musta pulled him aside and gotten on him. I can't believe Belinda is calling Joe T. "little boy" when he's forty-nine years old now, but that is what she used to call him when we were all kids. I guess I'm not the only one tripping down memory lane.

"I just don't understand! Why didn't she tell me about the tumor? I'm her sister. Her only sister."

Brain tumor! That's right. I was in here for them to remove a tumor the size of an egg from my left frontal lobe. I wonder how the operation went?

"Aunt Kitty, why you gonna say something like that? You know my mother told you. And she said that you promised to be there with her when they took her into the operating room. But you weren't."

"Well, I got busy and forgot what day she said—"

"Yeah, Kitty, I bet you were busy. So busy chasing crack and dick you forgot your own sister was having an operation to remove a brain tumor. You're just pitiful."

"Uncle Joe T.! Stop."

"Why you gotta act like such an asshole, Joe T.? You don't think I love my own twin? Of course I love Ke-Ke. I may have forgotten but it's not because I was chasing anything. I love my sister. I love my family. And I mean all my family. I'm not like you—selective about who you love. I even love you with your mean self. Even though sometimes, like now, you make it hard."

"Oh, just shut up, Kitty."

"Come on, Uncle Joe. Come on, Aunt Kitty. Both of you need to calm down. It's not doing Mommy any kind of good to hear the two of you arguing like this."

"You know what, Joe T.? She's right. We should be here trying to figure out what we're going to do when she dies. Like, who's gonna—"

"Aunt Kitty!"

"I'm sorry, Camille, but look—"

"Shut up, Kitty. Our sister's not going to die. Ke-Ke's strong, and she's going to pull through."

"Yeah, that's what you said about Mommy, remember?"

"I said shut up, Kitty!"

seven

*M*ommy got real sick right before I turned thirteen. She was getting stomach pains so bad she would cry and vomit and sometimes even pass out. It was scary as shit. The doctors couldn't find out what was wrong with her even though they gave her all these different tests. Upper GI. Lower GI. All kinds of shit. Then they started giving her all these different kinds of pills to try and treat her, but they ain't know what the hell they were doing. Medicaid doctors. So you know how that was. None of the specialist kinda doctors that knew what they was doing accepted Medicaid, so Mommy had to keep going to the same damn doctors over and over again, and they kept prescribing all these damn pills.

By the time I was fifteen she got even more sick, and not just her stomach. She started getting real weak and dizzy all the time and was forever getting headaches. The doctors kept prescribing even more pills, but nothing seemed to be working. Soon Mommy couldn't hardly get outta her bed, and we'd even had to help her to the bathroom. Mommy was dying and everybody seemed to know it but them damn doctors.

I wanted to quit my acting class so I could get a part-time job to help out with the bills, but Mommy wouldn't let me. Said she wasn't going to slow down my future 'cause her future was almost over. You can imagine how I felt, her saying that. I tried to tell her she still had her whole future ahead of her, but that just made her feel bad. She said she wasn't no kind of mother to be saying things that would make me feel hurt and scared like that, and maybe she just wasn't a good mother at all. She started crying, and I left the room, because I was going to start crying and that would make her feel even worse. I was feeling really helpless. All us kids was.

Joe T. started sleeping on the floor in Mommy's room, and wouldn't hardly budge outta there even in the day. He never cried, but he never smiled or said much either, except saying over and over that she was strong, and she was going to pull through. She just needed some time. He would stay up in Mommy's room looking at her, and whenever she moaned or something he'd yell for me or Kitty to come quick to help her.

David even started sticking around the house after Mommy got real sick, and he wasn't stealing no more. At least not from her.

Then one morning we saw that Mommy's eyes were all yellow, and I mean really yellow. Mommy was light-skinned, almost cream-colored, but now her whole complexion was taking on a dull yellow color. Mommy was conscious, but really weak, and was mumbling something we couldn't understand.

David yelled for me and Kitty to get Mommy dressed and he ran downstairs to get a cab so we could take her to the hospital.

Well we got to Harlem Hospital in about ten minutes and David carried Mommy in, but the nurse told us since Mommy wasn't bleeding or unconscious to have her take a seat and wait her turn because there was people ahead of us. David started yelling at the woman, saying his mother was dying, but the bitch hardly even looked up from her desk when she said, "If she was that sick she woulda come by ambulance."

Me and Kitty started yelling at the woman, but David propped Mommy up in a chair and ran out the door. He was back in, like, two seconds, dragging an ambulance attendant in by the back of his collar.

"Here's the ambulance guy. Now get my mother a doctor," he yelled, then pushed the ambulance guy over the nurse's desk.

Meanwhile Joe T. had run past the emergency room doors and rushed back in with a gurney, and me and Kitty started trying to put Mommy up on it. She was really really weak, but she kept trying to tell us to stop making so much noise and stop being rude.

Two big security guards ran in and jumped on David and wrestled him down to the ground, so then Joe T. picked up a chair and started hitting the security guards over their backs, all the time yelling at the top of his lungs. Don't ask me what he was yelling, because I don't know, but he was yelling and almost frothing at the mouth like he was gonna turn into his hero, the Incredible Hulk.

Me and Kitty started wheeling the gurney into the inner part of the hospital and bumped right into a doctor, knocking him down. He got up and looked like he was going to start cursing, but I grabbed him by the sleeve and started crying. "Please. You gotta help us. Our mother's dying."

He gave me an annoyed glance then turned to look at my mother, who by this time had passed out on the gurney.

"Oh my God," he said in a thick accent that I couldn't identify, then he shoved me and Kitty out the way and started poking at her with his stethoscope. After a couple of seconds he pulled open my mother's eyelids, then let out an audible breath.

"Get her in here quick," he said.

I don't know who he was talking to, but when me and Kitty started trying to wheel the gurney again he pushed us aside and took over, quickly propelling the gurney through the swinging doors, and yelling something about an IV. Me and Kitty tried to follow him, but someone pushed us back into the emergency room.

The police had come by that time and was trying to haul David and Joe T. away, so then me and Kitty started arguing with them that they ain't do nothing wrong. The nurse started shouting that David had tried to kill her or some shit, and I was getting ready to haul off and punch the shit outta her when the doctor flew back into the nursing room.

"What kind of medication is your mother on?" he asked in that thick accent.

"I don't know," I answered, forgetting about the nurse for a minute. "Maybe my brother knows." I turned and saw the police had David and Joe T. in handcuffs and were dragging them out the door. "Doctor, they're arresting my brothers and they ain't even do nothing."

"They assaulted me," the nurse broke in.

"No, they didn't. They was just mad 'cause you wouldn't let my mother see a doctor," I spat at her.

Even the other people in the emergency room who had been waiting to be seen jumped on our side, and said the nurse was wrong and they should stop picking on us kids.

The doctor glared at the nurse, then stepped to the police. "This is just a misunderstanding, and I would appreciate it if you would let the young men free. I take full responsibility."

The nurse sucked her teeth and started mumbling something about "them damn African doctors," then walked back to her desk and started shuffling papers around.

The police just shrugged and let David and Joe T. go and

then left. They ain't really give a shit one way or the other. The doctor waved for us kids to follow him and then led us to a little room and started questioning us, but all we wanted to know was where our mother was. He told us that other doctors were working on her, and for us not to worry, but he had to know everything we knew about her medical history. We told him about her bad stomach aches, and then he asked if she had been to the doctor before. We said yeah, and told him the name of her main doctor. The African doctor actually winced, and then shook his head.

"Okay," he said finally. "I know him. I'll give him a call now."

He started out the room and then stopped and looked at us. "Do you have any adult relatives you can call to come over here? Right away?"

I nodded. "We can call my Aunt Pat." He took us into another room that had a telephone, and I made the call.

But by the time Aunt Pat got there Mommy was dead. Liver failure. Not from heavy drinking or some shit, but because of all them damn pills the Medicaid doctors had been giving her.

Now ain't that some shit?

The African doctor—his name was Dr. Adefumi—let us in to see her. She was lying up on that white hospital bed looking like she was asleep. We was all crying. I huddled up in a corner of the hospital room just looking over at her. Aunt Pat was holding Kitty in a hug while she cried, and Joe T. just stood in the middle of the room glaring down at the floor and not saying anything. But David . . . David took one look at my mother and crawled into the bed with her and buried his head in her shoulder and sobbed.

Me, I sat quietly, huddled in a corner, just thinking. I

wasn't thinking about anything in particular, but I really was thinking hard.

Thinking real hard.

Blinking back tears.

Rocking my body back and forth.

And thinking real hard.

About nothing in particular.

I wasn't angry, I wasn't sad, I was . . . I don't know what I was. I just was.

★ ★ ★

"And if you care about her so much how come you wasn't here for the operation, Joe T.? How you gonna criticize me when you knew your sister was dying and you go off gallivanting halfway across the world?"

"Shut up, Kitty. You know damn well if I had known she was sick I woulda been right here."

"Aunt Kitty, stop talking about my mother's dying. I mean it. I'm going to call the nurse and tell her you can't come back in here."

"Humph! I'd like to see some damn nurse try to put me out."

"Kitty, Joe T. done told you to shut up a dozen times, and Camille's told you a dozen more. I swear I'm going to get up out this chair and knock you out so I know you won't say nothing else—getting on everyone's nerves like you ain't got good sense."

"But Belinda—"

"Don't 'Belinda' me. Shut the hell up. And now."

They were right, Kitty really should shut up, but I hated that they were yelling at her like that. I do remember now, though. I was hurt when I checked into the hospital for the operation and Kitty was nowhere to be found. But that was Kitty. She was fighting her own demons.

eight

*T*he family had a conference to discuss what was going to be done with us kids now that Mommy was dead. As I said earlier, my mother was an only child. Her father had died when she was twelve, and her mom passed in, like, 1963, so it was up to the Quinones family to take charge, and they had no problem doing so. God bless them, it wasn't a money thing with them, and they was actually arguing because each of them wanted to take in at least one of us. Aunt Pat was there, Aunt Bernice was there, Aunt Cora, and my mom's friend, Miss Teri, was also there. Joe-Joe was in Bellevue again so he wasn't at the meeting. They had let him out for Mommy's funeral, but then escorted him right back to the hospital that same day.

Aunt Cora was the oldest, and she said she would take us all in, but the family vetoed it. Her own daughter, Arlene, had recently died and she was already taking care of her five grandchildren. Bernice was the next oldest—she was Belinda's and Sister's mom—and she said that she should take in David, since he was the hardest to handle. Everyone agreed. Aunt Pat said she would take in me, Kitty, and Joe T.

Then Miss Teri piped up and said, "Well, me and my husband talked about it, and we'd like to take Kitty in."

I thought Aunt Pat was gonna just jump up and punch her in the mouth, but instead she just spit on the ground and said, "You ain't family. Stay out this shit."

Now, Miss Teri had known Mommy for, like, twenty

years, so she knew all of my aunts, and she knew that Aunt Pat wasn't one to be fucked with. Aunt Pat was a hard-drinking, hard-fighting woman who would beat the shit outta you and ask questions later. She was the meanest of all the aunts, but also the sweetest. All the kids in the family loved her because she was always giving us hugs, kisses, and candy, but more than that, the grown-ups were scared of her because she had a volatile temper and would jump on someone in a minute if she even thought they were trying to insult her or one of us kids.

Aunt Cora said, "Now, Pat, don't be so mean. You already have your own two kids to worry about along with the ones you're taking in, and Teri doesn't have any kids. And you know she loves children."

Aunt Pat just said, "Well, then let her have her own. Our kids stay in our family."

Well, there was a pretty big argument about it, but finally Aunt Cora put her foot down and, since she was the oldest of my father's sisters, that was that. Aunt Bernice would get David, Aunt Pat would get me and Joe T., and Miss Teri and her husband would get Kitty.

So, that afternoon David went home with Aunt Bernice on 128th Street, Kitty went home with Miss Teri to 117th Street, and me and Joe T. went home with Aunt Pat to 143rd Street, her cursing all the way, saying she was gonna kick Miss Teri's ass as soon as she got her alone.

At first I thought it would be cool. Like all the kids in the family, I adored my Aunt Pat. But see, Kitty was my twin, and she and I had never been separated before. I missed her. I missed the shit outta her.

Kitty and I were fraternal twins, so we didn't look exactly alike, but we looked close enough that friends often mixed us up. But other than our looks, we were as different as night and day. I loved to read, and had what my mother and Joe-Joe called "intellectual curiosity." For instance, if I was reading a book or watching a television show that mentioned a subject—even in passing—I hadn't heard about, I would go to the library and take out every book on the subject so I could learn about it. Kitty, on the other hand, was smart, but she never cared about learning. If she didn't know something that was cool with her. And she was ditzy. If she was white, Kitty would no doubt be a dumb blonde. And her ditziness used to irritate the shit outta me. She was always asking stupid questions, and running her mouth causing all of us to get in trouble, like when she told Miss Lovie Mae that we weren't playing with the landlord, but were robbing him. If Kitty knew any of your secrets, watch out! She never tried to get anyone in trouble, but she couldn't help herself. She just couldn't keep from running off with the mouth. Often her mouth would get her in trouble with people outside the family, and I wound up in a bunch of fights defending her. If they had known, David or Belinda would fight for her, too, but after they'd fought for Kitty they woulda turned around and beat her up, too; because there wouldn't have been a fight if she hadn't been running off with the mouth. So I never told them when Kitty's mouth got her ass in trouble, I would just jump in and whip ass for her. 'Cause even though she was a ditz, she was still my sister—she was still my girl. Another thing I didn't really like about Kitty, though, was she was boy crazy. She and a set of her friends were always giggling about some cute boy or the other, even though she never really talked to them. Me, I was the opposite. I decided early on that although I didn't really like boys, they could be put to good purpose. I would flirt shamelessly if I needed something one of them could provide. Nothing big, but for instance if I needed bags carried home from the supermarket I would bat my eyes and give a huge smile, and soon I would be walking aside some guy with bulging muscles hauling my groceries. Soon as we got to my building I would try to brush him off, often by giving him a fake telephone number. Soon as the guy was no longer of use to me, I wanted nothing to do with him. And if a guy refused the easy brush-off, well, I then would call in my secret weapon—namely David or Brucie. Both were extremely protective of me, and would beat the shit outta any guy they thought was trying to make time with me. But Kitty liked getting attention from boys.

Still, with all of her faults—being a ditz, having a big mouth, and being boy crazy—Kitty was a real sweetie. She was always nice to everyone, sharing her candy or any other thing she got, even with the few kids who ain't like her. She just hated seeing someone doing without. And she just loved animals. She was always bringing in stray dogs and cats, and going out to feed the pigeons and shit. And she really looked up to me, even though she was the older twin by one minute, and that made me feel good. She thought I was the smartest person on earth, and I never did anything to discourage that belief. And when she got scared in the middle of the night, after watching a scary movie or something, she'd hop into my bed and grab my feet and sleep with me for the rest of the night. Kitty worshipped me like I was her patron saint, and I adored her like she was my personal angel. A troublesome angel sometimes, but my personal angel, nonetheless.

I didn't even last one night at Aunt Pat's house without Kitty. About midnight, when I was in the bed I started missing her so bad I snuck out the house and walked the twenty-six blocks to Miss Teri's apartment on 117th Street.

Miss Teri was hesitant to take me in at first, but when Kitty and I grabbed each other and started crying she got on the phone and called Aunt Cora, who then called Aunt Pat and smoothed things over.

I missed David and Joe T., but I just couldn't stand being away from Kitty.

Staying with Miss Teri was great, too, because that allowed me to still be with my friends from the block, and for the first couple of weeks everything was cool. But then I noticed there was a little something too cool going on with Kitty and Miss Teri's husband, Mr. Leroy. I never did like the man. He was from Bermuda, a tall, good-looking man, at least twenty years older than Miss Teri. He always tried to be nice, but I just never did take to him, not from when I first met him at age seven when he and Miss Teri got married. I thought there was something sneaky and nasty about him, though he never actually did anything to warrant my dislike. Still, I instinctively knew he was not to be trusted. Him and Kitty always got along, but I shrugged it off as her just being a bad judge of character.

But now that we were all living together, I started getting uncomfortable with their friendship. He was always giving her money, complimenting her, and buying things for her. It didn't seem to bother Miss Teri, she kept commenting on how well they got along, but I ain't like the shit at all. Especially when he got into the habit of walking by her, reaching over, and then tickling her under the arms. Kitty would roll over in hysterical laughter, but weren't shit funny about it to me. After I witnessed it a couple of times I got really fed up.

"Why don't you just leave her alone?" I snapped at him.

He looked at me in surprise, then looked at Kitty like he was waiting for her to defend him or something. Miss

Teri said something about he was just playing, and I said, "Yeah? Well maybe he should stick to playing with people his own age."

Miss Teri got mad at me and told me to apologize. I just sucked my teeth and rolled my eyes. Mr. Leroy told Miss Teri to leave me alone, that I was still just adjusting to everything that happened in the last few weeks, but Kitty never did say nothing. She just lowered her eyes and slinked out the room. I decided then and there I needed to keep a closer eye on her and Mr. Leroy. I started staying in the apartment more, rather than hanging out with my friends, but I never did catch them doing anything else that I could jump on him about.

Then one Sunday Miss Teri said she needed me and Kitty to go with her to Delancey Street to do some clothes shopping. She wanted to go early because she wanted to get home in time to bake a cake and make a big dinner for Mr. Leroy because it was his sixtieth birthday, March 21. Kitty begged off, saying she wasn't feeling well. I then said I couldn't go because I wanted to stay home with Kitty, but Miss Teri made me feel guilty, saying she couldn't bring all the bags on the subway without me. I finally agreed to go. Mr. Leroy wasn't home, anyway, because he was at some lodge meeting and wouldn't be back until the late afternoon. I figured me and Miss Teri would beat him back to the apartment.

But when me and Miss Teri were walking to 116th Street to catch the number 2 train, we saw Mr. Leroy walking toward us. He told Miss Teri that he'd forgotten his lodge ring and was going home to retrieve it. She kissed him on the cheek and said she'd see him later. I ain't say shit. We bought our subway tokens and since it was a Sunday and trains were running slow we had to wait almost fifteen minutes for the train. But just as we was getting ready to board, a funny feeling came over me. I ain't say nothing to Miss Teri, I just turned around and ran back to the apartment, ignoring her shouts for me to come back.

I hauled up the stairs to the building, used the key that Miss Teri had given me when I moved in, and entered. The apartment was quiet at first, then I heard Kitty giggling, and the giggling seemed to be coming from Miss Teri's bedroom. I felt nauseous, like I was going to vomit, but I took a series of deep breaths, tiptoed to the room, and threw the door open.

There was Kitty laying naked on Miss Teri's bed, and Mr. Leroy's head buried between her legs.

I stood paralyzed for a moment that seemed like eternity. Then, just as I was getting my wits back and getting ready to shout, or attack, or something—I don't know what—Kitty looked up and saw me. She hurried up and pushed him off her and sat up in the bed. We stared at each other for two or three minutes while Mr. Leroy jumped up and started scrambling around putting on his clothes; we stared but said nothing. I was paralyzed again. Finally I was able to move, and I just walked out the bedroom and went to sit on the couch in the living room.

Through my daze I could hear Mr. Leroy telling Kitty to put on her clothes. Through my haze I could hear Kitty walk into the bedroom we shared. Through my fog I could hear Mr. Leroy come into the room with me and start babbling something about it wasn't what it looked like.

That he and Kitty were just horsing around. That I shouldn't tell anyone because they wouldn't understand. That he would be willing to pay me to keep my mouth shut. That I shouldn't be walking into people's bedrooms without knocking first.

Finally, after getting no response from me, he left the apartment. I was left alone to try and figure out my next move. My first instinct was to tell my relatives and the police what happened, but I wondered if I did would I be getting Kitty in trouble. After all, it wasn't like he was holding her down, raping her. But still, I couldn't let him just get away with it, could I? Maybe, I thought, I should just go find Brucie and tell him that Mr. Leroy tried to get fresh with me so Brucie could beat him up. But beating him up wouldn't be good enough. I didn't know what to do. But I knew I had to do something.

I was still sitting on that damn couch two hours later when Miss Teri came home with an armful of bags, yelling at me for abandoning her like that. I didn't say anything. When she walked into the kitchen to prepare dinner I followed her, sitting at the kitchen table, watching her as she cut up a fryer chicken, then started mixing cake batter. She'd only been home about twenty minutes when the telephone rang. She told me to answer it, but I didn't move. She muttered something about "not knowing what's wrong with the child," then went and answered it herself. From the sudden cheerfulness in her voice I could tell she was talking to Mr. Leroy, though I couldn't hear what she was saying. She came back in the kitchen all happy and shit and said that Mr. Leroy would be home in about an hour. I waited for another forty-five minutes, then walked into me and Kitty's bedroom.

She looked up when I walked in, then looked back down and started flipping through the *Jet* magazine in front of her without saying anything. I walked back in the living room and picked up the telephone.

"Aunt Pat, you need to get over here real quick. Something

bad just happened," I said in a dead voice. Before she could ask me what was going on, I hung up. The phone rang two seconds later, but I just picked it up and hung up without putting it to my ear. It rang again, and I did the same thing. I was hanging up for the third time when Mr. Leroy came through the front door. He looked at me as if he wanted to say something, but then just walked into the kitchen to talk to Miss Teri.

After five minutes I walked in and found him in the chair I was sitting in earlier, and Miss Teri just merrily prattling away while using one of the icing design thingees to write "Happy Birthday" on his cake.

"Miss Teri," I said in a surprisingly calm voice, "when I got home this morning I found Mr. Leroy in your bed with my sister."

She froze, and Mr. Leroy fell backwards in his chair onto the floor.

"What did you say?" Miss Teri asked.

Before I could answer, Mr. Leroy jumped up from the floor and shouted, "The girl's insane!"

"I found Mr. Leroy in your bed with my sister," I repeated calmly. "They were both naked, and he was licking her private parts."

"Ke-Ke, you must be mistaken," Miss Teri said frantically. "I know my husband, and he would never hurt a child. He's just not capable of anything like that."

"I know my sister, too," I responded. My temper was rising, though I was doing my best to keep it together. "And I didn't think she was capable of it, but I saw them with my own two eyes. He was eating her pussy."

Miss Teri's mouth dropped open. "You vulgar child," she

hissed at me. "Your mother would be ashamed to hear you use language like that."

"You're changing the subject. Your husband was molesting my sister," I said heatedly. "What are you going to do about it?"

Miss Teri looked at me for a moment and said, "I'm not doing a damn thing, including continuing to listen to your lies." She went over to the stove and started taking the chicken out of the frying pan. "And I suggest you not repeat them. Everyone knows the kind of man I'm married to, and they know he'd never do anything like that. Even if your sister was always trying to throw herself at him; which both you and I know she was."

I was getting ready to jump on her ass when I heard someone banging on the door. I looked at Miss Teri and Mr. Leroy and grinned. "Y'all hang on now. I'll be right back." I ran over to the door and swung it open. There stood my Aunt Pat, chest heaving from running up all the stairs, and behind her was her twin brother, my Uncle Pete, who had just returned from a long-distance moving job.

"Aunt Pat," I said, "I caught Mr. Leroy in bed with Kitty and I told Miss Teri and she said she ain't gonna do nothing about it." Then I stood aside and pointed to the kitchen. "They're in there."

Uncle Pete and Aunt Pat almost ran over each other trying to get in the kitchen. There was about ten seconds of screaming and shouting, and then I heard a howl. I walked into the kitchen just in time to see Uncle Pete bent over Mr. Leroy, pummeling him while the man lay on the floor. Aunt Pat had Miss Teri pinned against the stove and was choking her. She was already turning blue, and her eyes were popping out. As I was wondering how long it would take for her to die, I suddenly heard a piercing shriek. It was Kitty. She had finally come out the room and was standing in the doorway screaming at the top of her lungs. Aunt Pat made the mistake of letting go of Miss Teri and running over to grab Kitty in a bear hug. But as soon as Miss Teri was loose, she grabbed the frying pan off the stove and threw the hot grease on Uncle Pete's back. Thank God it was March and he was wearing a leather jacket, so the grease just rolled off him, but he did get a few splatters on his hand and his face, and he let out a howl and stood up. Mr. Leroy scrambled up from the floor, opened up the window, and started scurrying down the fire escape like he was sixteen rather than sixty. Uncle Pete started climbing down after him, and as I rushed over to the window I heard him shouting, "Nick! Nick! Get him. Get the bastard coming down the fire escape."

Wow! My Uncle Nicky was downstairs! Now, my father was crazy, but my Uncle Nicky was crazier. I mean really loco, and not in a nice way like my father. Uncle Nicky was crazy like going around cutting up people who looked at him the wrong way. As I watched from the window, Uncle Nicky took a straight razor from his back pocket, his favorite weapon, and ran under the fire escape to wait for Mr. Leroy to finish his descent. Well, Mr. Leroy stopped and looked at Uncle Nicky below him, and Uncle Pete above him, and he just started crying. He was still one level above the street when he jumped. Don't ask me why he decided to jump, because to this day I don't know. Well, he hit the ground and I think he broke his leg because he lay there for a moment, struggling to get up. Uncle Nicky ran over and grabbed him by the collar, then hollered up to Uncle Pete, "I got him. What you want me to do with him?"

"Slice that muthafucka up," Uncle Pete hollered back.

And good old Uncle Nicky, not knowing what was going on or what Mr. Leroy had done to deserve his fate, just started slicing.

I moved over from the window to see what was going on in the kitchen and saw my Aunt Pat stomping Miss Teri, who now lay on the floor unconscious. The cast-iron frying pan was lying next to her, and I guessed Aunt Pat had used it to crown her a couple of times. Aunt Pat finally got tired of stomping her and just stood there for a few minutes catching her breath, and then barked at me and Kitty to get our coats because we were getting out of there. I ran and got our coats, but Kitty just stood there, still crying. Aunt Pat had her in a big hug trying to comfort her, saying that she was not going to let anyone hurt her anymore. Then would you believe Kitty had the nerve to say that no one had done anything to her? Aunt Pat looked at her, then looked at me. Her eyes narrowed, and she said, "Which one of you is lying?"

I didn't say anything, I just pointed to Kitty. Aunt Pat stood up and slapped the shit out of her, sending her reeling across the room. It was the first time she had ever hit one of us kids, and it was a fucking wallop. Then she walked over and grabbed Kitty by the collar, almost choking her, and said, "You listen to me. Don't you ever lie to me, don't you ever lie to anyone to protect a man, and don't you ever think about lying to cover up for a fucking no-good, muthafucking pervert who molested you."

I could hear police sirens downstairs. "Aunt Pat," I said, tugging at her sleeve. "We gotta get outta here."

We all ran downstairs, Aunt Pat dragging Kitty by the arm, and hauled ass out the building. And wouldn't you know we ran smack into a police officer? He asked us why we were running, but before Aunt Pat could think of a lie Miss Hattie, from across the street, sprang into action. Miss Hattie used to run with my Aunt Pat back in the day, so even though she didn't know what the hell was going on, she was going to protect her running partner.

She jumped between us and the police officer and started screaming, "Oh my God. I seent it! I seent it all. These two teenagers cut that poor man up." She pointed to the bloody mess on the sidewalk that was Mr. Leroy. "I tried to stop them, but then they pulled their knife on me and they snatched my pocketbook. And it had all my rent money." She motioned behind her back for Aunt Pat to get the hell out of there.

"And they cut me. They cut me! See!" she yelled. She whipped open her coat, ripped her blouse down the middle then took one of her massive titties out of her bra. "See! Right here," she said, pointing to an imaginary cut. "They knifed me right here!" Then she collapsed on the ground.

Well, while the police were trying to tend to her, and calling an ambulance for Mr. Leroy, Aunt Pat hailed a cab, shoved me and Kitty inside, threw a five at the driver, and told him to just drive, but fast. We headed back uptown to Aunt Pat's place on 143rd. When we got to about 122nd Street we saw Uncle Pete and Uncle Nicky walking like nothing happened, even though Uncle Nicky's jacket and pants were covered with Mr. Leroy's blood. We stopped the cab, and told them to get in.

After we settled into Aunt Pat's house Kitty wanted to go straight to bed, but Aunt Pat called all the aunts and uncles for another family conference, like the one right after my mother's funeral. They questioned Kitty for hours, and it turned out that Mr. Leroy had seduced her when she was only eleven, and they had been sneaking around since then.

All my aunts were crying, and my uncles were all cursing, talking about they should go to the hospital and make sure Mr. Leroy was dead, and if he wasn't they wanted to make sure he soon would be. No one was afraid that either Miss Teri or Mr. Leroy would tell who had attacked them, because if they did he'd be arrested for child molestation. And the family also decided not to go to the police and report the molestation because as far as they were concerned, street justice was the best justice of all.

Turned out Mr. Leroy didn't die, but he was so sliced up he had to stay in the hospital for a month. When he was released he hightailed it back to Bermuda before Uncle Nicky or Uncle Pete could get to him. Unfortunately for Miss Teri, he left her behind. And for months, whenever Aunt Pat got too much rum in her she'd jump in a cab and go over to 117th Street, kick in Miss Teri's door, and beat the hell out of her. The only reason Aunt Pat eventually stopped going over there was because Miss Teri moved in the middle of the night, not letting anyone know where she was moving to. We figured she finally raised enough money to join her pervert husband in the Islands.

As for Kitty, no one in the family talked to her anymore about what had happened, and the decision was made not to tell David, Joe T., or any of the cousins about it. The aunts and uncles didn't want to embarrass Kitty.

But Kitty changed from that night on. She was still sweet, still loved animals, and was still generous, but now she was generous with more than just her candy. Kitty became an out-and-out slut, sleeping with any man who showed her the least bit of attention. The poor girl obviously needed counseling, but black folks weren't really much into sending kids to psychologists back in the 1970s. They figured with time everything would just work itself out. But as time went by Kitty just got worse.

Kitty was fucked up. And I was fucked up over her.

On March 21, 1974, I lost my twin.

* * *

"Yeah, Kitty, you do know that was messed up. If it was the other way around, you know Ke-Ke would have been there for you."

"Belinda, I love Ke-Ke just as much as she loves me, but I—"

"Look, Kitty, you don't owe me any explanation. I'm not trying to get on you like Joe T. is. I'm just saying."

"Cousin Belinda, don't you think we should just drop it? You know Mommy would just let it go."

That's right, Camille. I sure would. They need to stop picking on Kitty. I hate it when they get on her like that. But hell, they don't know her like I do. They don't know what she's been through. I never told anybody that wasn't there that night what happened with Mr. Leroy, and she sure as hell ain't.

"Look, I'm going to leave, but I'll be back in about an hour. I didn't even have a chance to talk to Ayoka and let her know I was coming to the States. I'm going to see if I can arrange to get the kids."

"That would be cool, Uncle Joe, but just so you know, you're not going to be able to bring them in here to see Mommy. The hospital doesn't allow children in to see patients."

"Really? That doesn't make sense. Here their aunt is recovering from brain surgery and . . . Okay, well we'll see."

Ha! If I know Joe T., by the time he gets through talking to the hospital staff they'll not only allow him to bring in little Akinseye and Anike, they'll apologize for ever having a regulation prohibiting children in the first place. That's my little bro! I'm so proud of him. Always keeps his head in the face of tragedy, and I guess what's going on with me could be classified as a damn tragedy. And damn, I've seen so much fucking tragedy. Kinda beats you down after awhile, you know? It kinda just makes you wanna just . . . man, it just wanna makes you just . . . damn . . . for a while it got me so down I wasn't feeling angry anymore, I was just feeling whipped. Numb. I mean, how much tragedy can one person stand? Especially when they're just a kid.

Gosh, I'm feeling so weak right about now. Maybe it's just the aftereffects of the surgery, but I really feel down.

nine

I wasn't even sixteen, and my life was falling apart. Falling? Let me rephrase that—my life had fallen apart. My father was in the nut house, my brother was a junkie, my mother had died, and my twin sister was molested by a pedophile and was now hell-bent on being a slut. I thought things couldn't get worse.

I was wrong.

A few months after Mommy died, Joe-Joe called from Bellevue to say that he'd be let out the hospital in a few days, and he had a big surprise. One that would change his life and everyone else's in the family. He said he wanted everyone gathered at Aunt Pat's house on the day of his release so he could make the big announcement. And everyone came. His mother—whom we called Mama—my Aunt Cora, Aunt Bernice, Uncle Pete, Uncle Nicky, and all of their kids. His cousins, the Osarios—Gee-Gee, Chino, Alfredo, and all of their kids—were there, too. And of course me, Kitty, and Joe T. were there. David wasn't, though. No one knew how to get in touch with him. Even though Aunt Bernice did her best to reel him in he was still roaming the streets, living the life of a heroin-addicted stick-up kid, and would be gone for weeks at a time, only coming back to stay with her when things got too hot.

Joe-Joe also invited all of his friends; even though he'd lived his entire life in Harlem he had developed friendships with a lot of artsy folks in Greenwich Village, many of them white. There was quite a crowd there, waiting on Joe-Joe. He finally came through the door about 8:30 p.m. carrying a shitload of boxes. He'd bought gifts for all of us kids, and for all of his sisters and brothers. Gold watches for the men, and gold rings, bracelets, and earrings for the women—all expensive stuff. And even a mink coat for Mama.

"Damn, Joe," Uncle Pete said. "Where'd you get the dough to buy all this? What? You robbed a bank or something?"

"Nope," Joe-Joe answered proudly as he helped Mama try on her new fur. "I wrote a book."

"You're kidding," people started saying, and "Oh, I'm so proud of you." Everyone started crowding around him, slapping him on the back.

"What's the title?" someone asked him.

"What's it about?" someone else asked.

"When did you write it?" someone else questioned.

"I actually wrote it about five years ago, but I started sending it out to publishers about eighteen months ago. Then I got a call at the hospital saying one of the publishers was interested. They even gave me an eight-thousand-dollar advance. I just cashed the check today."

"Wow!" I shouted. "We're rich!" Everyone started laughing.

"Well, eight thousand dollars doesn't exactly mean you're rich," one of the artsy white folks said.

"Shit, it might not make you rich, but it makes us rich," Aunt Bernice said. She turned to my father. "What's the title, Joe? And what's it about?"

Joe-Joe smiled, then sat down. "I can't tell you."

"Why not?"

"Just because. The time isn't right. But I'm going to have a book signing in midtown next week, when the book is released. And I want everyone there. You'll get all your answers then."

"Well, what's the name of the bookstore?" Aunt Pat asked.

"I can't tell you."

"Why not?"

"Just because. The time isn't right."

"Well, shit, how we supposed to go the bookstore for a book signing if we don't know the name of the bookstore?" Aunt Bernice said.

"Calm down," Joe-Joe said sweetly. "I'm going to tell you, just not right now. I have to wait until I feel its right with the universe."

You do remember I said Joe-Joe was crazy, right? The only other thing he told us was that he wrote the book under a pseudonym.

Everyone in the family knew there wasn't any point to trying to get any more information from him, but some of his friends continued pressing him, asking him to at least tell them who the publisher was; but Joe-Joe wasn't giving up any more info.

We partied and celebrated until about midnight, then everyone started going home. Joe-Joe was staying on 115th Street at the apartment of a friend who was out of town, but he told me, Kitty, and Joe T. that he was going to go apartment hunting, and his plan was to take us to our new place straight from the book signing the following week. Then he gave Aunt Pat three hundred dollars for taking care of us since Mommy died, and gave Aunt Bernice a hundred for taking care of David. He gave us all goodnight kisses, then took Mama home in a cab, promising us he'd come over the next day to take us to the museum to see some exhibit on Peruvian artifacts. I could tell by the look on Kitty's face that she was going to come up with an excuse for not going, but I looked forward to the outing. I had recently taken out a book on Inca cave drawing from the library, so the subject interested me. Joe T. wasn't too thrilled, but then when Joe-Joe said after the museum he'd take us to a comic book convention they were having downtown he brightened right up.

I helped Aunt Pat clean up after they'd all left. She started talking about how good it was see that Joe-Joe was cleaning up his act, that it was about time, and how it was a shame that it didn't happen before Margie—my mother—died.

"But, you know, he always did the best he could, I guess," she said whimsically. "It's not his fault he's crazy. What they call it? Paranoid something or the other."

"Paranoid schizophrenic," I told her.

"Yeah, that. But even though he's crazy, he's still the smartest person I knew. Your mom was smart, too. Me and Bernice used to eavesdrop outside the door whenever she came over to Mama's to see him. They used such big words we had to have a dictionary with us." She giggled. "But still, as smart as your mom was, Joe-Joe was smarter. Nope, doesn't surprise me the least he done wrote a book. Just too bad he didn't do it before she died. She'da been so proud."

"I hope the new apartment is on 117th Street," I said.

Aunt Pat looked at me and shook her head. "Girl, talk like you have some sense. If he got all that money he's gonna find you a nice fine place. Maybe downtown. Or even Long Island. 'Bout time you learned something about living outside of Harlem."

I didn't say anything, but I made up my mind to try and persuade Joe-Joe to get us an apartment on 117th Street the next day when he came to take us to the museum and comic book convention. I had no desire to leave Harlem.

But Joe-Joe didn't come for us the next day, and he didn't call. It wasn't like him, because Joe-Joe never lied, and he always kept his promises to us. I telephoned Mama's house, but she said she hadn't heard from him. I hadn't thought to ask him for the telephone number at his friend's apartment, and even though I knew the friend lived on 115th between Fifth and Lenox Avenues, I wasn't sure which building.

Two, then three days passed, and still no one had heard from him. We called the police, we called the morgue, and we even called Bellevue, but no one could locate him.

Then David popped up. We told him about Joe-Joe's visit, the book, and the promise he made to take us out, and that no one had heard from him since. But when I told him the name of the out-of-town guy whose apartment he was staying at, he said he knew exactly where the place was. Without another word, we got up and took the number 7 bus to 116th and Lenox, then walked one block to 115th.

The apartment was on the third floor, but as soon as we entered the building we could smell a foul stench. By the time we reached the third floor the smell was almost intolerable. The apartment was in the back, and as we walked toward it the smell became overpowering. Then I looked down at the foot of the door. There were flies buzzing angrily, trying to get inside. I fell back against the wall and started crying as David started kicking down the door. We found Joe-Joe in the bedroom, kneeling beside the bed, his hands clasped as if in prayer. His body had already started decomposing from the heat. It was June 20, the first day of summer.

It was also my birthday.

We never found out the name of the book Joe-Joe wrote, what pseudonym he used, or who his publisher was. No one doubted that he wrote a book, though. Joe-Joe didn't lie. He was crazy, but he didn't lie. For all we know that book might have been one that made the *New York Times* best sellers list that year. It might have made a million dollars in royalties. But because Joe-Joe was so secretive and so crazy, no one in the family ever benefited from it. We also don't know what happened to the money he had left over from his eight-thousand-dollar advance check. No money was found on him or in the apartment. I've always suspected he buried it in a hole somewhere rather than trusting a bank. It would just have been typical Joe-Joe.

★ ★ ★

"I'm with Joe T. on this one, Kitty. There's no way Ke-Ke's going to die. Brain tumor or no brain tumor . . . she's just too mean to die."

Huh?

"Cousin Belinda, don't say that."

"Aw, look at you smiling, Camille. You know I'm telling the truth."

"Well, okay, kinda, maybe, Cousin Belinda."

What the hell are they talking about? What's going on?

"Mean? No, I wouldn't say Ke-Ke was mean. She sure don't take no shit, though, never did. Our sister would haul off and beat your ass in a minute if you pissed her off. Right, Joe?"

"Yeah, I guess so. But like you said, she wasn't mean. She never bothered anyone who didn't first bother her."

"Okay, how about evil? I mean, not like wicked or anything, but Ke-Ke's one evil woman. People could just look at her and know not to mess with her."

"Yeah, I might go with evil, Belinda."

"Yeah, me too, Joe. I guess we could say Ke-Ke was evil. It was nice having an evil sister, though. Nobody messed with me 'cause they knew they had to deal with her.

"*Aunt Kitty, would you stop speaking in past tense? Dag. She's right here.*"

Now, see, I resent the fuck outta this. I ain't evil and I sure as hell ain't mean! Where do they fucking get off calling me some shit like that? And why would Camille let them get away with it? They're pissing me the fuck off.

"*You know, now that I'm thinking about it, Mommy wasn't mean or evil.*"

That's right, baby . . . you tell them!

"*You know what she is? Just what she always says she was, an Angry-Behind Black Woman.*"

"*Oh, go ahead and say it like she says it. An Angry-Ass Black Woman.*"

"*Yeah, Aunt Kitty. Even when she's happy and having a good time and smiling and everything, there is always something just below the surface just laying there waiting to boil over. Like she almost expects someone to make her boil over. I think that's what people sense, and why most people don't bother her. She's an angry woman, and they don't want to do anything to have her vent her anger on them.*"

"*Yeah, yeah, I think that's the best way to describe it, Camille. She's just what she says she is, An Angry-Ass Black Woman. That's your mother.*"

"*Yeah, uh huh, Joe. I can go along with that. Ain't that something? I think Camille hit it on the head. Something always there just below the surface. But you know, Joe, Ke-Ke wasn't always like that. Remember when we was real young she might get mad at something, and she might fight, but she didn't walk around with a chip on her shoulder. I wonder exactly when and why she turned angry.*"

Shit, if I could move I could tell Kitty when, why, and how it happened. It was that same year, 1974. When . . .

ten

*W*hile I loved the acting lessons at the Negro Ensemble Company, some of the people I most admired there had started getting on my fucking nerves. I don't know how many times I had listened to them go on about how they weren't gonna let "the man" keep them down and shit; but when I challenged them on who the hell "the man" was, they just said, "You know . . . the man."

"No, I don't know. What man?"

"Just the man," the pretty, high-yaller, aspiring movie star responded.

"But who are you talking about? Who's the man? Do you mean the white man? You mean the white man is trying to keep us down?"

"Well, yeah," she said hesitantly.

"Well, didn't you tell us one day that your grandfather was white? So is he trying to keep you down?"

"Well, no. I mean, not all white men. And it's not necessarily just white men."

"Okay. So then who's the man?"

"Forget it, Ke-Ke," she finally said. "You're too young to understand. You're just a kid."

"Yeah? Is that it? Or is it that you're too stupid to explain?" I challenged her. "Or is it that you heard someone else say it and it sounded fly so you decided to say it, too, even though you don't even know what the fuck you're talking about? Shit, I might be a kid, but at least I ain't no ventriloquist's dummy."

That didn't go over too well with her or the rest of the class, but Kris Keiser, Beverly's husband and the instructor of the class, thought it was funny as hell. Later I told him that I had at least some idea about who she meant when she talked about "the man." See, Joe-Joe was big into socialism, and really into Leon Trotsky—one of the architects of the Russian social revolution—and Fidel Castro, so I grew up learning about capitalism and how it's set up so that the working class has to be kept oppressed so that their labor can be exploited by the people who owned more than 90 percent of the capital of the country, even though they represented less than 10 percent of the country's population.

"So, if you know all that, why'd you jump on that poor girl?" Kris Keiser asked me.

"Because I hate people who go running off with the mouth and don't even know what they're talking about."

Some of the people who were there I really liked, though. Like Sarah Dash, from the singing group LaBelle. She was gorgeous, both inside and out. And, God, I really liked Kris Keiser. In fact, I had a crush on him. I'm sure he knew it, but to his credit, he never took advantage of it. He was always the perfect gentleman around me. Even took me under his wing as a protégée. Funny thing is, the whole time I knew him I never referred to him as "Kris," or "Mr. Keiser," I always called him by his full name, Kris Keiser. Don't ask me why. Hell if I know.

One of the biggest highlights of my life was when he decided to make me a production assistant on a film he was producing and directing called *The Portrait*. It starred one of the girls from the acting class, Alicia. Can't remember her last name. I do remember she was very pretty. It also costarred an older black actor whom everyone seemed to know and respect. His first name was Cornelius. Can't remember his last name. There was also a guy who was the gaffer—the one who did the lights—whose name was Toby. His name I remember. Toby MacBeth. As soon as I saw him it was like, forget Kris Keiser, I had a new crush. Ooh, Toby was fine! I was like, fifteen, and he was like, twenty-seven, with light-brown skin, an afro, thick eyebrows, and the dreamiest eyes I'd ever seen. I had more than a crush on him. I actually wanted to be his woman. I wanted to give him my fifteen-year-old cherry. I wanted to one day be his wife and bear his children. I wanted to grow old with him. I wanted to . . . well, you get the picture.

The problem was Toby didn't get the picture. Dude had to be blind.

Oh, he was real nice to me, and I know that the first day I met him I caught him looking at my ass, but see, Kris Keiser caught him looking at it, too. I can't prove that Kris Keiser talked to him about me, but I do know that was the last time Toby looked at me with anything that could pass for lust. Oh, we was cool, and we would hang out between takes on the stoop of the brownstone where we were filming, just shooting the breeze. He talked to me like I was a little sister, which I ain't like, but at least he was talking to me. When he asked me why I wasn't in school I told him about my experiences, and how my mother and father had backed me up in my decision. He thought about it for a while, and then said, "Well, you're not going to get too far without an education."

I replied that going to school didn't guarantee someone was getting an education, and he paused, and then said, "Yeah, you're probably right about that." Then he said that it was important that I didn't spend my time just goofing off and shit. I nodded. Then he asked if I liked to read and I told him I did.

"Oh, good. I have a book I'd like to recommend. You ever heard of Malcolm X?"

If it were anyone else I probably woulda looked at him like he was stupid, but I just said yeah. Then he said, "Well, you might want to read a book called *The Autobiography of Malcolm X*. It's pretty good."

And I said, "Yeah, it's real good. I read it a couple of years ago."

He looked pleased. Then he asked me what else I'd read. Shit, I didn't know where to start. I mean, I read everything from romance novels like Rosemary Rogers's *Sweet, Savage, Love* to nonfiction like Hitler's *Mein Kampf*. I decided since he was a kinda militant type of dude I could try to impress him by telling him about books I read written by black authors. "Um, I've read *Manchild in the Promised Land, Native Son, Invisible Man*—"

"Whoa. You read *Invisible Man*?"

I nodded, and continued. "Let's see, I've read everything by Langston Hughes—but I really like his Simple stories—and *Go Tell It on the Mountain* by James Baldwin—"

"*Invisible Man* by Ralph Ellison?"

I nodded again.

"And you're fifteen and you've read James Baldwin?"

"Yeah, I like him. I'm reading a novel written by him now." I reached in my little pocketbook and pulled out a copy of *Giovanni's Room*.

He looked at it and shook his head, then laughed. "Damn. I thought I was gonna give you a reading list, but I guess I should be asking you to recommend a few books."

We laughed, and after that he continued treating me like I was a little sister, but at least a very smart little sister. Me? I was still planning on making him the father of my children. I just had to figure out how. The first thing I had to do was remind him I wasn't a little girl, but a fine-ass teenager with a banging body. So I showed up one day wearing a white halter top and red hot pants. Kris Keiser took one look at me and sent my ass home to change. I was pissed. Toby hadn't even gotten a chance to see me. At that point I was like, "Fuck it, I'll just wait until the film shoot is over to make my move." I didn't have Toby's phone number or address, and I was pretty sure he was never going to ask me for mine, but I'd heard him tell Cornelius that he hung out at a bar named Turk's up on Eighth Avenue near 117th Street. Yeah, I'd bide my time and snag that fine muthafucka. I had no doubt. Remember, I was the bomb.

The movie wrapped in just a couple of weeks, but I didn't hit Turk's right away. I wanted to make sure that my shit was so tight that Toby's mouth would be watering when he saw me. That meant I had to save up some money to get some real fly clothes. I figured I'd be straight in a month or so. That was cool.

Unfortunately Beverly and Kris Keiser moved to Los Angeles right afterward, so that was the end of my free acting classes at the Negro Ensemble Company. I kinda missed going, but only kinda. I really missed the money I made babysitting, though. I guess I coulda got another job babysitting for another couple, but I didn't want to. I didn't like kids. Malik—Beverly and Kris Keiser's kid—was the only exception. For some reason I loved that kid, even though he was spoiled as hell. I think I missed him more than Beverly and

Kris when the family moved to Los Angeles. I sure as hell missed him more than I missed most of those so-called "enlightened" adults in the acting class.

I was still living with Aunt Pat, along with Kitty and Joe T.; Aunt Pat's daughter, Avis; and Uncle Peter's daughter, Tanya. I loved living there because Aunt Pat was real cool, and could cook her ass off. There were times, though, she got on my nerves. Like when she got drunk. Which was every weekend. She'd come home, and she'd grab whatever kid was around and hug them until their eyes almost bulged out, talking about she loved them. Now, yeah, it could have been a whole lot worse. I mean, shit, I know kids who would hide when their parents came home drunk because they know they was going to get the shit beat out of them.

I also had a problem with some of Aunt Pat's rules. Like having to be home by midnight. I mean, all the kids my age hung out all night. Well, at least all the kids I knew. Which means all the kids on 117th Street, where I still hung out whenever I could. This one particular Saturday night, I got permission from Aunt Pat to stay at my friend Trina's house, so at 1:30 a.m. I was out in the street with my friends, sitting on a car talking shit when another bunch of kids walked by, whooping and carrying on like they were at a party even though they was strolling through the streets. They had almost passed us when I realized I recognized one of the girls. Michelle. She lived in the Bronx, and I'd met her when I was going to junior high school out there. She and I almost had beef because she thought I liked her boyfriend. Truth was, he liked me, but I had no talk for that ugly mug. Anyway, she'd gotten up in my face, and we almost got into a fight but then some grown-ups broke it up. I hadn't seen her since.

So, as they're passing me by I turned my head real quick so she wouldn't see me, but I was too late.

"Hey, y'all! This is my best friend," Michelle said to her friends, giving me a great big hug. She stank of cheap wine and reefer, and I quickly pushed her off me.

"What's wrong with you?" she said with an attitude.

"Nothing. I just ain't know I was your best friend," I said with just as much 'tude.

"Shit, you know I always liked you."

"Yeah?" I eyed her up and down. "Then what's my name?"

"How the hell do I know?" Michelle started laughing, showing off her yellow decaying teeth. Yuck. She laughed so hard she fell into me, knocking me into the side-view mirror of the car I'd been sitting on. So I shoved her off me.

She looked like she was about to jump bad, but then one of the boys she was with pulled her away from me, and looked like he was about to say something to me. Of course, Brucie got in his face.

"What the fuck you gonna do?" he said with a grin.

Now, Brucie looked tough when he was six, but he looked downright dangerous at sixteen. His hair was cut real short, and its reddish brown color matched his complexion almost exactly, which really did make him look like a pit bull terrier, especially since he had dark, round eyes with a little hang at the bottom just like a puppy. He was still short, shorter than some of the girls in the group even, but he just looked like if you jumped the wrong way you was dead. It was obvious the other boy was high, but not high enough that he didn't recognize death when he saw it standing in his face. He started backing up, saying, "Man, I don't have any beef with you."

Brucie cocked his head to the side like he was deciding whether or not he should destroy him anyway, but I stepped in. "It ain't even all that serious," I said, moving in front of Brucie, much to dude's relief.

"Yeah, I remember your name," Michelle said suddenly. "It's Ke-Ke, right?"

"Uh huh," I answered.

"See, I told you you was my best friend," Michelle said triumphantly. "You don't remember Harry?" She pointed to the boy who'd almost met his death. I took a good look at him and shook my head.

"What?" Michelle said dramatically. "Come on! You don't remember my brother, Harry? Y'all was going with each other since you was, like, two years old."

"What the fuck you talking 'bout?" my girl, Trina, asked. "I've known her all my life, and I woulda known your brother if she'd been going with him."

Michelle squinted her eyes at Trina, as if trying to place her. "Well, I don't know what you talking 'bout. Ke-Ke lived right next door to me since she was born, and I don't know your ass."

"How the hell she live next door to you when she was born and raised right here on this block?" another one of my friends asked.

"Man, you don't know what you're talking 'bout," Michelle said, waving her off. "Ke-Ke lived in the Bronx. Matter of fact, she still does. Lives right next door to me. Right, Harry?"

"Nah, I don't even know her."

"Yes, you do! Stop playing!" Michelle punched him in his shoulder.

"I'm telling you, Chelle, I don't know her. And she don't live next door to us!" Harry insisted.

Michelle squinted her eyes again and looked at me again. "She don't? Damn. I must really be fucked up."

Brucie shook his head. "Man, you need to give me some of what you smoking."

Everyone started laughing. So then we all started clowning around and getting along. It was pretty cool, and I came to the conclusion that Michelle wasn't really that bad. So when she and Harry suggested we join their crew and go to some party in the Bronx, me and my friends said okay; especially after they told us there would be free reefer and liquor. I didn't drink or smoke at that time, but all my friends did. And hey, I liked going to parties. So we all walked over to the subway station on 116th Street to catch the number 2 train.

While we were waiting for the train Michelle and one of her girlfriends started passing a reefer. Like I said, I didn't really fuck with reefer like that, and I don't know why I decided to try it that night, but I did. I just took a couple of puffs, though, and passed it on, thinking the whole time that it was the skinniest joint I'd ever seen but putting it down to Michelle just being stingy with her shit. But let me tell you something, that shit was strong! By the time we got on the train I was floating! I know it had to take, like, thirty minutes to get to the Freeman Street station in the Bronx, but it seemed like thirty seconds. And when we got off the train and onto the platform I realized everyone was just as fucked up as me. We was laughing, even though no one had told a joke, and I mean really laughing, like tears streaming down our faces and shit.

The Freeman Street station is a platform station, you know, elevated tracks. So we're skipping and shit and getting ready to walk outside the station house and walk down the stairs to the ground when all of a sudden someone grabs my arm. It was Harry, Michelle's brother.

"Hey, Ke-Ke. Let's be smart about this."

"Huh?" I squint up at him. "What you talking about?"

"I'm talking about that." He pointed to the stairs everyone else had started down.

"What you mean?"

"They taking the long way." He pointed to the stairs again. "We gonna be smart and take the short way." He walked over to the platform railing and looked down at the ground, then looked back at me. "You see what I mean?"

I looked over the railing, then I looked back at him. "You mean, you think it would be faster to jump over the railing than to take the steps?"

He shook his head: "No, we don't jump over the railing. We just climb up on it, then step down. Then we only have one step, when they got, like, two hundred." He pointed to the stairs again, then tapped his head and said, "'Cause we're smarter than them."

Now, I was admittedly fucked up, but I wasn't *that* fucked up. It had to be a hundred-foot drop to the street! "Naw, I'm going down the stairs," I said, backing away.

"Okay, I'll see you when you get down there." Before I could stop him, and to be honest, I can't say I remember having any real urge to stop him, he climbed up on the railing, gave a smug smile, and stepped off.

I remember reading somewhere that even if a person intends to commit suicide by jumping from a height, they can't help but involuntarily give a yell on the way down. Well, I swear, not one sound came out of Harry's mouth. I didn't want to look down over the railing, but for a moment I wondered if he'd actually been right. Then I heard someone screaming down on the ground. I took my time going down the stairs; the rest of my crew had already made it down. When I reached the street I saw a crowd of people standing around Harry. He wasn't dead. He wasn't even unconscious. But he was real fucked up. One leg was bent under him, and the other was sticking out at a very unnatural angle. But you know what? This fool actually looked up at me, with blood streaming out his nose, ear, and from the back of his head, and said: "I told you I'd beat you down."

Well, that started me and all my friends laughing hysterically for a few minutes before it hit me. We were acting really weird. I mean, shouldn't one of us have been screaming or running around frantically looking for a pay phone to call 911 for an ambulance? I stopped laughing, and shared this really deep insight with the rest of my friends. And they all got quiet and nodded their heads. Then we started loudly lamenting what horrible friends we were.

"And you!" I shouted at Michelle. "You're his own sister!"

"You're right!" She started nodding her head frantically, her eyes as big as two dinner plates. "Wait! Maybe I'm not his sister!"

By this time Harry had passed out. And thank God there were other people in the street because one of them called for an ambulance. When they came and put broken-up Harry in the back, we had to actually toss Michelle in there with him. She was really convinced that she wasn't his sister! When the doors slammed shut and the ambulance took off I turned to Brucie and said, "I don't know what the hell is wrong with us. We're all acting strange."

Brucie nodded, then cocked his head, and without saying a word he took off after the ambulance. I mean, he took off like he was superhero or something. I almost imagined him leaving smoke in his wake. Do you know he actually managed to catch them before they got to the corner? He grabbed one of the back door handles while it was still in motion and he pulled himself up and started banging on the door. (Yes, yes, I know this sounds unbelievable, but it really all happened!) The ambulance finally stopped, and he pulled Michelle out and dragged her back to where we was standing.

"Where did you get that reefer?" he demanded.

"From right here," she said, patting her pants pocket.

"Well, where did you buy it?" Brucie grabbed her by the shoulders and started shaking her, and her head started limply rocking back and forth like a Raggedy Ann doll.

"Brucie, stop!" I managed to get Michelle away from him. "Now, please, just tell us where you got the reefer."

"Some guy gave it to me," she finally answered. She handed over the bag, and me, Brucie, and the rest of my friends took turns looking at it. We all agreed that it looked like regular marijuana to us.

"Then how did we get so messed up after sharing a couple of skinny joints?" someone asked.

"Oh," Michelle said slowly. "Oh," she said again. "Oh!" she now said loudly. "He sold me the nickel bag, but he had two skinny joints already rolled up in the bag. Said it was a gift."

"Shit!" Brucie exclaimed. We all turned and looked at him.

"What's wrong?" I asked in a low voice.

"I was wondering why that shit smelled funny. This bitch done got us smoking angel dust."

"What!"

It was 1974. Angel dust, or PCP, had just hit New York. It was some kind of drug—elephant tranquilizer or some shit—that was mixed into marijuana so it could be easily smoked. We'd heard of it, but not one of us had ever seen or smelled it, and we sure as hell ain't smoked it. But we'd heard the stories. As a matter of fact, just a few days before there was a news report about some guy on 119th Street who smoked angel dust and killed his mother, then wrote on the wall in her blood, "I Love My Mommy."

Brucie looked at Michelle. "Bitch!" he shouted. "I'm going to kill you!" She took off running, and he took off running after her. I started running after them, but I lost them after a few blocks. That's when I looked around and realized that none of the kids were behind me.

I walked a couple of blocks thinking about what exactly I should do. By the time I figured out I needed to get my ass home I decided to try and find the train station, but couldn't find that. Somehow I wound up in the middle of Crotona Park, and by this time I was sleepy as hell. I saw a bench, and decided to take a nap. Bear in mind that here I was, high for the first time in my life, and I was high off angel dust, so I wasn't thinking straight. So, yeah, I laid my ass down on the bench and took a nap.

The next thing I knew someone was nudging me. I rubbed my eyes and sat up and saw this middle-aged Puerto Rican guy looking at me. "Why you sleeping in the park?" he asked me.

"I ran away from home," I replied, for some strange reason.

"Oh. But you shouldn't be sleeping in the park."

"I ain't had no place else to sleep," I said.

"Well, you can sleep at my sister's place. She's a real nice person and she likes company. I'm on my way to work, but I'll stop you over there, okay?"

"Nah, that's okay. I'll be all right."

"Well, are you hungry? You want me to buy you something to eat?"

As soon as he said that, my stomach started grumbling. He started laughing, and I did, too. I asked him where we could get something to eat and he said we could walk a couple of blocks to a bodega that some of his friends owned. He told me his name was Tony, and I told him mine, and then we walked over to Intervale Avenue, and he had me wait outside while he went in the store.

I sat on a car and started dozing off again. He nudged me when he came out the store and handed me about a dozen slices of hard salami wrapped up in waxed paper, and a small box of soda crackers. Now, being that my father's side of the family is Puerto Rican, I was familiar with soda crackers—which are like saltines but a lot drier!—and I knew that a lot of folks used them to make sandwiches, so I quickly made a few. But boy, after eating just one I was thirsty as hell, and I told Tony so. I asked him if he had enough money to buy me an orange soda, and he nodded yes and went back into the store. He came back out with a can of Ballantine beer. I was like, "Nah! I don't like beer." But before I could get the words totally out my mouth right, he opened the can.

"Man, I can't take it back now, 'cause it's opened, and I don't have no more money," he whined as he handed me the can. I was thirsty, them dry-ass soda crackers had my mouth devoid of saliva, so I wrinkled up my nose and took a couple of sips. Then I ate a couple more soda-cracker-and-salami sandwiches, and started steady sipping on that beer until it was gone. I didn't even realize he had gone back into the store until he came out and handed me another beer, which I gratefully took as I was still wolfing down the soda crackers and salami. Didn't occur to me to ask why he bought another beer when I told him I didn't like it. Didn't occur to me to ask why he lied and said he didn't have anymore money. The beer on top of the angel dust I'd smoked made sure that shit didn't occur to me. And by the time I drank down that second can of beer my head was spinning, but I was feeling fine.

"So, you want me to take you to my sister's house?"

I shook my head. "I changed my mind. I'm not running away from home anymore."

"Why'd you want to run away home from anyway?" Tony asked me.

I shrugged my shoulders. "I don't know."

Tony looked at me strangely for a few moments, then said, "You want me to walk you home?"

"Naw, I'm okay."

"You sure? It's two-thirty in the morning. You shouldn't be walking home by yourself."

"I don't live around here. I live in Harlem, so I gotta get on the subway," I explained. "But, um, you could loan me some money 'cause I don't have any money to get on the train."

"Yeah, okay. Oh! I don't have any money, remember?" he said. "But wait right here, I can get some from my friends who own the bodega." So he walks back into the store, then comes back out a few minutes later with another beer. "They said okay, but they want us to wait, because they're getting ready to close the store," he said, handing me the can. "And when they do they're going to count up the money in the register and then give you some money to get home."

"But I don't need but thirty-five cents to get on the subway," I whined.

"I told them that. But they said it was too late for a young girl to be getting on the subway by herself, and I agree—so they're going to give you five dollars so you can catch a cab."

I nodded, as I drank the beer. Hell, if they were going to spring for a taxi, I'd wait a little bit. Hell, I was feeling more than a little woozy, so being jolted back and forth on a train didn't appeal to me, anyway.

It was just a few minutes later that Tony's friends locked

up the store. I nudged him, figuring that since they were pulling down the metal gates, they must have already counted up the money, and so they could give me the cab fare home. It was starting to rain, so I really wanted to hurry up and get out the weather.

"No, they gotta go upstairs to count it. They never count it in the store."

"Upstairs where?"

"Right there," he said, pointing to the building above the store. "They own the building. We can go up with them, get the money, and then I'll catch a cab for you."

"Man, I don't know them dudes. They might be rapists or something. I'm not going to their apartment." I was getting frustrated.

"No, no, they don't live there," Tony said quickly. "They own the building, so they're going to count the money in one of the vacant apartments, and then give you the money and everyone can be on their way."

"I don't know—"

"Come on, it won't take a minute, they count fast. And I gotta go to the bathroom."

Now that he'd mentioned it, I had to go to the bathroom, too. I guess it was all that beer. Reluctantly, I agreed. We walked upstairs to an apartment on the fourth floor, and when they unlocked the door I could see it was indeed a vacant apartment, though there was three folding chairs and a card table that had an adding machine on it. It seemed legit. The two friends pretty much ignored me, as they sat down and started pulling cash and food stamps out of a money bag and placing it down on the table. I turned to ask Tony where the bathroom was, but he was gone, he'd beat me to it. I leaned against the wall and waited for him to come out, crossing my legs as my bladder swelled to an enormous size and threatened to burst. He finally came out, and I darted in. Oh, good, it felt good to relieve myself. So good, that I must have fallen asleep on the toilet. I woke up when I heard someone knocking on the bathroom door.

"You okay in there?" Tony asked through the door.

"Yeah, I'll be right out."

But when I came out I found that the two guys had left. Only Tony was left in the apartment.

"Oh, man, please tell me they didn't leave without giving you the money!"

"No, no, I got it," Tony said in a quiet voice.

I breathed a sigh of relief. "Great, let's get out of here. I got to get some sleep."

"Yeah, I heard you snoring in there." Tony laughed, and I joined in.

"Say, why don't you rest up here for a little bit, so you don't fall asleep in the taxi?" Tony said, suddenly, as if the idea just occurred to him. There's a little cot in the back room, and—"

"No, no, no, that's okay," I said quickly.

"Why not?" Tony stepped close and started rubbing my neck. Now I was getting freaked out, and I tried to push by him and run out the door; but he grabbed me by the arm before I could get away.

"Hey, what's the matter?" he said soothingly. "Don't worry. I won't leave you here by yourself. I'll sleep out here on the living room floor while you take a nap in the bed. I promise I won't let anyone bother you."

"No, that's okay. I'd rather just go home," I insisted, still trying to pull away.

"Why?" He roughly pulled me so close to him I could

feel his breath against my face. And then he pulled me even closer, and suddenly I was pressed against his body.

"Please, let me go. I just wanna go home." I started crying.

"Now look, why you crying, *mija*? You scared? I'm not going to hurt you. I just want to look after you."

"I don't need looking after," I insisted. The more I pulled away, the more he pulled me toward the bedroom. So now I stopped doing the little-girlie whining, struggling thing . . . I hauled off and smashed him in the nose. He let me go for just a moment, and I darted for the door. But there were three deadbolt locks on the damn thing, and all of them were locked and I couldn't get them undone in time. He grabbed my hair from the back, swung me around, and slapped me in the mouth, then a few more times across the face. I tried to bring my knee up to smash his balls, but he kept me off-balance, using my hair to swing me one way and then the other. Somehow, I managed to clamp my teeth into his arm, and I was determined to take a chunk of meat out of it, but he jammed his free fist into my face so hard I actually saw stars. Up until that time I thought that was just a figure of speech, but I literally and actually saw stars. I started sinking to the floor as he continued to punch me, now in the chest and stomach. I was no longer fighting at that point. I was just doing my best to cover up. He picked me up and carried me into the back room, with me still trying to get away. The next thing I knew I was being thrown on the cot. I let out a scream and tried to get up, but he punched me in my right eye. Again, I saw stars, but I was determined to fight through them, and I punched him back as best as I could, and tried to bite him again. So that's when he started choking me. I clawed at his hands around my throat, but he just tightened his grip. Things began to go black. I passed out. I came to, and my pants and panties were gone, and he was standing over me unbuckling his pants. I tried to jump up, but he pushed me back down again, one hand choking me, the other pulling his pants down. I fought him as hard as I could, I swear I did. I was trying to either break free, or to make him mad enough to choke me hard enough to kill me. I was unsuccessful at both.

Pain. Throughout that entire fight, the stars, the blacking out, and the choking I had not actually felt any pain; I guess my adrenaline level was too high. But as he started pushing into me I felt the most excruciating pain I'd ever felt. I was fifteen and a virgin, but I was not naïve; most of my girlfriends had already had sex and I'd read enough books to know that when a female had intercourse the first time it was supposed to hurt, but I had no idea it would be that painful. It wasn't a sharp pain; it was more like someone was trying to bore a hole in my body with a blunt instrument. If that wasn't bad enough, I could barely breathe, because he was still choking me with one hand. All I could do was cry silently and wait for it to be over.

Finally, it was. He collapsed on top of me, releasing my throat. By now I was so weak I couldn't even push him off me. He finally rolled off, but he still wouldn't let me out the bed. I turned my back to him and, facing the wall, I just cried and cried.

"I'm sorry. I didn't know you was a virgin," Tony said quietly. He started stroking my arm. I ignored him, and just kept sobbing. "I thought we liked each other, and that you was just playing hard to get.

"But I should have known you was a virgin. You're such a good girl. Such a good little girl." He started kissing the back of my neck, and I tried to turn around and get out the bed, but he shoved me against the wall. "Such a good little girl.

Such a sweet little girl. You gonna be my girl, okay?" I panicked as I felt him pressing his body against me. I tried to use my arms to push back against the wall and get away, but he managed to grab one, and then the other; then pulled them above my head as he entered me from behind. First he raped me vaginally, now he raped me anally. I screamed until I was so hoarse that I lost my voice. This time it took longer for him to finish. When he did, I was so traumatized I didn't even try to get up.

Tony lay next to me for a few minutes, then he slowly got up. "You want some water? Or some juice?"

I didn't answer.

I didn't move.

I couldn't.

I was shattered.

I hurt all over, the pain from the beating I had taken and the double rape I'd experienced was overwhelming, and added to that was my mental and emotional pain; after all, I had brought this all on myself. I lay there and went over in my mind all of the mistakes I had made that led to me being violated. Was it the angel dust that clouded my judgment so much that I would have gone off with a stranger? Why did I drink that beer? And if he had bought it by mistake, and didn't have enough money to buy me the orange soda that I wanted, how could he have bought me the second beer? And the third? And why couldn't his friends have just given him five dollars from the register, and then just added that to their total when they added up their receipts? How could a girl as smart as me be so damn dumb?

I jumped at the sound of Tony's voice, then turned around and sat up in the bed. He'd refastened his pants and was holding a can of orange soda.

"Look at what I found in the refrigerator," he said sheepishly, handing it to me.

I nodded, avoiding his eyes. "Can I get dressed now?"

"Oh, yeah, of course," Tony said, as if it hadn't occurred to him that I would need to ask. As if he hadn't been holding me a prisoner. As if he hadn't just beaten and raped me. Go figure.

I got up and dressed, not bothering to wash up beforehand. I just wanted to get out of there. When I finished, Tony—who'd been sitting on the bed watching me—grabbed me by the hand.

"So, you going home now?"

I nodded.

"You don't want to be my girlfriend?"

I hesitated. I didn't want to piss him off, but I couldn't bring myself to tell that big a lie. I bit my badly swollen lip and softly said no.

"I didn't know that. I wouldn't have made love to you if I didn't think we were going to be boyfriend and girlfriend. I'm not that kind of guy."

Make love? Did he really call what he'd done to me "making love?" I should have been furious, but I was too tired, too drained. I just wanted to go home.

"Um, Tony, did they leave that five dollars with you?" I asked, timidly.

He looked at me strangely, then took a wallet out of his pocket and pulled out fifty dollars. "Here. You can have this. I thought I lost my wallet, but I had it in my pocket the whole time. This is enough for you to catch a cab and have something left to buy some new clothes, *verdad*?"

I took the money.

I was back on 117th Street less than an hour later, close

to five-thirty in the morning. Dawn had begun to break by the time I had the taxi drop me off on the corner, and slowly walked toward Tina's building, tears streaming down my face. I got to the building, and suddenly I couldn't take another step. I sat on the stoop, buried my face in my hands, and just started sobbing hysterically.

"What's wrong with you?"

It was Brucie's voice. Where did he come from? I turned away with my head still lowered and softly said, "Nothing."

"What do you mean, 'nothing?' Why you crying, then? And where you been? I was worried about you," Brucie said, sitting down next to me. "Man, that shit we smoked had me fucked up." He started laughing. "I never did catch that girl. Then I turned around and you was gone. How'd you get back downtown to Harlem?"

I shrugged, but still avoided looking at him.

"Man, you can be really stupid sometimes," he said, then playfully shoved my head.

I jumped up and started screaming, or the closest I could get to screaming since I still barely had a voice, and started running.

"What the hell?" I heard Brucie say before he took off after me. He caught up with me in just a matter of seconds, and swung me around to face him. "Girl, have you . . . *Oh my God, what the fuck happened*?"

It had never occurred to me that I must have looked like I'd been run over by a truck and then fallen off a cliff. Later I found out that I looked worse. I had two black eyes, swollen lips, knots all on my forehead, and bruises all over my body.

"Ke-Ke, what the fuck happened to you?"

If I wanted to get revenge, this was my opportunity. Brucie woulda went up to the Bronx to hunt Tony down and kill him—and kill him slowly at that. Then he would have set both the store and the building on fire.

"Ke-Ke, tell me—"

"Nothing. I just got jumped by some girls." I chickened out. I couldn't do it. As much as I wanted Tony to die, I couldn't bring myself to tell Brucie what happened. I was too ashamed. I mean, after all, I was partly to blame.

"Some girls jumped you?" Brucie said incredulously. I don't know why he'd think I was lying, but I could tell he did. Then without a word, I confirmed his unvoiced suspicion. I started crying hysterically, and tried to bury myself into his broad chest.

"Whoa, whoa, come on now, girl," Brucie said soothingly, patting me on the back as he led me back to the stoop.

Comforting was not Brucie's strongpoint, but God bless him, he did his best. He kept pressing me to tell him what really happened but I refused. Saying it was nothing, just a stupid beat down by some girls who said I was on their turf. I thought it sounded believable, because there were all kinds of gangs roaming around the Bronx back in the seventies—The Black Spades, The Royal Knights, The Savage Skulls—and they all had their female counterparts who were extremely territorial. But Brucie wasn't going for it.

"Ke-Ke, just tell me what happened for real. You don't think I can take care of it? Man, I wanna fuck a nigga up over this shit."

"No, just sit here with me a minute, okay? I'll be alright."

So we sat there on the stoop, silently, Brucie's arm around my shoulders pulling me close to him. We must have been there a half hour or so when people started coming out the different buildings, heading to work.

"Oh God, I can't let anyone see me like this."

Brucie stood up, and pulled me up with him. He grabbed me around the shoulders again, and started walking me toward his building. "Come on, my mom's not home. You can hole up over at my crib for awhile."

"No!" I stopped in my tracks, and threw his arm off me. "No! You can't fool me. I'm not going into no house with no boy."

Brucie looked at me, and his mouth opened as if he was about to say something, but then he stopped and let out a gasp. I could see it in his eyes. He knew. And a wave of shame enveloped me so tightly that I actually fell to my knees and started crying again.

"Goddamnit! Goddamnit!" Brucie ran over to a car and started punching it and kicking it, then ran over to one of the large steel garbage cans filled with trash, lifted it over his head, and threw it down on the ground, spewing rotten food, empty cans, and dirty diapers on the sidewalk. "Fuck! Shit! Goddamn! Fuck!"

It was enough to bring me back to my senses, and I ran over to Brucie to try to bring him back to his. "Brucie, please calm down. I—"

"Who did it?! Huh? Who did it?" Brucie backed away from me, and I could see there were tears in his eyes. "Why don't you tell me?" He closed his eyes and lifted his head up toward the sky, stamped his feet one after the other, and shouted at the top of his lungs, *"Why won't you tell me?"*

"Brucie, let's get out of here, please." People were looking, and while I knew they wouldn't have the nerve to approach Brucie themselves, someone might call the cops. "Come on, let's go to your place. Please, come on."

We took turns dragging each other the twenty or thirty feet to his building, saying nothing; me with tears streaming down my face, his tears threatening to overflow the puppy-like sag in his eyes.

"I don't wanna know what happened, okay? I really don't," Brucie said in a calm voice once we were in his apartment. "All I want to know is who. Just tell me who."

"Let it go, Brucie."

"I ain't letting shit go!" Brucie shouted. He stood there, breathing hard, looking at me as if he was going to punch the shit out of me. Instead he turned and punched the shit out the wall. Put a big hole in it. Thank God it was plaster and not cement. He woulda broke his fist.

"How you gonna tell me to let it go? You're my friend. You're like my sister," he wailed.

"Then treat me like a sister! Be my friend!" Now I was hysterical again. "Goddamn, motherfuck, let it go! You just making me feel worse. Brucie, stop it! *Be my friend, damn it!*"

He ran over to me and pulled me into his arms, and just let me cry. He led me to the couch and we sat, him still holding me, me still crying.

I woke up seven hours later. There was a basin of water on the coffee table, with a rag floating in it. The rag and the water were both a pale pink. I reached up and touched my face. Brucie had washed it while I was asleep. I got up and went in the kitchen, and found Brucie there on the phone. He hung up when he saw me.

"You okay?"

I nodded. "I guess so."

"I got you some clothes since yours are, you know, so fucked up." He pointed to a couple of blouses and three pairs of pants that were folded over a kitchen chair, their price tags dangling. There were even three packs of panties. I didn't bother asking him where he'd gotten them. Just about everyone on 117th Street knew how to boost clothes from stores. I went into the bathroom, took a shower, and put on the new clothes. Only then did I look in the mirror. I still looked like shit.

Brucie rode back in the cab with me to Aunt Pat's house and stood there silently as I once again blamed my appearance on a stray bunch of girls. Aunt Pat believed the lie, thank goodness. She fussed over me, and made me get into bed immediately.

For the next three weeks Brucie came over to Aunt Pat's house every day, and wouldn't let me out of his sight. If I went to the store, Brucie went with me. If I went to the park, Brucie went with me. If I went job hunting, Brucie went with me. If I went to 117th Street Brucie was there to escort me, and take me back. At first it irritated me because it was a reminder of that horrible night, but after awhile I didn't want to go anywhere without Brucie. He never mentioned the incident again. Neither did I. I never told anyone what really happened.

One day Brucie didn't come over. By evening time I was so worried I went over to 117th Street to find him. No one on the block knew where he was. His mom was still down south with his brothers, so I couldn't ask her. I went back to 117th Street the following day, and it was Sheila who broke the news. Brucie was dead. He was walking down the street on the Upper East Side, near 61st and Second Avenue, when a couple got mugged. The police pulled up on Brucie, but he didn't run since he hadn't done the robbery and didn't know anything about it. Well, the cops jumped out the car and told Brucie to assume the position, and he complied. Knowing Brucie, he probably shot off his mouth a bit, but he complied. This was all according to witnesses, mind you. Well, when one of the officers frisked him he must have touched him the wrong way, or said something to him, or some kind of crazy shit happened because according to what witnesses told the newspaper, Brucie turned around and pushed the officer. That's when the dude's partner shot Brucie dead. They called it a justified shooting since Brucie had assaulted the officer by pushing him. I don't know if they ever caught the real mugger.

I was wondering what the hell Brucie was doing up on 61st and Second Avenue at 5:30 in the evening—the Upper East Side was where the rich white folks lived. I found out, though, when Brucie's mother came up from South Carolina and got his belongings from the coroner's office. There was a long thin jewelry box, with the name of a jeweler's on 57th Street. Inside the box was a beautiful gold chain with a pendant that said "Karen" in script. I didn't know that Brucie even knew my real name.

A couple of weeks later I was in the dentist's office getting one of my wisdom teeth pulled because it was impacted. It was a welfare dentist, of course. And I should have known better, even if he did have a midtown office in a nice neighborhood. He gave me gas to knock me out while he pulled the tooth, but then wouldn't you know the bastard started yanking on the tooth before I was fully under? The real fucked-up thing was I under enough to not be able to move or scream out, but not enough so that I didn't feel the pain, and it was horrific. Fucking welfare dentist.

But then the weirdest thing happened. My brain started reeling, and I felt like I was spiraling downward into some other dimension or astral plane or something. Then when I got to the bottom there was a girl who looked just like me. I mean identical, down to my hairstyle and the clothing I was wearing. I stared at her for a minute, then said, "Who are you?"

She started laughing, then said, "You wouldn't know, would you?"

I shook my head no, still trying to figure out what was going on.

Then she said, "I'm you, but I'm better."

"What do you mean?"

"I'm you like you oughta be. Like you would be if you had any kind of sense. I'm the you who knows how take care of herself, and take care of anyone who tries to fuck with her. I'm the strong you. I'm the you who fights."

"I know how to take care of myself, and I know how to fight," I protested.

"No, you don't. You just know how to fight back." She started laughing. "I'm the one who fights, and who will make sure no one fucks with me. How do you like that?" She got up close to my face. "And I'm tired of you just accepting shit like it's okay. Me? I don't accept shit. I take. And I'm tired of your stupid ass acting lately like everything is just fate." She started jabbing me in the chest with her finger, and each jab felt like a hot poker going into my heart. "I make my own fate. I make my own way. You got that?"

I nodded, too intimidated to say anything else.

"In fact, I'm so tired of your ass that I'm going back instead of you."

"What do you mean? Going back where?"

She looked upward. "When the gas wears off I'm going to be the one sitting in the chair. You're going to stay here where you belong."

"No!" I shouted.

"Yes!" she shouted back.

"No!"

"Yes!"

I went to grab her, but just as I did I started feeling dizzy, and the next thing I knew I was coming out from under the anesthesia.

I groggily stumbled out of the dentist chair and onto the street, wondering if I was me, or the other me. Which one of us had made it back?

I felt too out of it to take the bus from midtown to Aunt Pat's house, so I decided to take a cab using the money I had. There was an empty yellow cab stopped at the red light, and so I just hopped in. "One Forty-third and Seventh, and don't give me no fucking shit about you don't want to go to Harlem."

The driver turned around and looked at me in surprise.

"Miss, you don't have to curse at me. You don't know I was going to say anything about going to Harlem, now did you?"

"No, I didn't," I snapped. "But if you did I would have been pissed. And better you be pissed than me. Got that?"

The driver pulled off without another word. And as we drove uptown I now knew. I knew who had come back.

I was suddenly, and forever more, An Angry-Ass Black Woman.

★   ★   ★

What? Get the fuck outta . . . Yeah, you'd better back the fuck up, bitch! Thinking I'm fooling around with your ass or something? Shit! Come on back this way, trying to whisper in my ear that I should just let go so the pain will stop. Yeah, motherfucker . . . I got your "let go" right here. Just 'cause I can't see you, and I can't move, don't mean I won't beat the shit outta you! Didn't you hear me before when I said if Death came pulling on my sleeve I would kick her ass? Think just because I had a brain tumor you could fuck with me? Go ahead and try me again, bitch, and see what happens!

"Camille, girl, you look beat. Girl, I know you must be tired. Umph. Look at your eyes all bloodshot and shit. Girl, you better be careful or it's gonna be you all laid up in the hospital and us worrying about you. Did you have anything to eat? Did you eat breakfast? Girl, I stopped at Dunkin' Donuts and got some coffee and hash browns. You want some?"

"That's okay, Cousin Sister. I'm fine."

Breakfast? Huh? How long did I drift off for? It was evening the last time I heard them talking. And who's here now? Wait! Did I hear Camille say Cousin Sister? Oh, great! Sister is here! I should have expected her to come see about me. Even though she and I weren't very close growing up, she was my girl once I was old enough to start hanging out. She always looked out for me. Thank God for Sister.

"Ooh, girl, your mother looks bad. I mean, I wasn't expecting her to look like no beauty queen, but I didn't know she was gonna look like that. Girl, did they shave off all her hair? And why is her face all bruised? Camille, girl, you don't look much better. Girl, you slept in the chair? Why didn't you just tell the nurse to wheel you in a cot or something? Girl, I bet if you asked they would do it."

"I was okay, Cousin Sister. Don't worry."

"Yeah, okay, girl. I just hate to see you being all worried like this. Did my sister make it over here yesterday?"

"Uh-huh. Cousin Belinda was here for a couple of hours. Uncle David, Aunt Kitty, and even Uncle Joe was here, too. You can just move those books to the night table so you can sit on that chair."

"Joe T. was here? Girl, I thought he was still in Africa somewhere. But I know how he is about Ke-Ke, so I bet as soon as he heard he got on a plane, huh, girl? What about your father?"

"My father?"

Huh? Why would Sister suggest Camille call him? The fuck???

"Yeah, your father. Girl, you didn't call and tell him that your mother just had brain surgery? I mean, I know y'all don't necessarily get along, but still."

"Cousin Sister, I don't think it's a problem me not calling my father. He probably wouldn't care all that much, anyway."

"Well, girl, how's that going to look? You not calling him?"

"Believe me, Cousin Sister. It's okay."

Shit. Camille knows the deal. Why the fuck would I want that bastard to know what's going on in my life? He can kiss my ass!

eleven

*H*e hit me! This big-ass fucking bastard just slapped the shit out of me! I lay there on the floor for just a moment, trying to get my head together, and the stupid motherfucker made the mistake of walking away. Did he really think that was going to be the end of it? I leaped up, grabbed a hammer from the counter, and tried to kill my husband.

He was six foot three, and I was five feet—so though I tried to smash the back of his head in, my blow only landed on his shoulder. He yelled, and I hoped I'd broken it, but no such luck. He swung around and lunged at me. I raised the hammer to try and knock the shit out of him, but he managed to grab my arm, pull the hammer from my hand, and throw me across the room. I landed on the floor next to the coffee table, and as he rushed toward me I picked up the telephone and smashed it into his face. *Bam!* That got results.

"You bitch, I'm going to kill you!" he yelled as he backed up. Both his nose and lips were bleeding.

"Yeah, motherfucker, I got your bitch right here," I taunted while swinging the telephone receiver by its curly cord. "Come on and get some more of this!"

He lunged again, and I took that receiver and started going upside his head like I was banging on a set of steel drums. He was punching me, and I was banging on him. We went like this for about five minutes, then somehow we retreated to mutual corners. It was our first fight, but it wouldn't be our last.

I married him in January 1985, a month before I got out of the U.S. Navy after doing five years' active duty. I did my military time in Keflavik, Iceland; Mountain View, California; Port Hueneme, California (which is where I first met him); and lastly Lakehurst, New Jersey. And when it came time for me to get out, I had no idea what I would do with my life. He was in the navy, and a Seabee—meaning he was in the highly respected Construction Battalion unit of the navy. He was two years younger than me, and he was crazy about me. I'd met him in 1982, and even though we weren't always in the same duty station, he always stayed in touch by phone or by mail. We'd occasionally visit each other for a weekend or something, but it was nothing serious. I never even mentioned him to my family, and as far as I knew he'd never mentioned me to his. So I was shocked when, one day—just two weeks before I was due to get out of the military—he proposed to me. I thought about it, and figured, why the hell not? If I married him it would mean that I would at least have health insurance since he was still in the navy. And I figured he just wanted to get married because by doing so he would be picking up a dependent and would be eligible for BAQ—bachelors allowance for quarters—which added an additional two hundred dollars a month to his paycheck to support a family. When I mentioned that, though, he insisted that wasn't the reason. He wanted to get married because he loved me. Getting married seemed like a good idea to me at the time. And I think I loved him. No, in retrospect, I actually *don't* think I did. But at the time, I did think I loved him.

He was romantic, compassionate, and charming. And he could fight. I hate to admit it, but one of the things that has always attracted me most to men was their ability to kick ass.

I guess I needed to believe that if it were needed, they could throw down on my behalf.

Another thing I liked about hubby was that he was mean. Yeah, kinda crazy, huh? But I've since given it some thought, and realized I wanted someone who was the opposite of my own father. Joe-Joe was one of the nicest people anyone ever wanted to meet, but he was weak. Not weak physically, but mentally. I guess that I equated niceness with weakness. And I equated meanness with strength.

Now understand, although one of the major requirements I had for men was that they be mean, it was important that they never be mean to me. Mean to someone in front of me; but not mean to me. Mean to someone because of me; but not mean to me.

And hubby followed the rule up until we got married. Then he switched the hell up on me.

In addition to being a Seabee, hubby was also an aspiring musician. He played a mean bass guitar, and was decent on a number of different musical instruments, including the trap drums and piano. He was also the only person I knew who could not only read music, but could also write it. That shit impressed the hell out of me! What didn't impress me was hubby's drinking. I didn't realize until we were married how heavy a fucking drinker he was because he hid it from me. I thought he was a social drinker like me; I could keep gallons of various liquors and wine in my apartment to serve to guests and they would last for months. Not after I married hubby. It was like he had some obsession with drinking every ounce of liquor in the house. So I stopped buying liquor. So he started buying it himself. When I confronted him about it, he swore he didn't have a problem and would prove it by simply stopping his drinking, period. And I was impressed.

For a whole two weeks.

That's when I flushed the toilet and found there was a problem with the flushing mechanism. I lifted the lid off the tank and found about fifteen miniature liquor bottles—like the ones you get on airplanes—bobbing and floating in the water inside. Damn.

I took the bottles and lined them up on the living room coffee table so hubby would see them when he came home from work. He came in about an hour later, grabbed a beer out of the refrigerator, sat down on the couch, and put his feet up on the coffee table. He took a swig of his beer, then kicked the bottles onto the floor. Yeah, so he didn't care.

Shit! I was married to a fucking alcoholic. I figured I'd just have to live with it since he seemed like he was at least a functioning alcoholic. Pretty bad, but, yeah . . . I could live with it.

But then, about three months into our marriage I got a wake-up call. I was reading one of those women's magazines, and they had an interview with actress Zsa Zsa Gabor. In it she said, "A woman who has never been hit by a man has never been loved by a man." I laughed and read the quote to hubby, adding, "Is she crazy, or what?"

Well, my dear husband rubbed his chin, and said, "Well, I don't know. She might have a point."

"What?"

"No, let me explain," he said hastily. "I think what's she trying to get across is that if a man really cares for a woman he'll do anything to make sure she's safe. And sometimes when a woman is going in the wrong direction, and she won't listen, you have to hit her for her own good. Because you love her, and you don't want to see her hurt."

"You're kidding," I said, while slowly realizing my ass was in trouble.

"No, I'm serious." Then he caught the look on my face and quickly added, "I'm not saying I'm like that. I'm just saying I know what she means."

Yeah. Right.

Our first fight? We were living in Atlanta, Georgia—even though I was no longer in the navy, he was still enlisted, and was stationed at the Seabee Battalion Center at Dobbins Air Force Base in Marietta—in a small apartment that hubby had rented before I moved down from my last duty station in New Jersey. He'd been drinking rum, beer, wine, and . . . I don't know . . . something else, while working on a song on his two-thousand-dollar keyboard. On his two-thousand-dollar keyboard that I had charged on my American Express card because he swore up and down that he had to have it and he'd have the money to pay the credit card bill before it arrived in a month because he was expecting some back money that the navy owed him. Of course the money never came through, I couldn't pay the bill, and my card privileges were revoked since American Express didn't play that waiting shit.

So anyway, he was drinking and writing this song on this keyboard, and it was late and I wanted to get some sleep. Hubby, however, wanted me to stay in the room with him while he wrote so he could keep asking me how this sounded, or how that sounded. And I wasn't feeling it. I wasn't feeling being forced to stay awake. I wasn't feeling that I had to listen to the keyboard that always reminded me his fuck-up (intentional or not) had cost me my American Express card. And I damn sure wasn't feeling the song he called himself writing.

Finally, at about two a.m., I said I really needed to get to bed because I had to work in the morning. He was upset, but I could see he was trying to deal with it, and I was grateful for that because I really wasn't up to arguing. But as I was leaving the room, he kinda tugged on my arm and said, "But honestly, Karen, what do you think of the song so far?"

I shrugged and said I guessed it was okay, but I wasn't that much into jazz so I wasn't a good judge.

He said, "But come on, Karen. Do you like what you hear so far?"

I said, "I guess it's okay."

He said, "Just okay? Does that mean you really don't like it?"

I said, "I'm not saying I don't really like it. I'm just saying it's not really my kind of music."

He said, "Come on, Karen. I want your honest, honest opinion. If you don't like it, just say so."

I said, "I'm being honest. It sounds okay. But really, I've got to get to bed. I'm bone tired."

He said, "I'm not letting you go to bed until you give me your honest opinion. Tell me if you like my new song or not."

I said, "Okay, you want me to be honest? I don't like it. It sounds like you're just playing the same thing over and over again, and it's boring. Now, I'm going to bed!"

Then he took a step back and said, "Oh, really?"

I took a step toward the bedroom, and said, "Really."

And then he said . . .

Pow!

Or at least his fist did as it smashed into my face.

And then it was on.

After we finally stopped fighting I was bruised up pretty damn bad. He was, too—I had managed to give him a black eye, a busted lip, and a bloody nose in addition to a bruised shoulder and a couple of lumps on his head. Still, my wounds were worse. In fact, I had to go to the hospital because my coccyx was bruised. Hubby took me, and as soon as we got to the hospital, they knew what was up. Both of our faces were swollen, our lips were busted, hubby had a black eye, and I had a bruised ass—I mean, coccyx; and every time we looked at each other we rolled our eyes or growled.

One of the nurses took me aside and said, "Listen, did he hit you? You can tell me, and I promise I can get you some help." I shook my head no, and said nothing. She asked me again, and once more I simply shook my head no. She finally said, "Okay." But as she was leaving the room I heard an orderly say to her in a low voice, "Maybe you should ask the husband. He looks as battered as her."

Wanna know how stupid I am? That statement made my chest swell with pride. And it stayed swollen for the duration of my combative marriage. Oh, hubby and I went at it on a regular basis, but I actually fooled myself into thinking that I wasn't a battered wife because, shit, I gave as good as I got. But what the hell kinda marriage is that?

And there were other things wrong with the marriage.

For instance, hubby resented my intelligence. Which is kinda funny, because he was a really smart dude himself, and knew it. In fact, he always used to tell me that he hated stupid girls, and needed to be with someone on his intellectual level. But I guess he found out he didn't like girls who were too intelligent.

I remember one day some of hubby's musician friends were over, and one of them was a guy whom everyone else seemed to really look up to. And the guy was just going on and on about music, and inspiration for songs, and this and that . . . and really just enjoying listening to himself talk.

"Musicians, especially black musicians in this racist country they call America," the music guru said, solemnly, "are like caged birds. And like one of America's greatest poets, I know why the caged bird sings." He paused, I assumed, to let the weight of what he'd said sink into his disciples. "I know everyone here knows what poet came up with that line."

"I do," I said.

Hubby hugged me, proudly. "Yeah, of course you know, babe. But let one of these other guys come up with the answer."

I gave him a kiss on the cheek and waited.

There was an uncomfortable silence as all of the disciples looked at each other, and then back at the music guru. He shook his head in fake frustration.

"You guys should be ashamed of yourself," he said, letting out a deep breath. He looked at hubby. "You know, right?"

"Of course, it's—"

"Maya Angelou," the music guru finished.

My irritation wasn't faked. What a showoff. He couldn't even let my hubby have the spotlight for even a second.

"Actually, you're wrong," I said.

"I beg your pardon," the music guru said.

Hubby squeezed my shoulder, a little too hard for it to be interpreted as show of support.

"Maya Angelou did not originate the line," I said, ignoring hubby's hint.

The music guru looked around the room and gave a little chuckle. "Actually, you're wrong," he said, mocking me. "It was the title of her 1966 autobiography. I would have thought you'd know that since your husband is always boasting about how smart you are; after all, it's a well-known classic. You should read it sometime; it's very inspiring, especially for African-American women."

How patronizing. There must have been something about the way my body stiffened that warned hubby that I was about to pounce, because he squeezed my arm even tighter. I smiled, removed his arm from my shoulders, and then turned to the music guru.

"Actually, you're wrong again. Maya Angelou's autobiography came out in 1969." I stood and walked over and picked up an empty beer bottle that sat in front of one of the disciples. "Would you like another?"

"Yes, please," the disciple answered softly, his eyes wide and darting between me and the music guru.

"I remember the year because I had just turned eleven, and Wilbert Tatum—you know, the executive editor of the New York *Amsterdam News*—sent me a copy in 1979 and asked me to review it for his paper for the book's ten-year anniversary," I shouted from the kitchen as I retrieved a bottle of Heineken from the refrigerator.

"Tatum asked a twenty-one-year-old girl to do a book review, huh?" the music guru said.

I walked back in the room just in time to see him sharing a "she's full of shit" grin with his disciples. "Twenty-one-year-old woman, thank you. Unfortunately, I couldn't do it because I had a bad case of mononucleosis and wouldn't have made the deadline."

"That's funny, because I've known Tatum for years, and he never mentioned it. I'll have to ask him the next time I see him," the music guru said with a smirk. "I go to New York quite often. In fact, I'm sure I'll see him at the NAACP luncheon next week."

"I'm sure you will, since he's one of the keynote speakers," I answered. "But you don't have to wait." I went over to my pocketbook, pulled out my address book, and started flipping through the pages. "We can call him right now."

The music guru's eyes almost popped out. He managed to

keep his voice calm, though. "It's Sunday. I'm sure he's not in the office."

"True, but I'm calling him at home." I looked over at hubby and saw he was grinning. I gave him a wink, and then dialed the number. I hung up a couple of seconds later. "The line is busy. But I'm sure you know Abiola Sinclair. She's one of the columnists for the *Amsterdam News*. Let me call her real quick."

"That won't be necessary—"

I ignored him and dialed Abiola.

"Hey, Abby. This is Ke-Ke. How are you doing? . . . Good. Listen, I'm sorry to bother you, but . . . Yeah, yeah, I heard about Rachel. But anyway . . . Okay, I'm sorry I haven't called you in so long, but listen, do you remember how old I was when Tatum asked me to do that book review of Maya Angelou's book? . . . I know it was before I joined the navy, but do you remember my exact age? . . . No?" I took the receiver from my ear and looked at the music guru, who had a wonderfully mortified look on his face. "She doesn't remember exactly how old I was, but she remembers it was before I joined the navy, and I can prove I enlisted when I was twenty-two. Is that good enough?"

"Yes, of course," he said sullenly.

"Cool." I put the receiver back to my ear. "Okay, thanks, Abby . . . Oh, no, I hadn't heard about James . . . Listen, let me call you back later tonight, okay . . . I promise I'm gonna call. Dang . . . Okay, I'm sorry. Love ya." I hung up, and then turned back to the music guru. "Oh, I'm sorry, I should have asked if you wanted to speak to her. You do know Abiola, right?"

"No, I don't." He turned back to the disciples. "Anyway, as I was saying—"

"Right," I interrupted. "You were talking about the title of Maya Angelou's book, *I Know Why the Caged Bird Sings*." I walked over and sat down next to hubby, but out of arm's reach. My shoulder was already sore. "She borrowed that line from Paul Laurence Dunbar's poem, *Sympathy*.

> "*I know why the caged bird sings, ah me*
> *When his wing is bruised and his bosom sore*
> *When he beats his bar and he would be free*
> *It is not a carol of joy or glee*
> *But a prayer that he sends from his heart's deep core*
> *But a plea, that upward to Heaven he flings*
> *I know why the caged bird sings'*"

I only recited the last stanza of the poem—my favorite by Dunbar—since it was the one that contained the exact line, but the smiles and nods from the disciples said it was a hit. I turned and looked at the music guru.

"*Sympathy* was written in 1898. No, I think it was 1899. Shoot, I can't remember. Let me call Abiola again, I'm sure she has a copy." I reached for the telephone.

"That won't be necessary," the music guru said quickly. His face was red, and his eyes were narrowed.

"Are you sure?"

"Look, you've made your point, okay? Damn. I can't stand smart-mouthed women!"

"Whoa. Hold the fuck up right there! I know you're not in my house talking to my wife like that!" Hubby slowly stood up. I started preparing for a fight. I moved toward the newly purchased glass coffee table to move it out of the way, but then one of the disciples jumped in between hubby and the music guru.

"He didn't mean anything by it," the disciple said quickly. But then the music guru stood up. He was about hubby's height and weight, and he seemed unafraid of a possible fight.

"What the hell is the problem, Miller?" he said with a definite growl in his voice.

I moved the coffee table, then tugged at one of the disciple's arm. "Would you move the stereo system, please? It's too heavy for me."

"My problem, asshole, is what the hell you just said about my wife." Hubby took one arm and flung the disciple, who'd jumped between them, across the room. That must have served as a reality check for the music guru, because as hubby advanced toward him he retreated, holding his hands in front of him in a placating manner.

"Hey, I'm sorry. I didn't mean to disrespect you," he said, not realizing he was backing himself into a corner. And I mean literally backing himself into a corner. He was obviously not a fighter, because if he were he would have looked around before backing up to make sure he had room to swing if he needed to do so.

"Yeah, okay, I accept your apology. Now apologize to my wife, and you'd better hope *she* accepts it."

The music guru, by this time, realized he was in the corner, and you could actually see his Adam's apple move downward and back up as he gulped.

"Karen—"

"Mrs. Miller to you," I said quickly.

"Mrs. Miller, I apologize for disrespecting you in that manner. I hope you forgive me."

I crossed my arms, threw my hip out to the side, and tapped my foot. I wanted him to sweat for a few seconds. And he did, and again, literally. Beads of perspiration sprang up on his forehead.

"Yeah, okay. I forgive you," I said finally.

Hubby didn't automatically move, and a couple of disciples looked at me like I should say something to get him to back off. Fuck that. I was still ready for a show. But eventually hubby walked over and grabbed the music guru's backpack and threw it at him. It hit the music guru in the stomach, and he grunted. Then he shrugged his shoulders and started walking toward the front door. He walked out, and as soon as the door closed behind him, hubby and I burst out laughing.

Later, after all the disciples had left and hubby and I were on the sofa sharing a bottle of wine, he pulled me close to him and said, "You are something else. Man, as soon as you said he was wrong, I was like, it's on now. Shit, to tell you the truth, I thought Maya Angelou was the author, but when you said she wasn't, there was no way I was going to bet against you."

I smiled and snuggled against my strong, protective, loving husband.

"That guy thought he was so smart, but you sure as hell showed him." Hubby took a sip from his wineglass and kissed me on top of my head. "You know what? I started to show him up myself. You heard that crack he made about America being a racist country? How stupid was that? I shoulda busted him right there. America is a continent, not a country." Hubby started laughing, but I just smiled. I guess he wondered why I didn't laugh with him, because he squeezed me tight and kissed the top of my head again. "Right?" he said.

I just gave a small laugh.

Hubby must have grown suspicious, because he repeated, "Right?"

"Well, technically, America isn't a continent," I said reluctantly. "North America is a continent, and South America is a continent. But it's the United States of America that's a country." I snuggled closer to him. It didn't work.

"Damn, Karen," he said, pushing me away. "Why you always gotta be correcting somebody?"

"I didn't *want* to correct you," I said defensively, "but you asked me to agree with you. And isn't it better that I correct you in private rather than someone else do it to you in public?"

"Oh, you mean like you did to Jeff this afternoon?"

Jeff? Oh, yeah. The music guru. "Yeah, like Jeff. But I just did that because he was acting like a jerk," I responded.

"So? Is it your job, now, to put jerks in their place? How much are you getting paid?" Hubby got up from the sofa, but I just lay there. I didn't feel like fighting. Especially since I knew it wasn't really my beef with the music guru—I mean Jeff—that we would be fighting about. It was about me correcting hubby.

Like I said, it wasn't that he resented me being smart, he just resented me being smarter than him. But even that wasn't the worst thing about my marriage. Although when you couple it with him hitting me, it was pretty bad.

I was really blown away when I found out he was cheating.

For some reason, it never occurred to me that any man I was with would cheat. Don't ask me why, I just didn't think they would. It wasn't because I thought I was all that beautiful (although I was), or that I thought I was that good in bed (although I was), or that I thought I was all that (although I was—and still am). I guess I just assumed that once a commitment was made, the man I was with would take that commitment just as seriously as I did.

So when hubby started staying out late and coming home smelling like perfume, I didn't worry. He said it was because he was at a club sitting in on a jam session and some girl or the other was leaning all over him while he was playing. I shook my head and said, "Some girls have no class."

When hubby stayed out all night and came home the next morning and went right to sleep, I didn't worry. He said that he'd gotten drunk and fell asleep on his friend's couch. I said, "Baby, please . . . you've got to watch your drinking. But, still, you did the right thing. I wouldn't want you trying to drive home drunk and getting a DUI."

When I found girls' telephone numbers in his pockets when I did the laundry, I still didn't worry. He said that a navy buddy of his had brought the girl around to his job because she needed a bass player to fill in for a party she was having. I said, "Ooh, that's so cool. You're getting paying gigs."

But my girlfriend Sandy wasn't having it.

I'd met Sandy shortly after hubby was transferred to the Seabee Base in Gulfport, Mississippi. I found a civil service job as a secretary working for the navy at the Ingalls Shipbuilding Plant in Pascagoula working with the civilian engineers on the ship that would later be named the USS *Wasp* (LHD-1), and Sandy was a civil service employee in another division. Like hubby, her husband was also a navy enlisted man, and like me, Sandy hated Mississippi. And I mean she and I *really* hated Mississippi. Pascagoula was just a few miles away from Mobile, Alabama, so I would often pick up a copy of the *Mobile Press* while at work. I couldn't believe it when I first turned to the classified section and found that people looking for babysitters, housecleaners, and handymen would often specify "white only." When I pointed this out to the engineers in my department, they didn't see anything wrong with it. They hastened to assure me they themselves had no problems working with blacks, but said they did think that people should be able to hire whomever they wanted to work in their homes. I agree, but I don't think you should exclude every race but your own.

That was bad enough, but then I got a part-time job as an answering service operator in Ocean Springs. It was a family-owned business, and the switchboard was actually located in the back of the family's home. They kept the place a mess. Oh, and I mean a mess. They had about six dogs and a good ten to fifteen cats, and there was animal feces all over the floor in the living area, and all of the sofa and chair cushions smelled of animal urine. I made the best of it because we needed the extra money, and I actually got along well with the family. Then one day the daughter, who was two years older than me, mentioned seeing an alligator at the lake nearby where she and some of her classmates were picnicking.

"You're kidding," I said with a shudder. "Ugh! I'm scared to death of alligators."

She laughed and said, "Well, I can understand that. Most black people are."

"Most black people? You mean white people aren't?" I said, eyeing her suspiciously.

"Not as afraid as blacks."

"You've got to be crazy," I said, now offended.

"No, for real! Everyone knows blacks are more afraid of 'gators than whites, because an alligator will go after a black person faster than a white."

"What?"

"It's true," she insisted. "Alligators prefer dark meat to white."

I rolled my eyes, thinking she was making a bad—not quite offensive, but bad—joke. But then when I looked at her face, I could see she was serious. To be certain, I actually asked, "Are you serious?"

"It's true," she said, nodding her head and looking over at her parents for confirmation.

I turned to look at them, too. After a minute or so, the father gave a deep sigh and said, "Karen, I hope you're not going to misconstrue this conversation to be that of a racist nature, but what Angela is saying is true. It's a scientific fact."

I paused. "Aren't alligators color-blind?"

He didn't miss a beat. "Yes, but they have an excellent sense of smell. Dark meat has a sweeter smell than white meat."

I had to admit, that one made me stop and think. I had to admit to myself that what he said sounded logical. Then I thought about it a minute more. And I had to stand up and say:

"Get the fuck outta here!"

Yeah, they managed to bring the Angry-Ass Black Woman up and out front.

There was a moment of silence as the family looked at me, and then at each other. The mother finally walked over and patted me on the shoulder. "Karen, I'm sorry. They were totally out of line."

"Damn right, they were," I huffed.

"Angela should never have brought up the subject of alligators," said this highly refined southern belle with the shit-loaded, urine-soaked, animal-fur-all-over-the-place, flea-infested, fucked-up house. "She should have known it's a touchy subject."

Instead of sitting down, I put my hand on my hip and gave

her the Angry-Ass Black Woman stare. "What do you mean she shouldn't have brought it up?" I said slowly.

She looked at me and slowly removed her hand, then turned and sat back down at the table that was cluttered with dirty dishes that couldn't fit in the filthy sink that was already filled to the brim with greasy dishes, pots, and pans.

"I don't know why you people are always so touchy," she said.

Yep.

She went there.

She left me no choice.

I met her at the meeting place she set up.

"I find it disgusting that a whole family chooses to believe that black people are more afraid of alligators than white people are." I turned to the daughter. "When you and your friends saw the alligators, are you going to tell me you didn't get the hell out of there?"

"We ran, but . . ."

"So, okay. That means you were afraid. Correct?" I didn't give her a chance to answer. I turned to the father. "And you saying that alligators prefer eating black folks as opposed to white people because the meat is sweeter, and then calling that a scientific fact. Can you tell me where you learned this scientific fact?"

The father's face reddened, but he said nothing.

"That's what I thought." I looked them up and down, rolled my eyes, picked up my pocketbook, and turned to leave.

"Karen, I hate to say this because I really like you, but you are really making a big deal out of nothing," the mother said. "We didn't say nothing that was derogatory or nothing—"

"No, of course not," I snapped. "Not in your little mind,

anyway. I just need to get out of here because with all these funky animals in your house, in addition to having a person with sweet dark meat, there might be alligators on the way as we speak." I looked out one of the Mississippi mud-stained windows and exclaimed, "Oh, look! There are a couple coming up the road now!"

Only the daughter turned to look.

Didn't matter. I was out of there. They could all kiss my big, black, beautiful, round, alligator-frightened ass.

Yeah, I hated Mississippi.

But I digress.

Sandy was over one night, and we were enjoying a glass of wine when I found a yellow Post-it note on the floor near the coffee table. I picked it up and saw that it had the name "Jean" scrawled on it, along with a telephone number. I casually put the Post-it note on the coffee table, and continued drinking my wine. Sandy saw the note and had a fit.

"And what the hell is that?"

"Some girl's number. She probably wants hubby to play at some gig or the other," I answered.

"Probably? Probably is good enough for you?" Sandy leaned over and picked up the Post-it note. "Jean, huh? If this is a business deal why does it only have her first name?"

I nonchalantly took a sip of my wine before answering. "I have no idea. But it's no big deal."

"You're stupid."

I shrugged, picked up the television remote, and switched on *Dynasty,* trying to use the drama on the screen to drown out the drama Sandy was trying to create in my living room. Sandy opened her mouth to say something else but, before she could utter a sound, the phone rang. It was hubby.

"Hey, babe," he said. "Could you look on the night table

in the bedroom and get my address book? I need Richard's number." Richard was a navy buddy of his.

"Sure, no problem." I put the phone down and obediently went and got the phone book. As I was giving him the requested number, Sandy was waving the Post-it note in front of my face and mouthing the words, "Ask him."

"Hey, hubby, I just found a Post-it note on the living room floor with a name and telephone number on it. The name is Jean," I said calmly, while rolling my eyes at Sandy.

"Oh, yeah, that's my sister Jean," hubby said without missing a beat.

"Really? But she lives in Detroit. This is a Mississippi number."

"She was flying to New Orleans a couple of weeks ago and stopped over in Mississippi to visit some friends," he nonchalantly explained.

"Oh, okay," I said satisfied, and smirking at Sandy. "I fixed macaroni and . . . wait a minute." I now sat straight up in my seat. "Isn't your sister's name Janet?"

"Yeah, but we call her Jan sometimes and Jean sometimes. It's a family thing." Again, he said all this pretty matter-of-factly. He couldn't possibly have been lying. Except, I didn't know one damn person named Janet whose family called her Jean.

"Um, okay. Well, I fixed macaroni and cheese and meat-loaf. In case you get home after I'm asleep, I'll leave a plate for you in the microwave."

"Thanks, Karen. Love you!" He hung up.

I hung up.

And immediately after I hung up I picked up the telephone again. "Give me that number," I said, snatching the Post-it note out of Sandy's hand.

"What's going on?" she asked excitedly as I dialed the number.

"Damn! The line is busy. That sleazy bastard managed to get through before me." This was in 1986, and although the call waiting feature on telephones existed, you had to pay extra for it so most people didn't have it.

I bit my lip, then dialed hubby's office number. "Yep, his line is busy, too. He's calling her to get their stories straight, just in case I call!" I slammed down the phone and looked at Sandy. "You're right. The bastard is fucking around on me."

I called back every five minutes, but it wasn't until thirty-five minutes later that Jean's line was finally clear. "Hello, may I speak to Jean?"

The woman on the other line sucked her teeth. "I'm sorry, but Jean isn't here. She stopped by last week but she already left and went back to Detroit." She didn't even say the rehearsed lines like she was trying to fool me. The bitch obviously didn't care.

"Well, look. My name is Karen Miller, and my husband's name is—"

"So?" she asked, cutting me off.

"Miss, I don't know you, but I'm hoping we can talk woman-to-woman. I mean, I'm not stupid. I found your number on my living room floor and my husband is trying to pass if off like it's his sister's number." I was speaking calmly, but my heart was racing. And Sandy was sitting cross-legged on the coffee table in front of me, looking straight into my mouth as I spoke.

"Like I said, I'm not stupid," I continued. "I realize that you have some kind of dealings with my husband. Maybe you didn't know he was married. Maybe you just met him and you guys didn't even have a chance to speak on the phone until today, but I'm hoping you can let me know the real deal, so I can figure out what I need to do from here."

"Miss, I don't know you from dirt, and I don't know your husband," was the response I received.

"Look, Jean—"

"I don't remember telling you my name was Jean," the woman said coldly. "Now, if you don't mind, I have to go to work." *Click*.

I turned to Sandy and told all that had happened.

"What are you going to do now?" she asked, as she poured us each another large glass of wine.

"I don't know. But I'm going to do something," I told her. "Give me some time. I'll figure it out."

It only took me a day to come up with a plan, but I had to bide my time in order to put it into action. Two weeks after I originally found the damning Post-it note I called Sandy and told her to come right over. Hubby was on overnight duty at the naval base, so I knew we'd have the privacy needed to pull off my little scheme.

"Hello."

"Hello! Is this Jean?" Sandy said in a booming, friendly voice.

"Who's this?"

"This is Deborah Richards, producer of the FOX-107.5 morning radio show! Jean, your name has been picked from 1,500 entries and you've won a five-thousand-dollar gift certificate from Kay Jewelers! Congratulations, Jean!" Sandy looked over at me and crossed her fingers and we both held our breath.

"Oh my God! How much? Five thousand dollars! Oh my God! I've never won anything before in my life!"

She fell for it! We both exhaled.

"Well, you've won now, and won big! How does it feel?" Sandy winked at me, and I covered my face with a couch pillow to keep from laughing out loud.

"It feels great! I can't wait to tell everybody! Oh my God! A five-thousand-dollar gift certificate? I'm going to buy myself a bunch of bracelets and earrings!" There was a brief pause, then, "But wait a minute! I don't remember signing up for no contest."

"Well, if you didn't one of your friends must have signed your name to it, because I certainly have your information in front of me right here. Your name is Jean, right? And your telephone number is 601-___-___, right?"

Thank goodness I had prepped Sandy on what to say in case Jean said just what she did.

"Yeah, that's right. I don't know which one of my friends coulda did that, though. They ain't tell me nothing."

"Honey, remember the old saying, 'Don't look a gift horse in the mouth?' Well, I'd say it would apply here," Sandy said. "Of course, if you don't want—"

"No, no, I want it!" Jean shouted into the telephone. "Of course I want it. When do I pick it up?"

"Hold on, first we have to get some information," Sandy said, giving a nice radio-type fake laugh. "Alright, Jean . . . oh, darn. I can't read this handwriting. How do you spell your last name?"

"It's Robinson. R-O-B-I-N-S-O-N."

"Right. I couldn't tell if the second letter was an 'a' or an 'o.' And what's your mailing address?"

Ten minutes later we had her full name, age, Social Security number, home address, work address, how far she'd gone in school (11th grade), and her marital status (single).

"Okay, you can pick up your gift certificate at Kay Jewelers at the Edgewater Mall right here in Gulfport on Thursday at exactly 6:30 p.m. We're going to have two of the DJs from the station there to interview you, and it will be broadcast on Friday morning, if that's okay with you."

"Yeah! Of course it's okay with me!"

"Fine. But one more thing. Because you won this contest you're also eligible for our next contest, which is a trip for two to Hawaii. Are you interested in signing up for that one?"

"Oh my God! Yes!"

"Good, I thought you'd say that. Now, I just need a bit more information. Okay, you said you're single. I assume you have a boyfriend you'll be taking with you on the vacation?"

"Yes," she answered without hesitation.

"Wonderful. And what's his name?" Sandy and I crossed our fingers again.

She gave my husband's full name.

Sandy and I both jumped up and high-fived each other, then Sandy continued with her rehearsed script.

"Good. Now where did you and he meet?"

"At the Navy Non-Commissioned Officers' Club."

"Oh, is he in the navy?"

"Um, yes." There was another pause. "Is all this information going to be made public?"

"Let me assure you there's nothing to worry about. I need all this information per contest rules but nothing is made public. Listen, I'm a woman just like you so I can guess what's going on here. You just met, so you want to keep everything hush-hush until you decide how everything is between you, right? Nothing can mess up a relationship faster than friends and family getting all up in your business before everything's solidified. I got you, honey."

"Yes, that's it, exactly," the lying heifer said. Shit, she didn't want it made public because she knew she was messing with a married man!

Another ten minutes and we found out when she and hubby met (four months ago), how they'd met (he approached her and offered to buy her a drink), how often they'd seen each other (twice a week), how she felt about him (she really liked him), and whether she thought he was serious about her (he told her that although they'd only known each other a short time, he thought he was falling in love).

"So, what are you going to do with all this information?" Sandy asked me after she'd hung up and we finished laughing.

"I'm not sure yet. But I'm going to do something," I assured her.

One thing I did do, though, was drive over to the mall with Sandy at 6:30 on Thursday. Talk about funny! Here was this girl and about ten of her friends throwing a fit inside Kay Jewelers because no one would give her a five-thousand-dollar gift certificate. Jean—who, it turned out, was passably good looking, but not as good looking as me—stomped out of the store and went straight to a pay phone (this was before cell phones were available, remember?) and called the radio station. Sandy and I couldn't get close enough to hear everything she said, but when she got off the phone she announced to her friends that she'd made a mistake and she was supposed to arrive the following Friday. Jean was wiping tears from her eyes as she told them that lie, and I wondered what she would tell them the following week. I would have felt sorry for her if she wasn't an adulterous, lying, stupid heifer who was screwing my husband. But since she was, Sandy and I went straight to a club to celebrate our success in making her look like a fool, and to plot how I was going to get hubby for his betrayal. I didn't want to throw it up in his face, because that would be too easy. But I also didn't want to publicly humiliate him, because I wasn't sure if I was going to leave him—so I would wind up looking bad myself.

Two nights later, hubby came in from work and found me on the telephone, crying, with a yellow legal pad in front of me.

"What's wrong, Karen?" he said, rushing up to me.

I put my hand over the receiver and tearfully said, "There's some girl on the telephone who says she's two months' pregnant and you're the father." I then burst out in hysterical tears.

Hubby exploded. "What? What are you talking about? Give me the phone."

I shook my head, tears pouring down my cheeks, and my hand still over the receiver. "She made me promise not to tell you. She doesn't know you're here."

"Give me the phone," he said again, and tried to take it from my hand, but I backed away.

"Hello? I'm sorry. I'm sorry, I was away from the phone, but my dog was pawing at the door to get in. Okay, you were saying that he told you he was divorcing me?" I looked up at hubby with the most pitiful face I could make. "Did he say why? What? Oh God." I jerked the receiver from my ear and stood breathing heavily, looking at hubby all wild-eyed. The look of fear on his face was priceless, and I couldn't help but start laughing. Damn! But I was able to cover it up by acting like I was hysterical. After I managed to stop laughing, I threw the telephone receiver at him and yelled, "You no-good bastard! How could you?"

He ducked in time to miss getting conked on the head, then picked up the phone and yelled, "Who the fuck is this!"

A high-pitched scream loud enough for me to hear responded, "I told you not to let him know I called!"

Sandy did her job well. We figured if she screamed loud enough that he wouldn't be able to recognize the voice wasn't Jean's, and we were right.

"I said, who the fuck is this?" hubby demanded again, but now the phone was dead.

"Karen, I swear, I don't know who that was lying like that," he said, as he approached me with his arms stretched out in front of him as if to scoop me up in a hug.

"You don't know who it is?" I screamed at him while backing up. "Well, I do!" I picked up the yellow legal pad, and read from it. "Jean Robinson, she lives in the Oak Lane Apartments, her telephone number is 601-___-____, she's twenty-three years old, you guys met at the NCO Club where you bought her a sloe gin fizz, and she's six weeks' pregnant."

I paused to let all the information I threw at him settle, and I must say, I was enjoying the shocked look on his face.

"Pregnant?" It took a few minutes for him to gather himself behind that, but then he was right back at it. "Karen, I don't even know this girl!"

"Really?" I challenged him. "Then how did she know about the raspberry birthmark on your stomach? Or the scar on your thigh from when you fell on a piece of glass when you were a kid?" I was assuming, here, but I felt it was a pretty good assumption.

"Karen, I swear I don't know how she knows all this!" Hubby started pleading. "You've got to believe me."

"Hubby, the only way she could have known all this shit is if she's seen you naked," I pressed.

"How is she going to have seen me naked when I don't even know her?" hubby insisted. "Okay, maybe she's seen some naked picture of me or something. Maybe she snuck into the locker room and took them or something. Maybe she's some kind of stalker. Hell, I don't know."

"Oh, and I forgot," I finally said, with as much hurt as I could muster in my voice. "She told me that you told her that you loved her only three weeks after you met, and that you were trying to get a divorce because . . ." I collapsed on a chair and covered my face with my hands. "Because . . ."

Hubby walked over and knelt down beside me, and started rubbing my back. "Karen, you can't believe anything this crazy girl is saying. She's making all this up for some reason. I don't know her, so I haven't told her anything. You've got to believe me, baby."

I kept up my fake crying. "Well, she said you didn't love me, and wanted to divorce me because . . ."

"Karen, please stop. You know I love you," hubby said soothingly. I let him pull me up from the chair and into his arms. "I would never tell anyone I wanted a divorce from you. You're the love of my life. Don't you know that?"

"Well, she said you wanted to divorce me because . . ." I buried my face in his chest and finished, ". . . because I'm smarter than you. Oh hubby, I'm so hurt!"

"You've got to believe me, baby, I don't even know . . ." Suddenly hubby stopped, and stepped back from me. "What did you say?"

"I said, I'm so hurt," I said, wiping my eyes.

"No, before that. What did you say? I mean about why she said I wanted to divorce you?"

I grabbed a tissue from the night table, and blew my nose. "She said you wanted to divorce me because you couldn't stand the fact that I am smarter than you."

"*What?*"

I knew that would get him!

"Yeah, she said that you didn't come out and say it, but that she could tell by the resentment in your voice when you talked about me. She said she asked you what I was like and you told her I was intelligent and well-spoken, but it seemed like you were angry when you said it. And she said you told her it pisses you off that I'm always showing off how smart I am. And since she's been around you awhile, she said she knows you're not really the sharpest knife in the drawer and—"

"What?"

It took every ounce of strength I had not to bust out laughing.

"Look, I'm only telling you what she said," I said defensively.

"That lying bitch!" he shouted. "I never told her anything about you, and she ain't even ever ask. And how's she's gonna call me stupid? That bitch is the ditziest ass—"

"So, you do admit you know her!" I shouted.

"Huh?" hubby started stammering. "Um, yeah. I know her. But, uh, she's a friend of a friend. I don't even know her that well."

"Oh, it goes from you don't know her at all to her being a friend of a friend." I used both arms to shove him in the chest. "How stupid do you think I am? And if she's such a ditzy, lying bitch, why the hell would you be fucking her?"

"I'm not fucking her!"

"Then why the hell would she call me and tell me got her pregnant?" I threw a vase at him, and though I missed, the water and flowers flew all over the living room. "I hate you!"

He stood there with such a pitiful expression on his face that I almost felt sorry for him. But he was an abusive, lying—and to top all that off—cheating bastard. At the moment I detested him.

"You know what, hubby? You want a divorce? You got one!"

"But I don't want—"

"Look, either she's lying or you are, and at the moment I'm much more inclined to believe her." I walked into the bedroom and slammed the door after me. Only a few minutes passed before I heard the front door close. I walked back into the living room to make sure he was gone, locked the front door, then quickly called Sandy.

"Phase One went perfectly," I said, not bothering to say hello when she picked up. "Time to put Phase Two into action. You got the binoculars?"

"Check!" she said excitedly.

"Okay, he left not five minutes ago. It'll take him at least twenty minutes to get to her apartment complex. If you hurry, you'll be able to get there and have time to find a good lookout spot and be settled with about five minutes to spare."

"I'm on it. Don't worry, I won't let you down."

I hung up, turned on the television, and waited.

An hour and a half later, an out-of-breath Sandy called me. "Oh my God. I think he's in there killing her!"

"What? What happened? Tell me everything!"

"Well, I had just gotten settled, and like you said he pulled up five minutes later," Sandy told me. "So he runs over to her apartment and starts banging on the door. She opened the door wearing a bathrobe, and he pushed her back in the apartment. Did I say push? Make that shove. I actually saw her fall."

"Oh, damn!"

"Yep! Good thing you bought these binoculars, because the door was still open, and I could see him kicking her while she was still on the floor."

"Get outta here!" I covered my mouth with my hand. So okay, now I was feeling kinda bad. Just kinda, though. After all, she was fucking my husband.

"So, one of them finally slams the door, but then about ten minutes later the door swings open, and he storms out pulling the girl behind him. She's kicking and screaming, her hair is all over head and shit, and he drags her over to the car and throws her in. Then he gets in and they peel off. I do mean peel off. There was actually smoke coming from the tires."

"Where'd they go?" I asked, excitedly.

"Damn if I know. I started to go after them to see, but I didn't want him to recognize the car."

I sucked my teeth. "Oh, man."

"Oh, no. Don't worry! I stuck around just in case they came back, and it was a good thing I did. About fifteen minutes later he pulls into the same parking spot. He jumps out the driver's seat, and he has a small white paper bag, and he walks over to the passenger door and tries to open it, but she's got it locked. So I used the binoculars, and I can see that she's crying. Her lip is all busted, and her nose is bleeding, and she just looks real fucked up. So now he's yelling and telling her to open the car door or he's gonna kill her. The neighbors started opening their doors, and I swear, I thought someone was going to call the police."

I chuckled. "Not in that neighborhood."

"I guess not," Sandy continued. "So she finally opens up the car door, and he drags her out by her hair back to the apartment."

"Ouch!"

"Yeah, they've been there ever since, and it's been about forty-five minutes now. You think he's killed her and now he's chopping up the body?"

"Oh, Sandy, get serious!"

"I am serious," Sandy insisted. "If you saw how mad he was you'd know what I mean."

"Yeah, well, I don't think he's chopping up her body. What was in the paper bag?"

"Man, I don't know!"

"You said it was a white paper bag, right? Like a drugstore bag, maybe?" I asked.

"Yeah, it could be. Why?"

"Well, I'm thinking it might be he took her to buy a pregnancy test," I answered.

"Ooh, now that might be. But why is he still in there? It doesn't take but five minutes to take the test and get the results."

"Well," I said, "either my lie was the truth and she is pregnant—in which case, you're right and he did kill her and is chopping up the body—"

"Ew!"

"Or," I continued, "the test came out negative, and he's in there apologizing, but grilling her about the telephone call."

"Ooh, Karen. What do you think he'll do when he finds out you made up the whole thing?"

I laughed. "He's not going to do shit. What's he going to do to me? Admit he went over to this girl's house that he claims he barely knows and beat her up and made her take a pregnancy test? Hmph. I don't think so. Anyway, you can go ahead and get outta there. I don't think there'll be any more drama today."

Sandy hesitated. "You sure?"

"Yeah. Unless you wait around to see if he puts a plastic garbage bag dripping blood in the car trunk." I laughed.

"You're so sick. But look, make sure you call me when you can tonight to let me know what he did when he comes home."

"Bet," I said. We hung up.

I went back in the bedroom and tried to take a nap, but I couldn't sleep. Two hours later, I heard the key turning in the front door. I grabbed a magazine from the nightstand and pretended I was reading. Hubby walked in the bedroom, walked over to where I was sitting, and just stood in front of me, saying nothing. When I looked up at him I was shocked to see two long scratches on his left cheek. Well, I wasn't really shocked to see the scratches, I was shocked to see there were only two, and while his clothes were disheveled, there were no other signs of a fight.

Finally he gave a deep sigh, and sat down next to me on the bed.

"Karen, you wanna go out to dinner?" he asked, reaching over and rubbing my back.

I moved away. "Leave me alone."

"You still mad at me?"

I rolled my eyes and said nothing.

"What if I admit that I was having an affair, but I'm really sorry she called you. I never gave her my telephone number. I went over there after I left her and I told her I didn't want to see her anymore."

"So?" I said nonchalantly. "Why should I care?"

"Come on, Karen. Don't be like that. And she was lying. She isn't pregnant."

"How do you know?"

"Because she admitted to me that she lied."

I bit my lip, wondering how the fuck he still believed she called me. I knew she told him she didn't. Then it hit me. He didn't believe her because he couldn't figure out how else I had all that info. I found that so funny I actually laughed out loud.

Hubby smiled, probably thinking my laughter meant I was no longer mad. "Why are you laughing?" he asked, I guess to make sure.

"Because you expect me to believe you instead of her." I got up from the bed. "I don't know why you came back here, 'cause you know you're not sleeping in this house. Go back to your bitch's apartment and sleep where you're fucking."

"Karen, I told you I broke up with her."

"Well, I suggest you make up with her if you want to get some rest."

Hubby stood up and tried to hug me, but I pulled away. "I'm not going any damn where," he said angrily. "I live here."

I walked over to the closet and started pulling clothes out.

"What are you doing now?" he asked.

"Well, if you're staying here, I'm not," I said as I pulled a suitcase from the upper shelf.

"Karen, don't be like that."

I said nothing.

Hubby stood there a few more minutes, watching me, then he suddenly sat down on the bed, put his face in his hands, and started crying. I almost stopped, because I had never even seen hubby with tears in his eyes before, and here he was sobbing like a baby. I almost stopped. I didn't stop. Instead I started throwing clothes into the suitcase.

It took a few minutes for hubby to pull himself together, but finally he wiped his eyes. "You don't have to go. I'll leave," he said in a hoarse voice. He stood back up. "Karen, I said I'm sorry and that I'm not going to see the girl again. I really love you, and I don't know what else I can do to prove it."

"There's nothing you can do to prove it," I snapped.

He tried, though. He bought me chocolates, flowers, and jewelry. But I didn't care. I was planning to divorce the lying, cheating bastard.

Until I found out I was pregnant.

★   ★   ★

"*You want Camille to call who? Have you lost your mind?*"

"*Calm down, Joe T. I just suggested she call her father. After all, Ke-Ke and him were husband and wife, even if just for a little while—*"

"*Damn right a little while! Sister, no disrespect, but you're out of line here.*"

"*Out of line? Okay, Joe, whatever. I'm out of it.*"

"*Like I said, Sister, no disrespect, but maybe it's good that you're out of it. I can't stand that bastard. After all he did to Ke-Ke? He'd better not show up here.*"

"*Uncle Joe, you know my father wouldn't come even if I did call him, and you know I'm not.*"

Hmph, thank God for that. Although, that would probably be just what I need to be able to move again. Because if I knew that no-good motherfucker was in this fucking hospital room I'd jump up out this bed and kick his funky ass.

"*Yeah, he'd know better than to show up, because I still owe that bastard. Your mother pissed me off by not letting me know what was going on so I coulda killed him years ago, but she wouldn't be able to stop me now.*"

Nor would I be inclined to.

twelve

*W*hat?"

"I'm sorry, but we can't go ahead with the abortion. I'm looking at your uterus, and I have to say you're well into your second trimester."

There I was, actually *on* the table in the abortion clinic, my feet firmly strapped into the stirrups, and the white-masked man in green scrubs who was supposed to be my savior was delivering the worst news I'd had in my life.

"That's impossible," I insisted from the prone position. "My husband just came back from deployment to Cuba six weeks ago, and he was gone two months. So I can't be more than a month-and-a-half pregnant."

The doctor pulled down his mask and looked at me skeptically. "Well, uh, Ms. Miller, you must have been intimate with—"

I sat up on the table. "Don't even go there! No, I haven't been messing around on my husband, okay? Damn! I can't believe you would even say something like that." I lay back down. "Just go ahead and do your job, please, and get this damn baby out of me."

The nurse looked like she was about to burst out laughing, but when she saw the look on the doctor's face she seemed to change her mind.

"Ms. Miller, I'm sorry," he said, pulling off his latex gloves, "but you're too far along to have the abortion done in a clinic.

You'll have to check into a hospital to get the procedure done." And with that he walked out the door.

I was pissed!

But I went from pissed to dumbfounded after going to two different doctors, only to have them tell me the same thing. I knew I wasn't insane, and I knew I hadn't fucked around while hubby was in Cuba. In fact, I hadn't fucked around on him during the whole of our marriage. Had not even been tempted. In spite of all his faults, hubby could be damn charming, and I have to admit through all our ups and downs, and all of our arguments, and even after the infidelity—I might have been angry with hubby, but I really still liked him. We were friends. I'm loyal to my friends. I was even more loyal to my husband. I don't know what I was more distraught about—the fact that it looked like I was an adulteress or the fact that I was pregnant and couldn't get rid of it.

Well, it actually was possible to get an abortion in the second trimester (which I knew I wasn't in!), but I would have to go into a hospital to get it done, and it would cost, like, eight hundred dollars; eight hundred dollars that I didn't have. I considered borrowing it from friends—knowing that I'd be able to pay it back as soon as they performed the abortion and found out that I was really only six weeks' pregnant and refunded me the money—but when I called the hospital to make sure I was right about that, they told me no. If they performed the procedure and it turned out I wasn't in my second trimester they would not refund the money because they'd performed the procedure as if it was, and so I would be charged accordingly. Damn! Borrowing was out.

Then I decided I would have to sell my car, a Honda Civic that I had bought a few years before I married. But when

I called to see just how much I owed on the car I was flab-
bergasted. Not only was I nowhere near paying off the car,
I was actually six months in arrears, and they were trying to
repossess the car. How the hell could that be? I had actually
doubled up my payments the past few months! I called my
bank to find out what happened, and found that my checking
account was $750 overdrawn. What the hell? I indignantly
asked why I hadn't been notified. That's when I was told that
they had been mailing me notices on a regular basis. And
that in fact, a notice was mailed the day before and should be
in the mailbox that day. I hung up, totally bewildered. Both
hubby and I had direct deposit, and I never wrote checks for
more money than I knew was in our account. That's when it
occurred to me I hadn't seen any bank statements for at least a
few months. To be honest, I never wondered about it before,
because I was never one to keep good track of my finances.
If I didn't get any notice anything was wrong, I just assumed
everything was right. And I picked up the mail every evening
when I got home from work myself, so why hadn't I received
any mail tipping me off that there was a problem?

I hung up, told my boss I had to take off for the rest of
the afternoon, and sped home. I got to our apartment building about 12:30 p.m., just in time to see hubby standing at
the mailbox going through the mail. I stayed in the car and
watched as he threw three envelopes and a postcard in a
nearby trash can, returned the rest of the mail to the box, then
hopped into an unfamiliar car and drove away. I got out the
car and went through the trash can. There was a bank statement, a postcard from the bank notifying me of a bounced
check, a credit card statement saying that my balance was
overdue, and a letter from my auto finance company saying
that a repossession was being ordered, and that I should turn

my car in. I went ballistic. I jumped back into the car to head to the navy base to confront hubby, but as I passed a 7-Eleven a few blocks away I saw the car that I saw hubby drive away in. I pulled in, blocking him in, and stormed into the 7-Eleven.

"Hey, Karen," hubby said when he saw me. "What are you doing here?"

I glared at him for a moment, and then asked, "Whose car are you driving?"

"Um, a friend of mine's . . . one of the guys at my shop," he said nervously. "He lets me drive it sometimes."

"So where were you driving it to?"

"Just over here to get a sandwich," hubby said. "Why? What's wrong?"

I crossed my arms and pursed my lips while looking at him and tapping my foot. "So, are you going to stop by the apartment?"

"The apartment? Why would I go over there? I wouldn't have time to go over there if I wanted to. I only sneaked out for a few minutes. The officer on duty is probably looking for me now." He laughed. "You were in the navy. You know what a jerk some of these guys can be."

"Not as big a jerk as you," I exploded—the Angry-Ass Black Woman once again emerging. I threw the mail in his face. "You dirty motherfucker! You're going to let them take my car away? You fucking bastard. You didn't have shit when I married you!" I was advancing on hubby as I talked and he was steady backing up. Let me be clear, hubby was *never* physically afraid of me, not by a long shot. I'm sure he was backing up because he was in shock and didn't know what I would do next. I didn't know either. I'd never gone off on my husband in public, but I was totally out of control that day, and didn't care that everyone in the 7-Eleven was gawking at us.

"You didn't have a car before you married me," I continued. "Your credit was so fucked up you couldn't get a credit card, so I had to buy that fucking keyboard on mine and you never gave me the money you promised to pay the bill. But that wasn't enough. Now you're trying to get my car repossessed. You bastard. You no-good bastard." I burst out in tears and ran out of the store, hubby following closely on my heels.

"Karen," he said grabbing me roughly before I was able to climb into my car and pull off. "What the hell is wrong with you? Let's go home so we can talk about this. *In private.*"

I struggled free. "I'm not going anywhere with you. I hate you!"

He grabbed the car keys from my hand, then snatched the unlocked car door open and threw me in the back, jumped in the driver's seat, and started the ignition. I jumped out the car and started stomping down the street. I had only gone a few feet before he got out of the car—leaving the car running—and grabbed me from behind. "Karen, get your ass in the car now before I get angry."

I managed to get free and turned to face him. "Get angry and do what? Hit me? You've done that before. Cheat on me? You've already done that, too. Steal from me? Well, we've got proof you've already been doing that for a while. What are you going to do now, hubby?" I spit on the ground. "I hate you. And I can't wait to get an abortion."

I didn't mean to say it, but boy, did that stop him in his tracks. Long enough for me to run back to my car and pull off.

I didn't go back to work, but I didn't go home either. I went to a bar and tried to figure out my next move. I finally went home after about six hours. Hubby was sitting in the living room with all the lights out when I walked in the door. I looked at him but walked straight to the bedroom, locking the bedroom door behind me. He stood outside the door for about an hour telling me how sorry he was, and to please not have an abortion. I finally had to unlock the door in order to go to the bathroom, and he grabbed me in his arms and started crying. Damn. I told him that I was sorry, but my mind was made up. I was going to the doctor to get an abortion, and then straight from there to a lawyer to file for divorce.

I took off from work the next day and went to one more abortion clinic, and told the doctor ahead of time that I knew I was only between six and seven weeks' pregnant and was willing to take a lie detector test to prove it. He looked at me like I was nuts, but told me to get on the examining table. He gave me a thorough examination, but came to the same conclusion as the others; I was too far along to get a first-trimester procedure. But this doctor was at least sympathetic, and I do think he really believed me. He finally suggested that one of the reasons my uterus might be as thick as it was—which is how everyone was judging me to be so far along—might be because I was having twins. Oh Lord! Now remember, twins run in my family. Not only was I myself a twin, I actually had five sets of living twins in my family, so the prognosis seemed feasible, but certainly was of no comfort. Damn! I didn't want one kid and now I might be having two? I was beyond miserable. I went home and found hubby once again sitting in the living room in the dark. Once again I went straight to the bedroom without talking to him. And, once again, he parked himself in front of the bedroom door, pleading. He was sorry for everything he'd done, and if I gave him a chance he would prove what a wonderful husband and father he could be. I finally opened the door and told him I'd changed my mind, and that while I was still upset with him about everything he'd done, I loved him and wanted to have his child. So, yeah, I lied. So what? It wasn't like he hadn't lied to me a million times over. And the bottom line was that while the thought of being a mother depressed me, the thought of being a single mother was more than I could bear.

The next couple of months were tolerable, but barely. For someone who said he was happy about the prospect of having a child, he certainly wasn't an attentive prospective father. If I had a yearning for something in the middle of the night—and I had a fierce yearning for tapioca pudding—then I had to get up in the middle of the night and run to the store to get it. Hubby used the excuse that he had to get up in the morning to go to work, not caring that I had to also. If I was feeling miserable, I still had to clean and prepare dinner every night, or else the apartment would be filthy and we wouldn't eat. And hubby went back to staying out late. By then the doctors had to admit they'd made a mistake about the length of my pregnancy after further testing during my prenatal care, but it was too late; I was stuck.

One Friday night in December when I was about four months' pregnant, I fell asleep on the couch and was awakened by a large crash about four in the morning. I jumped up and saw hubby standing over me, and the mirrored clock that we had was smashed to pieces on the living room floor.

"Hey! What happened?" I said, now wide awake, but totally disoriented. I got up from the couch and took a few steps toward him, when he suddenly rushed over and slapped the shit out of me. Before I knew what was going on, he'd pushed me back down on the couch and started choking me.

"You know what happened, you bitch!" he growled, while

I frantically struggled to pry his fingers open. "You ate up everything in this house because you want me to starve." I didn't know what the hell he was talking about, but I finally managed to get him to turn me loose by scratching his face. He pulled back from the couch, and I scrambled up and ran for the front door. I didn't care that I was half-naked, I was getting the hell out of there. He managed to grab me by the arm, though, before I could make it, and pulled me back to him, then threw me on the floor.

"You ate all the cheesecake, didn't you? You didn't even think about me!" he yelled down at me.

"What cheesecake? What are you talking about? We don't have any cheesecake," I said as I tried to get up.

He slapped me back down. "Yeah, because your fat ass ate it all. You don't care if I eat or not."

"We never had any cheesecake. And I have a plate of dinner for you right in the microwave. Let me get it for you," I pleaded.

"Then get it," he said, yanking me up so hard I thought he dislocated my arm.

I walked to the kitchen, turned on the microwave, and then when he wasn't looking, I pulled out a butcher knife.

"Look, I don't want to cut you," I said, edging away from him and back toward the living room, holding the knife in front of me, "all I want to do is get out of here."

"Oh, you're going to pull a knife on me now, huh?" he sneered.

"I swear. All I want to do is get out the door."

"Get the hell on out, then," he said. "See if I care."

I continued to edge away from him, and got to the front door and reached behind me to turn the knob to open it, since I couldn't take the chance of turning around and him jumping me. I didn't count on the door being locked. I took my eye off him for just an instant to unlock the door, and why did I do that. It was all the time he needed. He leapt on me, and managed to knock the knife from my hand.

"No!" I screamed, as his punch smashed into my left cheek, knocking me to the floor. "Stop! Please stop! The baby. Please remember the baby."

"I don't care about no damn baby," he shouted as he crouched above me, punching me in the face. "You only got pregnant because you knew I didn't want your ass no more, you bitch!"

I wanted so bad to reach up and start fighting back—I swear I did. But as much as I wanted to, I couldn't. There was some force, stronger than me, that made me curl up in a fetal position instead, and protect my stomach from his blows.

That night, hubby whipped my ass. And when he got tired of punching me, he stood up and started kicking me, while I continued to protect my stomach. This man, who swore he wanted me to have his baby so badly, seemed to be doing everything in his power to make me lose it.

The beating lasted about fifteen minutes, and finally hubby was tuckered out and plopped down on the couch to take a rest. I tried a few times to get up, but I couldn't. I just lay on the floor crying. Finally he stood up, reached down and grabbed me by my hair and dragged me into the bedroom and threw me across the bed.

"And now I'm going to fuck you," he announced. "And you're going to like it. I'm going to fuck you until you're sore."

I don't know if he did or not. God was kind, and at last allowed me to black out.

The next morning I woke up to find hubby gone, and that I was in excruciating pain. My head was throbbing, my throat was sore, my eyes were black, my ribs felt bruised, and I had black and blue marks all over my arms and legs. I tried to stand up and was unable. I had to slowly slide down the side of the bed and literally crawl on the floor and to the bathroom, where I filled the bathtub with the hottest water I could stand and climbed in. It was only then that I allowed myself the luxury of vocalizing the pain that I felt; I started groaning, then moaning, then screaming. Screaming and crying—pitying myself, and wondering what had I done to deserve all of this. Oh no, don't get the idea that I thought I'd brought the prior night's beating on myself—I was fucked up mentally, but not that fucked up! I was wondering what I had done for God to allow me to be in my situation. Was this some kind of karmic retribution for earlier evils I had done to others? I thought about all the guys I had used for their money in my wild teenage years; all the scams I had pulled off, all the drugs I had ingested, all the liquor I had drank, all the fights I had fought. Was this God's way of saying, "Nyah, nyah, nyah, nyah, nyah; I really got you good"?

I sat there for a while more feeling sorry for myself before finally getting out, grabbing a towel, and gently patting the water off of my still very sore body. But as I stood there, with the salty tears of self-pity still running down my cheeks, I started questioning God's reasoning. Yeah, I had used guys for money, but only dudes with a lot of money who flashed their wealth in my face—and even then I gave as good as I got. Yes, I had pulled scams; but none in which anyone got really hurt. Uh-huh, I had used drugs, but never hard drugs, and I had never developed a habit, or stolen money to buy them. Okay, I did my fair share of drinking, but never to excess. All right, I did a lot of fighting, but I never started a brawl or bullied someone just because I knew I could. I fixed myself to start cursing God for his injustice, then caught a glimpse of myself in the full-length mirror on the bathroom door. I was barely recognizable. I looked like shit. I looked like one of those battered women you see on television shows that always prompted me to say, "Damn. I'd never end up like that." But there I was.

As I stared at my hideous image, the anger I was beginning to feel toward God suddenly screeched to a halt, did a sharp U-turn, and zeroed in on the correct target for my hostility—that motherfucker I married. Here we'd been married less than two years, and he's committed every kind of marital violation there was—stealing, cheating, lying, and physical abuse. And to beat me while I was carrying his child! The kid he'd begged me to keep. Oh, that motherfucker. It only took me two seconds to go from a whiny battered woman to An Angry-Ass Black Woman.

I slowly walked back out to the bedroom and started getting dressed, trying to figure out my next move. Of course I had to get the hell out of there, but the reality was I had nowhere to go. Both of my parents were dead, my older brother David was strung out on heroin, my twin sister, Kitty, was strung out on crack, and my younger brother Joe T. was in the navy, on a destroyer out somewhere on the Pacific Ocean. And truth be told, I really didn't want to go back to New York until I knew where my life was going. I just needed somewhere I could go for four or five months so I could get my head together. But where? I realized I needed to get an apartment there in Mississippi; the rents were cheap, and I already had a job.

While I was contemplating my next move I heard the lock turn on the door. Now dressed, I hurried—as best I could—into the living room to greet my husband.

"Hey, sweetie," I said as he entered, wearing the same clothes he'd had on the night before. "Are you hungry? Let me fix you something to eat."

Hubby looked at me suspiciously, then walked over to the sofa and sat down. "What are you going to fix?" he said, crossing his arms behind his head in a leisurely fashion.

I cooked him a massive lunch, turned on the television and handed him the remote, then kneeled down and took off his boots and massaged his feet. I told him how sorry I was about my behavior the night before, and told him I was going to change. I was going to be the best wife in the world. Told him that I loved him, and that I knew it must have really hurt him to have to hurt me the way he did. He ate that shit up. I wanted to vomit. He eventually fell asleep in front of the TV, and I knew he'd be knocked out for the rest of the day. I looked down at him, and seriously considered going to the kitchen, getting a knife, and slitting his fucking throat, but changed my mind. I didn't really want to go to jail. Instead I went to the bedroom and called a friend from work, and asked her if she felt like shopping.

Corrine knocked on the door about a half hour later, and when I opened the door and she saw me, she let out a loud gasp and covered her mouth. I grabbed my keys and pocketbook and pushed her back outside. "C'mon," I ordered, "let's get outta here. I'll explain everything in the car."

I had met Corrine on my very first day at work, and while we were always friendly, it wasn't until I got pregnant that we started to get kind of tight. Corrine was a blond, blue-eyed, homespun woman from Minnesota with one son, and she loved children. She was the kind of woman who baked a cake or brownies to bring in to work every Friday. You know, the kind of oh-so-cheery woman who you wanted to slap just to make her stop smiling. When I got pregnant she started bringing me little gifts for the baby; stopping by my desk three or four times a day to see if I needed her to run to the store to get something; and buying baby magazines. She was much more thrilled about my pregnancy than me. At first she got on my nerves, but gradually I began to like her, and appreciate her attention. She was just a really nice young woman who liked making people happy.

We hopped into her car and I told her to just drive, and then I filled her in on everything that had happened the night before.

"Oh gosh darn [she really talked like that], Karen. What are you going to do?" she asked, staring straight ahead, but tears forming in her eyes.

"Well, the first thing I've got to do is get the hell out of there," I responded. "I don't want to go into a shelter, and I don't have enough money to get an apartment, but I've got to figure out how to get the money."

"How much money do you need?"

I reached over and patted her shoulder. "Naw, Corrine. I don't want your money. I don't want to wind up in debt to anyone."

"Well," she said cheerfully, "I didn't say anything about loaning you any money; I just asked how much you need."

I thought about it for a moment. "I've got nothing in the bank, but I get paid next Friday, and that's, like, $550. I could probably get a two-bedroom apartment for about $500, but everyplace wants the first month's rent, and the first month's security before they'll let you move in. I'm at least $450 short."

"Why do you need a two-bedroom?"

"For the baby," I said gloomily. "I'm probably going to be

there for a while, and I don't want the baby sleeping in my room."

She was silent for a moment, and then said slowly, "What about if you got a roommate and the two of you get a three-bedroom apartment for, like, seven hundred?"

"Hmm, $1,400 to move in, split in half, I'd still have to come up with $700, and I'm only able to come up with $550." I paused. "I'd only be $150 short then, but I don't know where I could come up with the extra money." I shrugged. "And where would I find a roommate?"

"Maybe your roommate could pay the extra money to move in, and then you just pay an extra $75 a month for rent for two months, and you'd be even."

I shook my head. "One, I don't know anyone who's looking for an apartment; and two, I don't know anyone who would be willing to make an arrangement like that."

Corrine pulled over on the road and stopped the car. "I do."

"Do what?"

"I know someone who might want to get an apartment, and wouldn't mind loaning you—I mean, fronting you—the extra money," Corrine said, suddenly eager.

I looked at her skeptically. "Yeah? Who?"

"Me."

I looked at her and laughed. "You? What do you need an apartment for? You already have a house. And a nice one at that. And wait a minute, what about you husband and son?"

Corrine bit her lip. "I'm leaving Tim. And it would make sense for Little Timmy to stay with his father. Like you said, it's a nice house, and the only one he's ever known. I could get him on some weekends, but I think it's best he stay there."

Now it was my turn to gasp. Little Miss Suzy Homemaker talking about leaving her happy home, and her child? I guess my reaction hurt a bit because she lowered her eyes. "I've been thinking about it for a while, Karen. I'm really not happy, and I just want to be happy. I got pregnant right out of high school and married Tim two months later. Now I'm twenty-six years old, and I feel like I've missed out on a lot of things. I've never had my own place. I've never been able to go out and have a good time. I've never had the luxury of sleeping late and not worrying about making sure everyone ate."

"Damn, Corrine! I never would have thought," I said.

She looked up and gave me a weak smile. "I sound like a really horrible person, huh?"

"No," I said slowly. "You sound a little mixed-up, but you also sound like if you don't make the move you're going to be miserable, and that's not good for you, your husband, or your child."

She let out a deep sigh. "I'm miserable already."

"Have you thought about marriage counseling?" I asked.

"I'd rather start counseling after I'm already out of the house," she said in a firm voice.

"You've really thought about this, huh?"

She nodded. "I have. I mean, I really have. Just this morning I thought about looking for a place to stay, and here I come pick you up and you're talking about the same thing! Well, golly gee! It's like a sign, don't you think? We could be like Kate and Allie," she said referring to the eighties television sitcom about two divorced women with children who lived together.

"Do you really think we'd get along as roommates?" I said skeptically.

"Oh darn, yes, most definitely!" She giggled. "I mean, I know you can be kind of . . . well—"

"Bitchy?" I offered.

"I was going to say grouchy. I swear!"

We looked at each other and laughed.

"Anyway," she continued. "I think we'll get along just fine."

I stuck out my hand. "Then it's a deal."

The two of us took vacation days the next week and used the time to look for a place to stay while our husbands thought we were at work. We finally found a nice spot in a safe neighborhood in Pascagoula, a town only ten minutes away from our jobs, for $650 a month. There were three bedrooms—two right next to each other, and the other a little further down the hall. That one, I told Corrine, would be the baby's room.

"But, Karen, why not put the baby in the room right next to you? I don't mind having the smaller room."

"No. I plan on feeding the baby, putting it to bed, closing the door, and then walking into my own room and closing that door so I don't have to hear the baby if it cries."

"Karen!" Corrine said, alarmed.

"Look, I said I would feed the baby first, and I'll make sure it has a dry diaper, but I don't plan on catering to a baby just because it wants to be held," I said firmly. "I'm not going to raise a spoiled brat, and it needs to learn early on that I'm not going to be waiting on it hand-and-foot just because it makes some noise."

Corrine looked at me, a worried look on her face, but she said nothing.

So we paid a deposit to secure the apartment. Now we just had to move. I continued being the sweetie-pie, lovey-dovey, doting wife, and hubby continued being an asshole; I guess he figured he had whipped me into shape. I spent a few days trying to figure out how to move out without hubby realizing what was going on—which would be difficult since

I'd decided to take all of the furniture in our apartment to furnish the new one. How to move the furniture out without him realizing what was going on? Some of his navy buddies lived in our apartment complex and worked various shifts, so if I tried to do it while hubby was at work I had no doubt that one of them would see what was going on and dime me out.

Then I had a stroke of luck.

My brother Joe T. called me one morning, and said that he was driving from his base in Long Beach, California, to Chicago to visit a friend over the Christmas vacation. I told him he was nuts to be trying to drive to Chicago in the middle of winter, when an idea hit me.

"Hey, Joe. You know what? You should swing by Mississippi and come by my place and pick me and hubby up. We'll drive with you as far as Detroit, and then you can drop us off to see his family and keep on going. And it'll be fun, seeing I haven't seen you in almost four months," I said, crossing my fingers as I spoke.

"Wow, yeah, that would be cool," he said without hesitation. "But I don't know when I'm driving back."

"No problem," I said, all happy as hell. "We can catch a plane back. This'll be fun!"

I hung up, prepared a nice meal for hubby, and sat down next to him as he wolfed it down. "Guess what," I said, rubbing his feet. Yeah, that's right. I was the one who was five months' pregnant, but I was rubbing his feet! "Joe T. called today. He's driving to Chicago and he volunteered to drop us off in Detroit if we wanted to take the ride. I thought it would be nice for your mom to see me while I'm still able to travel. You know, before I get too far along."

Hubby didn't have to even think about it before shouting, "Wow! Yeah! I'd love that. My mom always goes all out for

Christmas and Thanksgiving. You should taste her German chocolate cake."

"Mm, I can't wait." I didn't even like German chocolate cake, okay?

"When's he gonna get here?"

"He's leaving tomorrow morning, so he should be here in about twenty hours, because he's driving straight through," I explained. "I figured he should get a day's rest and then we'll leave early Wednesday morning."

"Bet," hubby said, pushing me away from him to grab the telephone and call his mother.

When Joe T. pulled into our apartment complex parking lot I ran out and greeted him with a great big hug, and showered him with kisses. I missed my little brother so bad, and wanted to cry on his shoulder and tell him everything I'd been through, but I managed to restrain myself. It was hard, but I did keep my mouth shut. Part of my master plan. Joe T. was so wonderful! He rubbed my stomach, and told me he was looking forward to being an uncle, then he and hubby exchanged high-fives as he congratulated my husband on the upcoming bundle of joy.

"Man, Ke-Ke must really love you. She always said she wasn't going to have any kids," Joe T. said as he, hubby, and I walked into the apartment. "You must be the man!"

"Yeah," hubby said, without batting an eye. Joe T. said that he wanted to be the godfather, and then asked hubby, "I know you're taking good care of her, right, man?"

Hubby put his arm around my shoulder and pulled me close to him. "Are you kidding? You know I'm not going to let anything happen to her. This is the love of my life!"

Yeah, right.

Joe T. slept for about twelve hours, and hubby and I spent

the time packing, and talking excitedly about our impending trip. Hubby was actually being nice to me for a change, and I made sure to do nothing to piss him off.

We were supposed to leave Mississippi at eleven a.m. on Wednesday and at nine that morning we were packing the car when the phone rang . . . on cue. I ran into the apartment to catch it, then came back out and gave the guys the bad news.

"I can't believe this," I said, wiping nonexistent tears from my eyes. "That was my doctor. He said I have to be on bed rest for the rest of the week or I risk losing the baby."

Hubby said, "Shit."

Joe T., on the other hand, dropped the suitcase he'd been holding and rushed over to me. "My God, Ke-Ke. Are you okay? Why did the doctor say that? Are you in pain? Do you need me to take you to the hospital?" he asked in a rush as he gently led me back into the apartment and sat me down on the couch. "Here, put your feet up." He grabbed some pillows from the love seat and placed them on the floor in front of me. "Are you sure you're not in any pain?"

Hubby came up behind Joe T., and stood there looking stupid for a minute. Then he asked, "What exactly did the doctor say?"

"Well, I went to see him on Monday because I was spotting—"

Joe T. jumped up. "Ke-Ke, did he say you're okay? What about the baby?"

"I'm fine, I'm fine," I said, trying to calm Joe T. down. "He just ran some tests, and said that it seemed I was under some kind of strain"—I looked at hubby pointedly, but he didn't even have the decency to avert his eyes—"and that I needed to keep off my feet for a few days. You know, just take it easy," I started fake sobbing, covering my face with my hands as I willed tears into my eyes. "I asked him if it was okay for me to take the trip to Detroit, and he said under no circumstances should I do so."

Joe T. sat down beside me and started rubbing my back. "Dag. But don't worry. We'll just stay here and take care of you. I don't mind."

"No, no, no," I said hurriedly. "There's no reason why you two can't go!"

Joe T. waved me off. "Man, Ke-Ke, you're crazy. There's no way we're leaving you here by yourself. Right, man?"

Hubby's mouth said, "Right," but his eyes were like, "Damn. I'm going to miss seeing my family because of this stupid bitch."

"Joe T. I'm serious. You two should go ahead without me. I swear, I'll get more rest without you guys here. I'll just lay here on the couch and read magazines and books and just relax. There's enough food here that I can just pop in the microwave, so I'll be fine. Please go."

"But—"

"No buts, Joe T.," I insisted. "You guys go on ahead. Just call me when you get there so I know you're okay."

It took some convincing, but Joe T. finally agreed to leave my side. Poor baby! Hubby, on the other hand, couldn't wait to get the hell out of there. I stayed on the couch, biding my time, reading and watching television until I got a telephone call a few hours later from Joe T., checking up on me. After I assured him I was okay, he said they'd already made it up to Georgia, and should be in North Carolina by the end of the day.

As soon as he hung up I called Corrine. "Okay, it worked. What time can the guys get here tomorrow?"

Joe T. called me the next morning to tell me they'd already

made it to Ohio, and then hubby called that afternoon to tell me he'd made it to Detroit. Joe T. was staying at hubby's family's house to get some rest before pushing off to Chicago, so he got on the telephone to see how I was doing, then hubby's mother asked to speak to me.

"You okay, baby? Your brother told me you weren't feeling well. You better take care of yourself and my grandbaby," Ma said in her sweet, caring voice.

"I'm fine, Ma. Just getting some rest," I assured her.

There was a pause. "You sure you're alright? What is it I hear in your voice? You been doing okay?"

I swear, that woman was psychic.

"No, no, I'm fine," I repeated. "Don't worry, okay? The doctor just wanted me to get some rest." I hated lying to her, because while her son was an asshole, Ma was one of the most wonderful women I'd ever met.

Hubby finally got back on the phone. "So, um, okay, seems like you're doing okay, Karen. I'll call you later, okay?"

"Cool. But you know what? Don't even call me back today, because I'm really tired and I'm just going to try and sleep for the rest of the day. Just give me a call sometime tomorrow morning or afternoon."

"Okay, then," hubby said. "I love you."

"I love you, too," I responded as I watched my coworkers lift the television and haul it off to the U-Haul truck. "And I can't wait for you to get home, baby. I have a big surprise for you."

That night I was in my new apartment, which now contained all the furnishings from my old place, enjoying a good night's sleep. I had the telephone company move the telephone number to my new apartment, so hubby had no idea that there was anything up when he called me.

The day that hubby was flying back to Mississippi I called him and told him I couldn't wait to see him, and verified that I'd be there to pick him up when his plane arrived at one a.m.

"And remember me telling you I have a big surprise for you when you got back? Well, believe me, you're going to be very surprised," I said, the smile evident in my voice.

"Yeah. Something I'm going to enjoy," hubby asked excitedly.

"Baby, I can promise you right now, it's a surprise you'll remember for the rest of your life."

That night, around midnight, I sat on the couch eating potato chips, watching Gregory Peck in *The Guns of Navarone* on HBO. At exactly 1:15 a.m. hubby called.

"Hello?" I asked, yawning, as if I'd just woken up.

"Karen! Why are you still home? You were supposed to be here to pick me up fifteen minutes ago," he shouted.

"What? Oh, my goodness," I said, making like I was disoriented. "I must have fallen asleep. I'll get dressed and be right on my way."

"You have to get dressed? What?"

"Um, yeah. I'd just taken a shower and sat down on the bed for a moment, and I must have conked out. It will just take me a minute to get dressed and get out of here. I should be there in about an hour."

"Shit. Well, hurry the fuck up." *Click.*

I popped another potato chip in my mouth. Gregory Peck was waiting to see if the explosives they set would blow up the big cannon-sized guns, and I wanted to see, too.

An hour and fifteen minutes later the phone rang again. "Hello," I said in as panicky a voice as I could manage.

"Karen! Your fat ass is still home?"

"Oh, I'm sorry! I fell asleep again. But I'm dressed, and I'm going to run out the door right now. I'll see you in about an hour." This time I hung up before he did. I used the remote to turn the volume on the television back up. *Force 10 from Navarone* was now on, and I was hoping the sequel was going to be as good as the first movie, even though Robert Shaw was now playing the Gregory Peck part and Edward Fox was in the role originated by David Niven.

At three-thirty a.m. the telephone rang again.

"Karen, you know what? I'm going to kick your ass," hubby roared into the receiver.

"Yeah? You're going to have to walk a long way to do it. Or do you think any of your drunk-ass friends is going to get up at this time of night to drive an hour to pick you up?" I couldn't resist it. I giggled like a little girl.

"What? What the hell kinda games are you playing?"

"You'll find out when you get to the apartment. Believe me, you'll find out," I said, now laughing as I talked.

"I'm going to kick your—"

Click. I got up from the couch and stretched. Just as I expected, Robert Shaw would never be the man Gregory Peck was, and I simply didn't find Edward Fox likable. I decided not to bother watching to see how the movie ended. I went to bed, but not before turning the ringer to the telephone off.

Bright and early the next day, about 12:30 p.m., I got up and turned the ringer back on. The phone rang within ten minutes.

"Hello."

"Karen, where the hell are you?"

"I'm home. Where are you?"

"I'm out in the cold at a fucking pay phone, is where the hell I am!"

"Hm, too bad. It's nice and toasty here."

"Where's all the furniture? What the hell is going on?" he demanded.

"Man, even you can't really be that dense." I sighed. "I mean, come on. What the hell do you think is going on?"

There was a pause, then all of a sudden I heard hubby sniffing. Then sniveling. Then letting out soft sobs. Then he broke into full-blown bawling.

"Karen," he finally managed to croak. "I know I've treated you like shit. I'm really sorry."

"Are you really?"

"Honest to God, I am," he said, still sobbing loudly. "I don't know what the hell is wrong with me."

I let out a deep sigh. "You know what, hubby? I don't know what the hell is wrong with you either."

"Karen. Karen. I'm so sorry. I'm really so sorry. Baby, please don't leave me."

"Listen, calm down. I understand what you're going through. I do. But calm down, I want to tell you something important."

"But, Karen—"

"No, come on, calm down."

"Okay."

"Are you calm?"

"Yes."

"Okay, listen closely now . . ." *Click!* I hung up the phone and turned on the television and found that *To Kill a Mockingbird* was playing on Channel 5. I settled in to watch my man Gregory Peck.

Fuck both hubby and Robert Shaw.

★ ★ ★

"Mommy, I know you can hear me, and I just want you to know that I realize you're just getting some needed rest. But don't rest too long, Mommy, because I miss you."

Oh, my baby!

"I'm the only one in the room now, Mommy. Cousin Sister was here, but she had to get to work, she just stopped by for a few minutes. And Uncle Joe called my cell to tell me that he'll be here in a few minutes. But right now, Mommy, we're by ourselves."

I can feel her rubbing my face.

"I hope you're not worrying about all the arguing going on in here sometimes, but you know how our family can be. Get two or more in a room and you have the makings of a fight, you'd always say. But I'm trying to keep it civil as I can without getting in the crosshairs myself, Mom."

I want to tell her that I understand, and to thank her, but I still can't move my damn lips! Oh, Lord, I want to reach out and pull Camille to my breast and rock her back and forth like I did when she was a little girl, but I'm still stuck. I'm still paralyzed.

"Mom, do you remember when you used to tell me that it's you and me against the world? Well, it kinda feels like that right now. I don't mean to be disrespectful, but some of our family is getting on my dang nerves right about now."

I know, baby, they usually get on mine.

"But that's okay, in a little while you're going to wake up, and I'm going to put you in the car and drive you home where I can take care of you all by myself. It'll just be me and you, Mom. Just me and you."

Just the way it's always been, babe.

thirteen

*K*aren, you've got to get to the hospital."

I glanced up at my roommate, Corrine, and shook my head no. I could see where she was coming from, though. After all, I was slowly moving along on all fours on the floor, panting like a dog suffering from sunstroke, and occasionally letting out howls that would have made any canine proud.

Labor is a bitch.

"Karen, please let me take you to the hospital," Corrine pleaded.

"No, I'm trying to wait until the pains are three minutes apart," I gasped. "I don't want to be sitting in a hospital room for ten hours just waiting."

"But at least they'll be able to give you something for the pain," my downstairs neighbor Rena (pronounced Re-NAY for some reason) said urgently. "I can't bear to see you like this."

"I'm not going to be getting an epidural. I'm having natural birth," I said, as one of my pains eased. "I read somewhere that the medicine can get into the baby's system and cause birth defects."

"Dag, you're a really good mom," Rena said while Corrine went to the kitchen and ran cold water on a hand towel. "That's love."

"Bullshit! Tell her," I barked at Corrine, who was following me around as I scrambled around the floor, trying to get the wet rag on my neck.

"She's only doing it because she doesn't want to be stuck with a retarded child," Corrine said wearily.

"Oh," Rena said, a shocked look on her face.

Corrine just sighed. She had been with me for the whole last four months of my pregnancy, and knew exactly how I felt. I had to have the kid, but I didn't have to like it. In fact, I had even called up adoption agencies to arrange for someone to get the baby while I was still in the hospital. But then—just by coincidence—I saw a news report about the dismal rate of African-American children being adopted, though white children were in high demand. The report said that most black children given up for adoption stayed in foster care for the rest of their lives. Having known some kids who had grown up in foster homes, even I couldn't be coldhearted enough to doom my child to a possible life of physical and sexual abuse. Yeah, I was pretty much stuck. My only hope was that I could force hubby to take the child once our divorce was final. I was even willing to pay child support. But in the meantime, I didn't want to do anything that might result in a physically or mentally damaged child. Hell, if I couldn't convince hubby to take her, I was going to be the one stuck taking care of her.

I had already picked out a name—Camille. Again, just in case I was stuck with her I was hoping to at least learn how to tolerate the kid, and I figured the odds of that happening would increase if I named her after my niece—David's daughter—who was the only kid I liked since Beverly and Kris Keiser's son Malik. I didn't refer to the thing inside my stomach kicking me and giving me heartburn by name, however. I simply referred to it as "the kid," "the child," or just "it." Every now and then I would refer to it as "the baby," usually just to make Corrine happy.

"Yeah, oh." Then a couple of seconds later, *"Ooooohhhhh!*

Oh God!" I rolled over on my back, and started pulling at my hair.

"Karen, that one was only three minutes after the last one," Corrine said, kneeling down next to me on the floor.

"You sure?" I eyed her suspiciously.

"Positive."

"Okay. Help me up. Let's get out of here."

It took the two of them to haul me up from the floor, and about fifteen minutes to get me out the door and downstairs to the parking lot. We headed for my car—Corrine was going to drive it since her car was in the shop—but when we got to my parking spot we found the car wasn't there.

"What the hell? Where's my . . . *Aughhhh!*" I grabbed my stomach and fell back on Rena, who then fell back on the side of a parked car. I moaned and groaned until the pain passed, then, panting, I pointed to my empty parking spot. "What the hell?"

One of my other neighbors came out the door to see what was going on and if she could help.

"Oh, this guy came over and got in the car. He had the keys, so I didn't think anything about it," the neighbor said after the situation was explained to her. "Tall, kind of athletically built, dark skinned, and oh, yeah, he had on a Seabee uniform."

Corrine and I looked at each other. "That motherfucking bastard husband of mine," I hissed. "I oughta wring his fucking neck!"

Rena didn't have a car. The neighbor's car had been totaled a week before. Corrine's car was in the shop. My car was stolen by my soon-to-be ex-husband. Even though I had phoned a few days before to inform him that the doctor said he thought I'd be delivering any day. Fuck!

The Pascagoula Naval Station was just a block away, and so I suggested that we walk over there. Rena was in the navy, Corrine and I worked for the navy; surely, we figured, we could get someone there to drive me to Keesler AFB Hospital in Biloxi, just twenty minutes away. If it wasn't a Sunday, Easter Sunday at that, we might have been in luck. As it was, there was only one person on duty at the time, and he wasn't cooperating . . . something about him facing court-martial if he left his post. Yeah. Whatever. I let out another howl as we hobbled outside, trying to figure out what to do next.

"Isn't that Joe over there?" Rena asked, pointing to a short, heavy-set man jauntily walking our way while whistling joyfully, seemingly lost in happy thought.

"Joe!" I yelled. "Please come here, quick!"

Joe was also in the navy, and after assessing the situation he agreed to a plan I had hastily put together. He went into the duty office, pretending to look for something he'd left there the day before, and when the sailor on duty wasn't watching he swiped the keys to one of the navy trucks. We climbed in, and fifteen minutes later (every yell I let out spurred Joe to ignore the speeding laws) I was being wheeled to the maternity ward.

I was in labor for more than twenty hours, some of which could be described as comical. Like when I told one of the nurses that I was going to be sick to my stomach, and asked if I could be given a plastic basin to catch my food waste. She said okay, but didn't seem to be in a rush to comply. So I asked her again.

"Mrs. Miller, it's not at all uncommon for women in labor to feel nauseous. You may think you need to throw up, but really, you don't," she said in a condescending voice.

"No, I'm really about to be sick," I insisted in between contractions.

"Really, dear, you're not. But if it will calm you down, I'll get you a bedpan in a moment."

I was getting pissed, watching her dawdle about the room, fluffing this, moving around that . . . and deliberately taking her slow time.

I motioned Corrine over to my bed. "Help me sit up further," I told her urgently.

A worried look crossed Corrine's face, but she complied. I then swung my legs so that they dangled over the side of the bed, prompting the nurse to turn to me and say, "Mrs. Miller, please don't tell me you're going to try and walk to the bathroom on your own."

I looked her straight in the eyes, shook my head, and then let loose. That chick in the movie *The Exorcist* had nothing on me. You would have thought I'd gotten a PhD in Projectile Vomit. The nurse was about three feet away from me, but I still managed to cover almost the entire front of her uniform. Rena busted out laughing, and even Corrine had to grin. Never again will that bitch deny An Angry-Ass Black Woman in labor.

We'd arrived at the hospital about ten p.m., but it wasn't until the following afternoon that the doctors decided my child should be delivered by Caesarean birth. Camille was born at one p.m.

I was so worn out that I immediately fell asleep, and didn't wake until the following morning.

"Oh, Karen, she's so lovely," Corrine cooed at me.

"We just got back from the nursery," Rena added. "She looks just like you!"

"Does she?" I asked groggily. "Dang, I'm hungry. Have they served breakfast yet?"

"Shoot, I wouldn't eat anything in this hospital if I were

you," Rena said with a big grin. "After you sprayed that nurse with vomit I bet she's paid someone in the kitchen to poison your ass."

We all cracked up laughing, then started talking about how crazy everything was that night, including my car being stolen, and then us turning around and stealing the navy truck. I was just getting ready to ask if Joe had gotten the truck back before anyone noticed it was stolen when a pretty young nurse walked in, sporting a clipboard and huge smile.

"Well, Mother, now that you've woken up would you like to see your little precious bundle of joy?" she said, coming over and preparing to take my temperature. "I can have someone bring her down from the nursery in just a moment."

I looked at her and shook my head. "That's okay. I want to finish talking to my friends. Maybe a little later." I turned back to Rena and Corrine.

"But, Mother, you haven't seen your baby yet, have you?" the nurse said before I could restart the interrupted conversation. "Don't you want to hold her?"

"No, it can wait," I said, not bothering to hide the annoyance in my voice. "There'll be plenty of time to hold her when I have to take her home." Out of the corner of my eye I could see Rena and Corrine exchange worried looks.

"But, Mother—"

"Nurse, please. My name is Karen Miller. You can call me Karen, or you can call me Mrs. Miller. But stop calling me Mother," I snapped.

The nurse took a step back as if I'd hit her. "Well, Mrs. Miller," she said carefully. "Don't you want to hold the baby and count her little toes and her little fingers?"

I glared at her, pissed that she was making my friends feel uncomfortable. "I'm sure if there were something wrong with her little toes or her little fingers someone would have already told me. Now, do you mind?"

Before she could answer, yet another nurse walked into the room. "Mrs. Miller," she said urgently. "We have it noted that you're supposed to be breastfeeding your baby. Is that correct?"

"Yes," I answered, rolling my eyes. "Why?"

"Oh, dear!" she said instead of answering me. "I'll bring your daughter in immediately."

"Why? I was just telling this nurse here I'd see the kid later."

"Well, when it's been noted that a baby is to be breastfed, the nursery is instructed not to give it any nourishment, because once a baby is given a bottle it will often refuse the breast." The nurse paused, and then took a deep breath. "That means your daughter hasn't had any nourishment since she was born yesterday afternoon."

"You're kidding!" Rena and Corrine said simultaneously.

The first nurse looked at me accusingly and then walked out the room, but I didn't care. Hell, it wasn't my fault the kid didn't eat. I didn't make or know about the stupid rule. Wasn't it the hospital's responsibility to keep track of these things?

"I'll be right back with the baby," the second nurse said.

"Hold on, I'm talking to my friends and—"

"Actually, we need to get out of here," Corrine said, tugging at Rena's arm. "We just wanted to stop in and see how you were doing."

"But we weren't finished talking," I protested.

"We'll be back later," Rena assured me.

I rolled my eyes at the nurse after they left. "Well, you may as well bring her in now since I'm not doing anything else."

She brought the kid in a few minutes later, and stayed and showed me exactly how to breastfeed, then waited in the room until I finished. Then she asked if I wanted her to bring in a portable crib so that I could have the baby sleep in the room with me.

"No, thanks," I said firmly, as I handed the baby back to her. "I'm going to be stuck with her for the next eighteen years; you guys can take of her while I'm here."

Back then mothers who had C-sections were kept in the hospital for four days; I planned to get as much rest as I could during that time. The next two days I only saw the baby when the nurse brought her in for feeding, and as soon as I finished I would hand her right off. On the third day, however, there was some kind of emergency happening on my floor, so the nurse didn't come right away after I rang the bell for her to come get the baby. I sighed and lay the baby on my stomach, then dozed off. A few minutes later I woke to find her nuzzled up under my chin. I reached down and moved her back to my stomach, and closed my eyes. Again I woke to find her up under my chin. How the hell is she managing to do this? I wondered. This time I stayed awake and watched as this little tiny thing just kind of squirmed and wormed her way up my chest, past my breasts, and up under my chin. I thought it was funny, so I lay her on my stomach and watched her do it again. And then again. The fourth time I kinda laughed and leaned down and kissed her on her head as I went to reach for her, but before I could touch her, her little head raised, her eyes opened, and she looked at me with what looked like a shocked look on her face. "Dang," I said with a little chuckle. "You act like you've never been kissed before."

And then it hit me.

She hadn't.

No one had ever kissed her.

Here she was a beautiful little baby, and she'd never been kissed.

Even her mother hadn't kissed her.

Suddenly my heart swelled so big with love I thought it would burst through my chest. Tears streamed down my face as I scooped Camille up and started smothering her with kisses. That's who she suddenly became to me. Camille. Not the baby. Not the child. Not the kid. She was Camille. My Camille. And I loved her. Oh, how desperately I loved her.

When the nurse finally came into the room to return Camille to the nursery she was shocked to find me protectively holding my child and insisting that they bring a crib into the room right away, as I was not letting my baby out of my sight.

The day I was due to be discharged I called the navy base and arranged for hubby to pick me up from the hospital. (He'd been at the hospital once since I'd given birth, but I'd barely spoken to him.) I asked him to pick up a baby's car seat from the Navy Exchange since the hospital wouldn't let a mother go home alone or without a car seat. I then called a girlfriend of mine, Sarah, and asked her to pick up Rena and then come to the hospital to bring me home, and requested that she be there fifteen minutes earlier than the time I gave hubby.

When he walked into the room he immediately started rushing me, saying he had to be back at the base in an hour because his office was being inspected by the base captain. I told him that it would take me a few minutes, and said he should just make himself comfortable. As soon as he took his jacket off, I told him that I just remembered that the hospital administration office needed him to fill out some paperwork for Camille's birth certificate. Just as I'd hoped, he left his jacket in the room when he went on the bogus errand, and as soon as the door closed behind him I dipped into the pocket and removed his copy of my car key from his key ring.

"Karen, I thought you said they needed to see me," he said when he walked back in five minutes later.

"I lied. You can leave now," I said with a chill in my voice that would have frozen Hell.

"Oh, yeah?" He looked over at Sarah and grunted. "Oh, I guess she's going to take you and the baby to your apartment, huh?"

"Nope, hubby. Sarah's going to take you back to your base. Rena's downstairs at the gift shop, but when she gets upstairs she's going to drive me home."

"What do you mean?"

"Just what I said. Sarah is going to drive you to the base in her car, and Rena is going to drive me home in my car." I looked at him with pure disgust in my eyes. "You are really the lowest of lowlife bastards. How could you steal my car when you knew how close I was to my due date?"

"I didn't steal it. I have a key, remember?" he said, smirking.

"Not anymore." I flashed the car key at him, and then threw him his key ring. "And if you make one threatening move toward me I'm going to call the doctor, and your ass will be up for court-martial before you can blink." That was one good thing about having Camille in an Air Force Base hospital—all of the doctors were military officers and could write hubby up if he made any trouble.

Hubby glared at me, and I could see in his eyes he wanted to smash my face in, but I stood there defiantly. Finally he turned to Sarah and said, "You ready?"

Sarah was a trooper; hubby could scowl and growl all he

wanted but she didn't care. She came over and gave me a quick peck on the cheek, grabbed her pocketbook, and without looking at hubby, said, "Well, come on," then marched out the door. Hubby gave me one more "I'ma fuck you up when I get the chance" stare before following her.

I chuckled for just a moment after they left, but only for a moment—I now had another problem. How was I getting home? Rena was called into work at the last minute so Sarah had arrived at the hospital without her. So I had the car, but no driver. The obvious solution would be for me to drive myself, but it was against hospital rules. I wasn't sure, but I think the hospital could, by law, keep Camille if I didn't comply since driving myself with a baby in the car might be considered a reckless act—especially after just having had a Caesarean section.

I managed to get through the check-out okay, saying my husband was outside waiting, and for some reason they believed me. Most new mothers are wheeled out of the hospitals with their newborn. I walked out the front door and into the parking lot. It was April, and it was hot . . . even for Mississippi. It took me about five minutes to find the car, five very hot, sweaty minutes, and the whole time I was praying that Camille stayed asleep. I finally located it, opened it up, and placed Camille on the front seat while I took the car seat out the box and set it up in the back. I started the car and turned on the air conditioner to keep her cool, but as I struggled with the car seat, beads of perspiration trickled down my neck, and the stitches from my surgery began to ache. It took another ten minutes to get it situated, and as soon as it was I climbed into the front with Camille and rested for a couple of minutes. When I had recovered slightly, I put Camille in the back passenger seat and prepared to drive away. That's when I discovered the next problem.

Hubby was six foot, three inches, so when he drove my little Honda Civic he always had the driver's seat pushed back as far as it would go so he could have enough leg room to drive comfortably. I was five feet even, and there was no way my feet could reach the brake and accelerator pedals with the seat that far back. Normally, it would have been simple to just sit on the seat, reach down between my legs, and pull the bar to reset the seat position, but when I tried I found I didn't have the strength to scoot the seat up. My stomach muscles, those needed to do the scooting, had been cut through in the C-section, and every time I tried to pull the seat forward it felt like I was tearing my body in half.

I tried jamming the seat release bar up, then getting into the back and pushing my legs against the front seat, but every time I tried the bar would spring back up and the seat would be unmovable. I was out there in that parking lot—pushing, pulling, praying, and silently crying—for a good half-hour before I collapsed in the back seat next to Camille.

I looked over at her, and saw that she was awake and looking at me with her big beautiful brown eyes. I wiped away my tears, and managed a weak smile. "Don't worry, baby, Mommy is going to do this. It's me and you against the world, but we're going to make it, Camille, we're going to make it."

And then it happened. Camille squinted her eyes and gave a little jerk of her head, as if to say: "I understand. Me and you, Mom."

That was all I needed. I kissed her (no shocked look from her now, because I'd been showering her with kisses for a bit by this point), raised the positioning bar again, and pushed the seat with all my might. Success!

"Camille, we did it!"

As I rolled our little Honda Civic out the parking lot and toward our home, Camille mouth gave a little twitch, which looked like a smile, and which I took as her acknowledging our victory.

We've been rolling like that ever since.

*   *   *

I didn't know someone could cry just on the inside, but damn if I ain't right now. I don't feel tears rolling down my cheeks, or my body being racked with sobs, but the cloudiness in my brain and the swelling in my heart that comes with crying—those I can feel. That bitch Death thought she could take advantage but one snarl from me sent her funky ass scrambling backwards again. That pussy.

"Mom, you've been here four days now—"

Four days??? I have? Shit!

"—and you wouldn't believe the number of cards and flowers your fans have sent you."

My fans! That's right, my fans. I've been so busy warding off this bitch, Death, that I forgot about my fans. Man, it's great they haven't forgotten about me!

"The nurse was in here yesterday saying that we're going to need a bigger room. Of course, you know Uncle Joe. He jumped right on it, saying that the hospital should go ahead and move you to the VIP wing since it was obvious that the community recognizes you are a VIP even if the hospital hasn't recognized it so far."

VIP wing? I didn't know hospitals had VIP wings. But, ahem, like Joe said, I'm a VIP. I love it!!!!!!!

"You could tell the nurse was sorry she said anything, Mom. She muttered something about her not knowing anything about a VIP wing, but we both know Uncle Joe, and he's not going to let it go.

Doesn't matter. By the time he gets everything straight and they decide to move you, you'll already be up and ready to get up on outta here."

I can feel small pieces of something cold and hard being rubbed across my lips. Oh. I guess my lips are chapped and Camille's rubbing ice chips across them. How sweet.

"I wouldn't be surprised if you opened your eyes right now, Mommy—"

Oh, I wish I could, Camille. I'm trying, babe!

"I know you can do anything, even if nobody else knows. Hey, I've witnessed it, right, Mommy?"

Ah, my baby kissed me.

Right, babe, I can do anything. At least when I'm doing it for you.

fourteen

"One hundred and twenty-five dollars? Um, okay, thanks. I'll see what I can do." I hung up, picked up my pencil, and tried to rework my budget to see if there was any way I could afford for three-year-old Camille to go to Washington, D.C., with her preschool. I was working as a secretary at the *Philadelphia Daily News,* in the operations department—which was a little office in the dark, dank garage where the daily dispatch of the delivery trucks was made—and earning $21,000 a year. Not too bad a salary for a secretary back in 1990, but still only enough to get through the bare necessities. I was doing okay financially, but not doing well. Not well enough to find an extra $125 for Camille to go on the trip.

"Karen, would you print out the expense report for me? And hurry up."

"Um, Ken, I'm on lunch right now. Can I do it when I'm off my break? In, like, thirty-five minutes?" I didn't bother looking up. Even for a boss, Ken was bossy. I can't say it was bad working for Ken Borders, though. And the whole office had a family atmosphere that I enjoyed, though I can't say I ever felt part of the family.

I'd moved to Philadelphia when Camille was only six months old. I had to get the hell out of Pascagoula, Mississippi, but I didn't want to return to Harlem because I didn't think it was a good environment to raise a kid. I picked Philly because Joe T.'s ship was docked at the Philadelphia Naval

Shipyard for an overhaul, and I thought it would be cool to be near him. My older brother, David, was totally strung out on heroin. Kitty was turning tricks to support her crack habit—Joe T. was the only sibling I had that seemed to have his shit halfway together.

It took him awhile to forgive me, though. When he found out what hubby had done to me, and that instead of telling him so he could beat him to a pulp I had used him to get hubby out of town, he was pissed! Don't get me wrong, I would have loved to sic Joe T. on hubby, but since he was in the navy, he could have gotten into real trouble if he seriously hurt hubby—and there was no doubt in my mind that he would have seriously hurt hubby. Joe T. had grown up to be a really big guy, and sported a purple belt in tae kwon do to boot! But as always, he did forgive me, and he and I had become closer than ever.

"Thirty-five minutes?" Ken looked at his watch and scowled. "You don't think you can—" He suddenly stopped. I looked up and saw why. His boss, The Suit, was walking in the office with one of his assistants, a long-legged willowy blonde—"Blondie." Ken was immediately all smiles. Not just because he was so happy to see The Suit, but because of Blondie—whom every man in the office had a crush on, including Ken. His was a harmless crush—Ken was a married man and was truly in love with his wife—but a crush nonetheless. He exchanged quick niceties with The Suit, then immediately turned his attention to Blondie. The Suit wandered around the office for a few minutes, talking to the different supervisors, and then stopped at my desk.

"So, Karen . . . what are you up to?" He peered down at the yellow legal pad I was writing on. "Doing a budget?"

"Yeah," I said wearily. "Camille's preschool is going to Washington, D.C., for the weekend, taking a tour of the White House and everything. I really want her to go, but I can't make the numbers work to make it possible."

"How much does the trip cost?"

"One hundred and twenty-five dollars, but . . ." I shrugged. "I'm going to make it work, though."

He patted me on the shoulder. "You know, I realize you want the best for Camille, but times are hard. Sometimes you just can't afford luxuries like sending your daughter on an out-of-town trip. She's young. She'll get over it."

I sighed and gave a little nod. He was probably right.

Just then Ken and Blondie walked over. "So, Jim was telling me you guys were looking at boats this weekend," Ken said to The Suit. "You thinking about buying?"

The Suit sat on the corner of my desk. "No, I'm not thinking of buying. I've just bought. A yacht."

"Get outta here," Ken said with awe in his voice. "How big is it?"

"Not very big, a fifty-footer. A real beauty. Can get up to six knots an hour," The Suit said, looking out the corner of his eye to make sure Blondie was listening. She was. "I plan to take her out a couple of weekends a month. She can sleep up to ten people, so I might invite a few people to come out with me every now and then."

"Wow!" Ken said. "How much does a baby like that cost?"

The Suit gave a dismissive chuckle. "I don't like to discuss prices, but let's just say boats like that go for about three thousand dollars a foot. You do the math."

I didn't even need a calculator. While I was trying to figure out how to swing the $125 cost for Camille to take a trip to

D.C., the man who just told me times were hard for every-body was boasting about spending $150,000 to buy a damn yacht. Damn.

I slumped down in my chair and put my head on my desk.

"Hey, ain't your lunch hour up?" Ken asked a few seconds later.

"Yeah, no problem." I was upset, and trying to beat back the unfounded resentment I felt. I figured work would take my mind off it.

I printed out the expense reports, then got busy doing payroll for the truck drivers, then went into Ken's office to do some filing. When I looked up it was 4:15 p.m. Forty-five minutes until quitting time. I walked back to my desk to fin-ish up some paperwork before I left.

The Suit, Blondie, and Ken were standing in a corner of the office, laughing, when Blondie looked at her watch and said she had to go.

"Where are you off to?" The Suit asked.

"I've got to take a contract to one of the sponsors for the Newspapers in Education program," Blondie said, while putting on her cashmere coat. "It's only a ten-minute walk. Down to Tenth and Callowhill Street."

"You're going to walk?" The Suit's brow furrowed. "You know it's already dark, and there's been a spate of muggings in that area."

"Absolutely no way you're going out there. You're a woman. Here, give me the contract," Ken said, slapping his hand on a desk. Blondie handed him a manila envelope, and I thought he was going to volunteer to make the trip for her. But oh, no! Instead he turned around, walked over, and placed the envelope on my desk. "Karen, walk this over to

Tenth and Callowhill. It won't take you but twenty minutes there and back."

I swiveled my chair around to face him, but he'd already started walking back over toward The Suit and Blondie. Since his back was to me, he couldn't see my face, but The Suit and Blondie did. Their sudden silence must have tipped Ken off, because he turned back to me to see what was going on. I slowly got up and walked over to him. Ken got a panicked look on his face; he must have realized what he'd just done. He opened his mouth to say something, but I beat him to it.

"So, it's not safe for her to walk over there," I said, pointing to Blondie, "but it's okay for me?"

"Karen, I—"

"You won't chance her getting mugged, raped, or murdered, but you don't care what happens to me?" I continued through clenched teeth.

"Now, Karen—" Ken began again.

"In the words of my beautiful black sister, Sojourner Truth, 'Ain't I a woman, too?'" I said, cutting him off once more.

The Suit took a deep breath and said calmly, "Karen, this is just a misunderstanding."

"A misunderstanding?" I looked at him incredulously. My eyes narrowed, and I was breathing hard. I turned around and started walking back to my desk to try and calm down, but suddenly stopped and swung back around to face The Suit.

"'That man over there,'" I pointed to Ken, "'says that women need to be helped into carriages, and lifted over ditches, and to have the best place everywhere. Nobody ever helps me into carriages, or over mud-puddles, or gives me any best place! And ain't I a woman?'" I was quoting from a speech Sojourner Truth made in 1851, and which I learned as a monologue while I was taking classes at the Negro Ensemble Company. I never recited it with more passion as I did then. I never felt it as much. I fought back the tears as I spoke.

"'Look at me! Look at my arm! I have plowed and planted, and gathered into barns, and no man could head me! And ain't I a woman? I could work as much and eat as much as a man—when I could get it—and bear the lash as well! And ain't I a woman? I have borne thirteen children, and seen most all sold off to slavery, and when I cried out with my mother's grief, none but Jesus heard me! And ain't I a woman?'"

"Slavery? What?" Ken sputtered. "Why are you talking about slavery?"

I ignored him, and continued to glare at The Suit. I was no longer the secretary taking orders from the man to whom he gave orders. I was An Angry-Ass Black Woman, and I was on a roll. "Yeah, it's a misunderstanding all right. The same misunderstanding that's been going on for hundreds of years in this United States of America; the misunderstanding that you white assholes have that your white women are more precious than black women."

Ken must have thought the heat was off him since I was addressing The Suit, because he came over and tried to put his hand on my shoulder. I jerked violently away, throwing him off-balance. "Don't fucking touch me," I snapped at him.

The shock on his face was priceless. I had never displayed more than minor irritation in the office, and had certainly never raised my voice or used profanity. "You punk. If you think it's unsafe for 'Miss Anne' here to walk out there, why ain't you do it your damn self? You've shown me what you think of me; now let me tell you what I think of you.

You're a fucking racist motherfucker, and you can kiss my black ass."

I then tossed my head, walked over to my desk and picked up the manila envelope, and threw it into the trash can. There was silence in the office as I got my coat from the coat rack and walked out.

When I returned to work the next morning nothing was said of the incident. But that week I had an extra $125 in my paycheck, marked as a bonus.

Camille made the trip to D.C.

It was about a year later when I submitted a piece to the "Letter to the Editor" column that ultimately changed my life. It was something I'd grown up doing; both my parents were avid readers, and between them they would bring in four or five different newspapers every day. All of us kids would read the papers just to have something to talk to Mommy and Joe-Joe about over the dinner table. They encouraged us to not only tell them what we read, but also tell them our opinions about what we read. And they also urged us to write the editor of the newspapers to share our opinions with them. It just seemed kind of fun to do and a familial bonding exercise at the time, but I now realize they were teaching us that our opinions mattered and should be heard.

Well, in early 1991, the *Philadelphia Daily News* devoted a quarter of a page to a women's rights demonstration in Boston or someplace, but only did two short paragraphs about a protest in Washington, D.C., held that same weekend about cutbacks in affirmative action—although it was a known fact that more than three thousand people from Philadelphia had taken part in the D.C. event. I thought the coverage unbalanced, so I decided to write a letter to the editor to let him know what I thought.

It was a three-page letter, and I put a lot of thought into it before sending it up to the Ivory Tower through interoffice mail. After I sent it, though, I didn't give it much more thought. I knew it was too long to be included in the "Letters to the Editor" section, but I just had to write it and send it to get it off my chest, and let the editors know what their readers think.

Then on Wednesday, I got a call from one of the secretaries in the editorial department, saying that an editor wanted to speak to me. I'd actually forgotten about the letter, so I asked the secretary why I was being summoned.

"Something about a letter you wrote," she answered.

"Oh!" was all I could say.

"I really appreciate your letter; it was well thought out and put together," the editor said at the meeting. "So many times we get letters from people accusing us of unbalanced reporting with nothing to back it up. You gave examples."

Hell, yeah, I did!

"The thing is," the editor explained, "people tend to be interested in writing stories that they feel affect the people around them. Well, if most of the news reporters are white, male, and live in the suburbs, they are going to be most focused on stories that may not reflect the lives and issues of black people. It has nothing to do with prejudice or racism; it has everything to do with lack of sensitivity, though."

I'd never thought of it like that, but, yeah, it kinda made sense now that he was breaking it down like that. "So," I said, leaning forward to ask this very important question, "what is the solution?"

"The solution," the editor responded, "would be to add more African-Americans, and people from inner cities to the news staff."

I actually applauded. "Right! So when do you plan on doing that?"

"Well, actually right now we have a hiring freeze."

I stopped applauding. "And how long will this hiring freeze last?"

He shrugged. "It's been on for three years so far."

I couldn't believe it. So why did he have me come up and see him then, I wondered. I screwed my face up, and was about to say something, but caught myself just in time. He was the editor. I did need my job. And what I'd started to say wasn't pretty. I couldn't stop myself from rolling my eyes, though. That was enough for the editor.

"Well," he said, rising from his desk, "it was nice meeting you. Thanks for coming up to talk to me."

Okay, I couldn't stop myself. "I can't help but thinking this 'talk' was a waste of time," I said as he escorted me to the door. "It's not like anything is going to change. What was the point?"

I may have a lot of Angry-Ass Black Woman in me, but I soon found out that he had at least a little bit of Angry-Ass Jewish Man in him. He turned and looked me up and down, crossed his arms, and said, "It's very easy for someone not qualified to write a news story to criticize someone who is."

I was like, damn, where did that come from? The fuck he mean I ain't qualified? Because I didn't go to college? Because I didn't go to high school? Maybe I wasn't trained in journalism, but formally educated or not I was good enough to see that his reporters were guilty of unbalanced reporting. I guess I was qualified to do that. Fuck him. All this cursing and carrying on was done in my head as I took the elevator down from the seventh floor, walked through the lobby, and out the back door to return to the garage. After all, like I said, I needed my job.

When I got back to my desk I saw that my work had piled up. Letters to be typed, reports to be filed, and telephone calls that needed to be made. I suddenly felt depressed. So very fucking depressed.

There was so much wrong with this world, man, and nothing was being done about it. Even when a little thing like unbalanced reporting in a newspaper was pointed out, and was acknowledged by the editor, nothing was to be done about it. No one cared. No one was looking out for the little guy.

But I cared. I always had. After all, I was one of the little guys, and I felt oppressed, ignored, and angry as hell about it. And this was besides the shit that came with being black and a woman! But what good was it that I cared when all I was doing was filing someone else's reports and papers?

I was angry, but I needed to channel my anger. I needed to let it propel me forward to not just lash out, but lash out to bring about change. Change some of the things that were wrong with the world, the things that made me angry. But it was hard to bring change when you were stuck filing other people's stories. And that's when I made my decision. Fifteen minutes later I walked into Kenny's office and handed him a letter of resignation.

The next afternoon, on my lunch hour, I took the bus up Broad Street to Temple University and took steps to enroll in their journalism program. Four years later I graduated magna cum laude with a GPA of 3.88. All in all, I'd say the only thing I'd missed by not attending high school was the prom.

I'm not going to say going back to school was easy, because it wasn't—especially since I was now a single mother *without a job* and doing the school thing full-time. But maybe that was the best thing for me, because it caused me to really get my hustle on.

I first approached a small start-up magazine in Philly called the *Freedom Forum* and told them I'd like to do articles for them, just so I could get the experience. The editors were a nice couple named Kenyetta Giles and Reuben something or the other. They were glad to have the help, and I was glad for the opportunity to get some clips. Joe T. by this time was already a student at Temple University and had started a group called Afrocentricity United, and somehow he persuaded me to head the group's political unit division. One of our duties was to write profiles on the various candidates running for political office in Philadelphia. With the clips from the *Freedom Forum* and the articles I did for Afrocentricity United I approached the publisher of the *Philadelphia New Observer,* Hugo Warren, and told him I'd like to do some political writing for him. He immediately named me chief political correspondent, and paid me something like fifty dollars per article for his weekly paper. Cool. I was in business. I tried my best to write at least two articles per week, but I always managed to do at least one. In addition, I was now on public assistance because I wasn't able to collect unemployment compensation since I had quit my job and had not been laid off. I didn't like the fact that I had to depend on welfare, but I didn't mind it too greatly, either. After all, I had been working since I was sixteen, and it wasn't like I was planning on spending the rest of my life on relief. I just needed a temporary helping hand. Fuck it. We all do at times, I figured.

With the clips I got from the *Philadelphia Observer* I was able to apply for—and win—the Golf Writers of America internship, which awarded students with financial need, a good GPA, and proven writing ability a trip to the Ryder's Cup golf tournament at the Doral Country Club in Miami, and three thousand dollars for two years to intern at any newspaper or media outlet that would accept them.

I picked *The Philadelphia Inquirer*.

They accepted me.

And I finally had a platform where I could let my anger loose, and for the good of the community, as I wrote about racism, reverse racism, sexism, sexual abuse, domestic abuse, child abuse—stories that made a difference. That helped bring about needed change.

Just one month after I started interning there I had my first front-page story. Even after I stopped receiving the internship money the *Philadelphia Inquirer* kept me on as a correspondent. They loved me, and I loved them.

After my graduation, I worked for the *Norfolk Virginian Pilot* for one year, then returned to the *Philadelphia Inquirer* on a permanent basis.

But . . . me, being me—meaning An Angry-Ass Black Woman—I did have some issues.

Like always wondering when they were going to find out who I really was. I mean, would the *Philadelphia Inquirer* really want someone with my background working for them? My childhood was no bed of roses, and the only reason I wasn't in prison even then was because I was lucky enough not to have gotten caught at most of the shit I'd done during my teenage years. Hell, some of the folks I was messing with in New York City were so infamous that when they got arrested the stories actually made it into the *Philadelphia Inquirer*.

I loved working at the *Inquirer,* but almost the whole time I was there, I was uneasy. Always doubting that I belonged. And I also felt that if the newspaper found out about some of my activities—hanging out with drug dealers, the occasional con game, the boosting every now and then, sporadic drug use—well, they might throw me out on my ass. So I was a little paranoid. Which made me a little defensive. I was one of those who was quick to get into an argument, even with my colleagues. I remember once I had just told a fellow journalist where she could get off and was walking back to my work-space when one of my friends in the newsroom said, "You know, Karen, you really do have a chip on your shoulder."

Without looking over my shoulder, and not missing a beat, I replied, "Better a chip on my shoulder than a knife in my back."

How fucked up was I?

One evening, in 1998, on my way home from work I stopped off at the video store and got a copy of *Set It Off*, starring Jada Pinkett, Camille's favorite movie star. She had Jada posters on her bedroom wall. She checked Jada's horo-scope every day. Her screen name on AOL was "Jada Fan." Camille loved Jada and was totally engrossed in the movie when we watched it that night, and unfortunately, it was run-ning longer than I expected. I looked at the clock on the wall, 9:15 p.m. Fifteen minutes past eleven-year-old Camille's bedtime. I took a deep breath and tried to calm my fidgeting so my daughter wouldn't notice. Finally, the film was over, and I jumped up and turned off the VCR.

"Okay, baby, time to get to bed."

"All right, Mommy. But wasn't that movie so good? And Jada Pinkett. Isn't she pretty?"

"Yes, baby, the movie was great, and Jada is very pretty. Come on, let's get ready for bed."

"Okay, Mommy. But Jada really is so pretty. And did you know that she and Will Smith are married, Mommy? And both of them are big movie stars. They're like the king and queen of Hollywood. Don't you think, Mommy?"

"Yeah, babe, they're like the Black Hollywood royalty. Hurry up now and go to the bathroom so we can get you in bed."

"I'm going, Mommy. But isn't it romantic? And they even have a baby, Mommy. Ooh! You know what, Mommy? They should do a movie together, Mommy! Jada and Will and the baby! They should all be in a movie together, don't you think?"

"Camille—"

"But they should, Mommy! I wonder why they haven't? Maybe they're trying to, huh, Mommy? Maybe they're looking for a good movie script that they could all play in. Maybe, someone should write them a script. Or maybe a book that they could turn into a movie, huh, Mommy?"

"Sure, Camille. Someone should write a book and then have it turned into a movie so that Will and Jada and their baby can play in it. But I'm really serious about you getting in your pajamas so you can get to bed."

"I am, Mommy. But since someone should write a book, and you're a writer, why don't you write the book?"

"Damn it, Camille! Whatever! I'll write the book so it can be turned into a movie and Jada, Will, and their baby can star in it, okay? Now get your butt to bed right now!"

Finally Camille was under the covers and fast asleep. I relaxed on the sofa for a while, then got up and picked out and ironed clothes for Camille and me for the following day, then went to bed myself.

When I woke Camille up the next morning the very first thing she asked me was, "So, did you start writing yet?"

Damn!

Now, anyone who has ever known Camille would know that it would be easier to write a book than to live down not doing something you promised her you were going to do. So that evening, after I put Camille to bed, I sat in front of the computer and wondered what the hell I was going to write about. Then, it seemed all of a sudden my fingers started moving, and the words began appearing on my computer screen. And I kept at it. For four months. I would rush home from work at six p.m. and spend some quality time with Camille before putting her to bed at nine p.m. At 9:15 I was in front of my computer and I stayed there until 3:45 a.m. I would then go to bed, wake up at seven a.m. to get Camille ready for school, then I was off to work. And the whole routine would start over again.

After four months I had a completed manuscript, which was titled *Satin Doll*. It was about a young girl from Harlem whose parents died, forcing her to drop out of school at thirteen, and who started hanging out with a fast crowd. She finally decides to get her life together and moves to Philadelphia and attends Temple University, where she majors in journalism. She becomes a successful journalist, but never feels like she really belongs.

So, okay, now you know it's true what you've heard . . . that most novelists' first book is heavily influenced by their real-life experiences.

I let Camille read the manuscript and she was like, "Mommy, this is good. Now we should get this published."

I was like, "Yeah?"

She was like, "Yeah!"

It then became our mission to get it done . . . you know, just another mother and daughter project—getting a book published. No big deal.

We knew nothing about book publishing, so I started reading everything I could about the subject. I found out that if we wanted to get my manuscript published I had to have a literary agent, and in order to get a literary agent, I had to write a query letter. A query letter, I learned, was a one-page letter that gives a brief—but tantalizing—synopsis of your manuscript, and asks the agent to represent you to publishers. If the agent is intrigued by your query letter she (or he) will contact you to request you send either a full synopsis, or the first three chapters of your manuscript.

So, okay, I typed up a query letter, let Camille read it to make sure she thought it was on point, then sent out thirty-five copies along with self-addressed stamped envelopes to thirty-five different agents. We believed when the thirty-five agents read our query letter, and subsequently read our manuscript, they would all ask to represent us. At that point, we figured, we could pick and choose which literary agent we wanted. That agent would then get us a six-figure publishing deal, and our manuscript would be turned into a best-selling book. What a life!

Every evening when we got home, Camille and I would rush to check the mail. The first two replies came in about four weeks. Three more followed the week after that, six or seven more the week after that, until all of the query letters were answered within a period of three months. In fact, we actually got *fifty* responses to the thirty-five query letters we'd sent out—it seems some of the agents were so affected by the query letter that they decided to reject me twice. No one, it seemed, was interested in representing us.

I was puzzled by the response we'd gotten to a perfectly good query letter about a magnificent book, and I turned to eleven-year-old Camille and asked what she thought of the situation.

"Mom," she said, "they're just plain stupid."

Sounded about right to me.

Of course giving up was not an option, and while we were put off by the agents' disinterest, we weren't totally fazed. Camille and I celebrate Kwanzaa, and try to live by the seven principles. The second principle is Kujichagulia, which means self-determination, and we were applying it to this situation—we were not going to allow a bunch of literary agents whom we had never met determine whether or not we were going to have a book published. Fuck that! It wasn't until September 8, 1999, that we decided exactly what our next step would be, though.

It was a Wednesday, and I was dropping Camille off at school when an idea suddenly hit me.

"Camille, what do you think about us going ahead and self-publishing *Satin Doll*?"

"I think it's a great idea, Mom," she answered, then gave me a kiss on the cheek and headed off into the school building. "Let's talk about it some more when we get home tonight."

I promptly went to Borders Books and bought every book I could find on self-publishing and started studying. Then I borrowed money from every family member I had who actually had any money (which was just one—Joe T.), and ordered three thousand copies of *Satin Doll* from the printer. I figured three thousand would be a good number to start with—I mean, I bought and read books constantly; even if people only buy half the amount of books I bought I'd move the three thousand in six months or so.

I was lucky in that I'd spoken to Kimberla Lawson Roby a few times the year before, when I was trying to get the *Philadelphia Inquirer* to let me do a book review on her self-published book, *Behind Closed Doors*. I'd read it and loved it, but when I approached the book editor I was told the *Inquirer* did not review self-published books. I later found that most major newspapers don't review self-published books.

But Kimberla was *extremely* helpful and forthcoming with information—helping me with figuring out things like book dimensions and especially telling me the importance of having a book launch party to officially announce the book release.

But boy, did I make some stupid mistakes. For instance, it never dawned on me that I had no place to put three thousand books, okay? This big-ass truck pulls up in front of my apartment building one Saturday morning, and I freaked out.

"Wait, wait, let me figure out someplace for you to take the books," I pleaded to the driver.

"Miss, my manifest says I'm supposed to be delivering to this address, and I'm delivering to this address," the driver said drily.

"But I don't have room in my apartment for all these books," I said frantically.

"And I'm not taking them to any apartment. I'm not hauling these books up any flights of stairs."

"Well, what are we going to do, then?" I asked.

He answered in a nonchalant voice that indicated that he didn't give a damn about my literary future: "Either I drive on and bring the books back to the printer, or I drop them off right here on the sidewalk."

And that's just what he did. My neighbors, thank God, helped me carry the books up to my apartment.

Yeah, eighty-six boxes of books up two flights of stairs to the one-bedroom apartment I shared with Camille. We wound up putting most of the books in the living room, but there were so many that we had to move the couch to the front stoop overnight while we figured out what to do with it. And then we woke up the next morning to find out that someone had stolen the fucking sofa. I mean . . . like . . . damn!

Although the books were delivered in late November, our plan was to have the actual book launch in early December. In the meantime, I had the opportunity to talk on the phone to Omar Tyree, one of the first successful self-published authors, and I told him I was also publishing my own book.

"Great, how many books did you print for the first run?" he asked.

"Three thousand," I answered proudly.

"Three thousand books!" he shouted into the phone.

I inwardly sighed, thinking the problem was that he couldn't believe I had printed such a small number of books. "Yeah, I know it's not a lot, but my thinking is—"

"Three thousand books," he repeated.

"Well, yeah, but what I'm going to do is take the money I make from these books and turn around and—"

"Three thousand books," he three-peated.

"Yes, three thousand, but my plan is to take the money I make from these three thousand and turn it around and buy five thousand the next time," I said in a rush, trying to finish before he interrupted me again.

"Karen, are you out of your mind? Do you know how long it will take you to sell three thousand books?"

I hesitated, then decided to answer on the conservative side. "Um, a year?"

Omar started laughing. When he finally stopped he said, "Girl, you'll be lucky if you sell a thousand books in a year. And you'll only be able to make that number if you're a good salesperson."

Me? A good salesperson? I never even sold a fucking Girl Scout cookie. And I needed to turn those books over a helluva lot faster than Omar was saying, because I had taken an unpaid leave of absence from the *Inquirer* to sell *Satin Doll,* I was already moving my car from one street to another trying to stay ahead of the repo man, and I was going to run out of rent money in another three months. See, for some strange reason I thought I'd sell at least a thousand copies in ninety days, and if I was lucky, maybe two thousand. So you know Omar's words freaked me the fuck out. And when I got off the phone and told Camille, bless her little heart, she freaked the fuck out, too.

We were so freaked out that we sold all three thousand copies of *Satin Doll* in just three weeks.

Yeah, that's right. We sold all three thousand fucking books in three weeks.

Oh great, I guess I now have to tell you how.

The first thing I have to say is that the best thing that ever happened to me was that I never took a business or marketing class. I had no idea what it would take to sell three thousand books in a year, so I just did everything I could hoping I'd make it. We didn't know when to stop, so we just didn't! Even before the book came out, Camille and I started printing flyers. Her bedtime was 9:00 p.m., so at 9:00 she'd put two hundred pieces of paper into the printer, and then go to bed. At 11:00 I'd take the two hundred flyers out the printer, put two hundred more pieces of paper in, and go to bed. Camille's alarm clock was set for 1:00 a.m., and she'd get up and take out the two hundred flyers I'd made, and put two hundred more pieces of paper in. At 3:00 a.m., I'd get up and take out the two hundred flyers she'd printed, then wake her up. We'd get dressed in dark clothing, pull dark ball caps down low on our heads, and we'd hit the streets with our eight hundred flyers. We would flyer everything that stood still, letting everyone know about the hot upcoming novel *Satin Doll* and promoting the upcoming launch party. We'd even put fifty cents into the newspaper vending machine and take out all the newspapers . . . then we'd put our flyers in the newspapers and put them back into the machine. Hey, we were fucking desperate, ya know? We even made up postcards and went into bookstores, and one of us would act as lookout as the other pulled down books off the shelves, opened them up and put our postcards inside, then put them back on the shelf. Anyone in Philadelphia; Wilmington, Delaware; or New York City who bought a Terry McMillan, Omar Tyree, Lolita Files, Eric Jerome Dickey, or E. Lynn Harris book in 1999 probably found a postcard telling them about *Satin Doll* and inviting them to the launch party.

I went on the internet every night trying to find local book clubs to send them messages about *Satin Doll* and invite them to the launch party. One book club, Eye of Ra, emailed me back and told me they'd love for me to come and read for them. Boy, was I thrilled, and scared shitless at the same time. I mean, shit, it's one thing to write a book, but I never really gave any thought to reading the book out loud to a group of people. I mean, shit, what if they didn't like it? I thought about declining . . . I really went back and forth about it. Finally I told Camille about the book club's offer, but didn't tell her my qualms. I thought she'd jump up and down with excitement, but instead she took a deep breath and said, "Well, I guess we may as well get it over with." Didn't sound very encouraging.

When the evening rolled around for the book club meeting I was more than a bundle of nerves, I was shaking in my boots. I was so antsy I was snapping at Camille to hurry up, and sit up straight in the car, even to stop breathing so loud.

But, Camille was a trooper—I guess as young as she was she understood what I was going through.

When we got to the book club meeting the members all introduced themselves and said how thrilled they were to meet a local African-American author. I looked at Camille like, "Oh my God, did I misrepresent myself?" She saw the look on my face and just turned away. After all the pleasantries were exchanged, we got down to the business of the meeting—me reading an excerpt from *Satin Doll.* I was given a seat in the center of the room, and I turned to the page that Camille and I had decided I should read from. For the next twenty minutes, I read the book I'd written. When I finally looked up, everyone started clapping, and Camille was beaming. Whew! On the ride home she told me, "See, Mom, I told you our book was good. I know you were nervous, and I was, too; but I knew it was going to be okay."

"You think it really went well, baby? You don't think they were just being polite?"

Camille snuggled up close to me in the car. "Mom, your job was to read, but I had a job, too. I watched everyone's faces while you were reading, Mommy. I wanted to see their reactions. And you know what? They were all up in it, Ma!"

"They were?" I asked, excitedly.

"Yeah! There was no one moving around in their seats, no one looking at each other and whispering or anything. They were all wrapped into what you was saying. For real, Ma! And I know because I was looking. I made it my job to look."

I looked at my eleven-year-old girl, whom I had given such a hard time that evening for no reason that had anything to do with her, and my eyes brimmed with tears. "Well, thanks for taking the job, Camille. And, listen, I apologize for being such a jerk—"

"Don't worry about it, Mommy," Camille said, cutting me off. "I get scared sometimes, too."

My baby.

The launch party for *Satin Doll* was held on December 7 (exactly three months from the day that we decided to self-publish) at Zanzibar Blue, one of the snazziest clubs in Philadelphia—and the place was packed! All the promoting Camille and I had done had really paid off. We'd even gotten Patty Jackson from WDAS-FM, one of the hottest female DJs in Philly, to emcee the event. Camille was one of the people at the door, steering everyone toward the books as soon as they entered the club. I was at the table signing until my fingers were numb, and still signing more. And when I went up to the microphone and did a reading, people who had already bought books went to the table and bought more.

Joe T. had been just as supportive of me in my dream of publishing a book as he had been in my being an actress twenty-five years before. He told everyone he knew about the book, he stopped people in the street and told them about the book, he called me every day to see if there was anything he could do as far as helping to promote the book. And he'd lent me more than a thousand bucks toward getting the books printed.

Well, we sold more than three hundred copies of *Satin Doll* at the launch party that night, and you should have seen Joe T.! Man, he was walking around the book launch party in a happy daze, smiling, slapping people on the back, and talking about, "Yeah, that's my sister. You know when she sets out to do something there's no stopping her."

Three hundred books at thirteen dollars a pop . . . we made almost four thousand dollars in that one evening. We were able to pay Joe T. back that same night. Woo-hoo! By the time we got home Camille and I were bushed, and happy. We managed to get a good night's sleep, and then it was back to promoting the next day.

We were out of books by the time February rolled around, and I had just contacted the printer about another larger order when my phone rang. It was Manie Baron, who was an editor with Random House at the time. Manie was from Harlem, and we knew each other personally, though not well. In fact, I'd sent him a query letter about *Satin Doll*, but he'd never bothered getting back to me. But now he'd heard about what was going on with *Satin Doll*, and he offered me ten thousand dollars for publishing rights to it and a second book. I would have jumped at the offer a year before, but now . . . naw, not so much.

"Look, Karen, I'm trying to look out for you because I know how hard it is to self-publish, and with you being a single mother. In fact, if my bosses here at Random House knew how much I was offering you I'd lose my job."

He was pissed at me turning him down, but I figured he'd get over it.

The next call was from Kensington Books. They offered fifteen thousand. I turned them down also.

Then I got a call from Simon & Schuster. They offered $83,000 for *Satin Doll* and a second book . . . okay? Yippee! I was celebrating inside, but I told them I had to think about it, and talk it over with my business manager. So I got off the telephone and immediately ran to tell Camille. To my surprise, she was happy, but insisted that I turn it down.

"Are you out of your mind?" I argued. "Do you know how much money that is?"

"But, Mom, I just have a feeling we can do better!" she persisted.

I thought turning Simon & Schuster down was simply stupid, but I reasoned that if it wasn't for Camille I would never have even written *Satin Doll* in the first place, so I might as well listen to her.

Then in May I got an email from a literary agent named Delin Cormeny . . . one of the many who had turned down *Satin Doll* back in my query letter days. She said she'd overheard an editor from Simon & Schuster talking about a book named *Satin Doll* but she figured they were talking about my book, and how they thought they were going to be able to pick up the book for cheap. She ended her email by urging me to get an agent. "You don't have to use me, but I really suggest you get someone so you're not cheated out of money," she wrote in her email. I emailed her back and said she was hired. But by this time there were so many publishers interested in purchasing the publishing rights to *Satin Doll* that Delin had to actually hold an auction.

The Book Expo of America was being held in Chicago that year, and I was already slated to go as a guest of Ingram Books—the largest book distributor in the country—to sign copies of *Satin Doll*. Book Expo is a convention for booksellers, but it's attended by booksellers, editors, publishers, agents, and authors. It's the biggest literary event of the year, and now I was going as a bona fide author. Even though I was still self-published, I had already made the *Essence* Best Seller's list, and word had spread around the publishing world about my success. I thought I'd be accepted as a bona fide peer. I was wrong.

When I got to the Book Expo I was surprised to find that I was not welcomed into the rank of authors with open arms. There were some established authors who thought since I had self-published *Satin Doll,* it meant I wasn't good enough to be accepted by a publishing house. Worse, there were some who had heard the buzz that publishers were interested in picking up *Satin Doll,* and resented me for it. One—a very well-known author—actually said within my earshot, "Simon and Schuster is interested in her? I guess they'll just let anyone on the plantation these days."

There were a few exceptions, notably Kimberla Lawson Roby, but not many. I continued to hold my head high, but my feelings were undeniably hurt. Still I was determined to act with dignity.

But finally, I'd had enough. Another *New York Times* best selling author made a snide remark, and I narrowed my eyes, looked that short stocky bastard up and down and said: "I know you're a man, but you know what? I think I can take you." With that I lunged at him, and that motherfucker hauled ass. I ran after him for about fifty yards through the crowded McCormick Center. I didn't catch him. If I had it would have been on!

Later that evening, at the end of a reception held for African-American authors at the Expo I was headed for the exit when I saw a group of editors, authors, and agents standing by the door whom I recognized from previous meetings. I squared my shoulders, lifted my chin, and prepared to pass by and ignore them just as I knew they were going to pointedly ignore me. I had just reached the exit and reached for the doorknob, when suddenly someone grabbed me from behind and swung me around.

"So you're Karen E. Quinones Miller! Girl, I heard about you, and I read *Satin Doll.* It was just great, and you're simply a wonderful writer. I'm so happy for your success! Girl, you have a magnificent future in front of you." And then he hugged me.

E. Lynn Harris, beyond doubt the best-selling male African-American author at the Book Expo—hugged me! And then chucked me under the chin. I stood speechless for a moment, and then mumbled, "Thanks so much, Mr. Harris."

"Karen," he responded, "my friends call me E. Lynn."

Tears came to my eyes, but before I could say anything else, I was suddenly surrounded by the group of literary insiders who had managed to go through the whole Book Expo without saying a kind word to me, and they were congratulating me, introducing themselves to me, and acting like I was an old friend. By giving me that very public hug, congratulatory salute, and chuck under the chin, E. Lynn gave me something even more—he gave me credibility. I will always love him for that.

The publishing auction Delin had set up was held on June 7, 2000, and the first bid was made by Random House. Remember, Manie Baron—my homeboy who was an editor at Random House—telling me he was doing me a favor by offering ten thousand dollars? Well, Random House's first bid was one hundred thousand. I was driving up Walnut Street when Delin called on my cell phone and told me. I had to pull over because I started hyperventilating. I immediately drove over to Camille's school and made up some excuse about her having a dental appointment so I could get her out of school and tell her the news. We just whooped and hooped it up in the car. Then we picked up some pizza and soda and waited until we heard word from Delin that the auction was over. The final bid came in late that afternoon. Simon & Schuster was the winner, and paid $165,000 for *Satin Doll*, and a second book yet to be written or named.

Yeah, we did it.

Me and Camille.

* * *

"I think I saw her eyelids move! Aunt Kitty! I think her eyelids flickered."

Did it? About damn time! I've been trying for the last . . . damn, I don't know how long. I remember Camille saying something about me being in the hospital for four days, but I don't even know how long ago it was that she said that.

"She stopped. Oh, no, she stopped. Come on, Mom! Please, keep trying. Open your eyes, please!"

"Camille, I told you not to get so excited. That was probably a reflex, her moving her eyes and all."

"No, it wasn't, Aunt Kitty. And please stop being so negative. You'd think you'd be pulling for her after all she's always done for you. She's always been there for you. Can't you just pull for her for a change?"

Yeah, Kitty . . . Camille's right. Come on and pull for me.

fifteen

*I*t's eleven p.m., Saturday, February 10, 2001. Do you know where your sister is?

I didn't.

I hadn't heard from Kitty since right after Thanksgiving, and I was having a nervous breakdown behind it. I had called all of my other relatives, and no one else had heard from her either. No one had any clue where she was. I was frantic.

Me and Kitty were forty-two years old now, soon to be forty-three, but she was no closer to being straight than she had been twenty-five years earlier. In fact, she was much worse. When crack hit New York City in the mid-eighties, Kitty was one of its first victims. And I gotta be honest, she wasn't just a crackhead, she was an out-and-out crack 'ho, selling her wares on 'ho-stroll.

You know what 'ho-stroll is? It's a street—or strip—where prostitutes walk and pick up johns. Quite often the johns come on the street looking for some pussy, and then the john and the prostitute would negotiate a price. But some 'ho-strolls were more aggressive than others, and the prostitutes would actually go into the street and hail cars as they drove by to find out if they were "looking for a date." The 'ho-stroll where Kitty worked was aggressive like that—Park Avenue between 127th and 128th Streets. My cousin Belinda lived on 128th Street between Park and Lexington Avenues and me and her stayed close even after I'd grown up, had a kid, and moved to Philadelphia. So I'd drive up with Camille to visit her two or three weekends a month. The thing is, coming from Philly we'd take the New Jersey Turnpike, get off at the George Washington Bridge, then get on the Harlem River Drive to the 125th Street exit. Then to get to Belinda's we'd have to go up Park Avenue—right past 'ho-stroll. So what I would do is, as soon as I got to the corner of 125th and Park (two blocks before we hit 'ho-stroll) I'd turn to Camille while I was driving and engage her in a serious bit of conversation, which would require her giving me her full and undivided attention—with total eye contact—and keeping her engaged until we turned the corner onto Belinda's block. It was dangerous, keeping her eye contact and still glancing forward to keep my eye on the road, but I did it because I never wanted to take the chance of Camille looking out the car window and seeing her aunt climbing out some john's car, or hailing vehicles down to see if someone wanted a date.

Please don't think that I didn't care about Kitty anymore, because that was far from the case. All my life I'd been told I had to take care of my sister—the overall sentiment being that she needed taking care of. When we were kids I'd simply fight people who messed with her. When she started using drugs I tried talking to her, and even tried getting her professional help. Didn't do much good; she would just tell me that she liked what she was doing and had no plans to stop, and she'd screw all the male psychologists who tried counseling her. When she started selling pussy on Park Avenue, I even called the New York City Department of Health and lied and told them that she had AIDS and was still hooking on the streets, and gave them her location. No one ever did anything to try to reach out to her.

Damn. I tried.

Whenever Kitty said she'd changed her mind and wanted

to straighten herself out I would help her get an apartment, buy all her household goods, and purchase a new wardrobe so she could go job hunting. We would be thrilled that she was turning over a new leaf, and would laugh and have a great time going from store to store, shopping for her clothes for upcoming interviews. One thing about Kitty, she had great job skills; she typed eighty wpm, knew teletype, and also how to run a switchboard, all very marketable skills back in the eighties and nineties. Kitty could land a job in a minute as a receptionist or secretary, and did whenever she wanted to. And man, she would grab some great gigs. Once she was a secretary for American Express—that job ended when they found out she was renting cars and charging them to the office credit card. Another time she got a job as a receptionist at the home office of a cruise liner. One of the perks was a free cruise for two every year once you were with the company twelve months. Well, as soon as I heard that stipulation I knew Kitty wasn't going to be doing any cruising. A grown-ass woman of almost fifty and—I swear to God—she has never in her life stayed a full year at any job. I think the cruise line job ended when they found her trying to smuggle a big electric typewriter out of the office in a paper shopping bag.

That was just Kitty. And when she didn't get fired for some illegal activity or the other, she'd just stop showing up. She'd land a job for a little while, then within a few months decide she was tired of working and wanted to start partying again. And for Kitty, "partying" meant smoking crack and treating other people to the pipe, too, when she had the money. But once she started partying she didn't know how to stop. She'd be up in the crack house for days smoking whenever she had enough money to do so. And when she didn't, she'd just go out in the street and make a few dollars and head right back to the crack house. She'd lose her job but she didn't care. She'd lose her apartment, and she didn't care. Then she'd be homeless again. And the cycle would start over.

There were the times, though, that Kitty would convince me that she wanted to get off of crack, but she needed a change in environment. I had her move out to Philly with me, much to Joe T.'s chagrin.

Joe T. couldn't stand being around Kitty, and I thought it was a shame because when he was real little she acted like a little mommy to him. I think seeing her all strung out really hurt him. And it didn't help that she had managed to go to bed with all of his friends once he became a teenager. She still tried to be sweet to him, but he didn't want anything to do with her, and criticized me for having her around Camille.

And it's true that Kitty was a ditz, and never bothered to leave the vulgarity of the street outside when she was in the house.

Like the time Joe T. came over to my house to have Sunday dinner with us, and after dinner Kitty said she wanted to give a toast. Joe T. asked what it was she wanted to toast, and she said she didn't have anything to toast but she didn't care because she had made up a toast and she wanted to use it. Joe T. rolled his eyes, then sighed and said, "Okay." Kitty picked up a glass of water and raised it and said: "Good food, good suck, good God, let's fuck." Then she burst out laughing.

My mouth dropped open, and Joe T.'s face started turning red. I could see he was struggling to keep quiet, but his silence lasted less than thirty seconds.

"What the hell is wrong with you, Kitty, huh?" he said quietly.

"What?" Kitty said defensively.

"Why would you sit here and say some stupid shit like that?"

"Oh, Joe T., don't make such a big deal about it. I thought it was funny." Kitty turned to me. "Didn't you think it was funny, Ke-Ke?"

I couldn't lie. "No."

She sucked her teeth. "Well, that's because I didn't give you guys no context. See, it's like this. I made up that toast with this guy I used to screw around with to make a couple of dollars. He took me over to his house and fixed me dinner. And then we started messing around a little, you know, foreplay. And well, he went down on me. And so then I was real ready I just said, 'Good food, good suck, good God, let's fuck.'" When she saw the look on my face, she added: "I thought it was cute."

Joe T. jumped up from the table. "Kitty! Why would you think something like that was cute?" He stomped over to the door and I thought he was just gonna storm out but he suddenly turned around to face her. "And I can't believe that you think telling us the story behind that stupid thing you called a toast would somehow make it better." He walked up close to her and said in her face, "You are really stupid."

"What? What? We're all adults in here. Camille's in bed. What's the big deal?" Kitty looked over at me for help.

I sighed, then said, "Come on, Joe T., she didn't understand before, but she does now. She won't do it again."

Joe T. shook his head. "That's not true, Ke-Ke, and you know it." He looked over at Kitty. "Is it?"

"Is what?"

"Is it true that you now realize that your so-called toast was inappropriate and you won't say it again," he explained.

"Well," she hesitated, then shrugged and said: "I think it would be safe to say that I won't ever say it again in front of you, anyway."

Joe T. snorted then turned to me. "I rest my case."

But that was Kitty.

The thing is, though, I would rather she be in Philly with me making dirty toasts while trying to clean up her act than have her out there on 'ho-stroll in Harlem, though.

Still, it didn't last long—she was with me about three months, then one day I came home from work and found she was gone, along with the uncashed paycheck I had left on the television the day before. And all the spare change I had in the house. And the money from Camille's piggy bank.

But still she was my sister, and I knew that most of her problems stemmed from what Mr. Leroy did to her. See, not only did that dirty old man seduce her, but he made her feel like she was just as wrong as him; like they were in on it together. She didn't realize that she was the victim. So she felt guilty. She thought she was a slut for screwing her mother's best friend's husband, so she was simply acting like the slut she was convinced she was. At least that's how I figured it. Kitty had been stuck in this cycle since, like, 1974, and I was stuck in the cycle with her. Her messing up, and me still trying to defend her.

But then in 2001, Kitty went missing.

Like I said earlier, no one had heard from her since right before Thanksgiving the year before. I was uncomfortable when I hadn't heard from her by Christmas, and started getting really fidgety when New Year's came and went without Kitty calling me. I waited a few more weeks and drove up to New York City and went and got Puddin', David's wife, and together we went looking for Kitty. Puddin' and Kitty used to hang out back in the day, and she was one of the few people who was as worried about Kitty as I was. The first thing we did was put in a missing person's report with the police department. Then together we walked over and talked to the girls on 'ho-stroll, but no one had seen Kitty in months. Same thing at the nine or ten crack houses we went to. We'd been looking about two days when Puddin' finally said the words I'd been trying not to think: "Maybe it's time we called the morgue."

We looked at each other right after she said it, and both burst into tears. It took us a good hour to get ourselves together, but at last I managed to get myself to call the morgue. There was no one there who fit her description. Thank God.

Poor Camille, she didn't know what to do . . . she was so worried about me being so worried about Kitty.

"Mommy, you know how Aunt Kitty is. She's disappeared before," Camille said, trying to soothe me. And it was true, Kitty had wandered off before without letting anyone know where she was, but she'd usually pop up after a few weeks and we'd find out she was shacking up with some guy she'd just met. But this had been a few months already.

"Yeah, she's disappeared before, baby," I told Camille, "but never this long. Never this long."

My nerves were so shot my hair actually began to fall out, and I started losing weight, and was always on the verge of tears.

I was still doing appearances for *Satin Doll,* and was scheduled to appear at a book club event in Harrisburg one Saturday. Camille and I drove up and everything was going fine until I got up to read. I stood up in front of all those people and started reading a funny excerpt, and right in the middle of it I burst into tears. I was really bad off.

We drove back to Philadelphia and I dropped Camille off at Joe T.'s house because I wanted to have the night to myself. I went into my office to continue working on my next book, *Timing the Moon,* which was to be the second book on my contract with Simon & Schuster. While working I gulped down a rum and Coke, and then another. And then another. And then another. And then another. And then another.

The next thing I knew it was morning—I had fallen asleep in the chair in front of the computer. I got up and took a bath, fixed myself breakfast, and then crawled into bed to try and sleep off the hangover. My telephone was ringing off the hook, but I didn't feel like talking to anyone so I finally unplugged it. I slept about three or four hours, and when I woke up I remembered the phone and replaced it on the hook. As soon as I did, it began to ring.

"Hello?"

"Karen? This is Delin. Are you okay?"

"Um, yeah. Why wouldn't I be okay?"

"Well, when I woke up this morning and read the e-mail you sent me last night I thought something might be wrong. Are you sure you're okay?"

"Yeah, I'm fine. But what e-mail are you talking about, Delin?"

"You don't remember sending me an e-mail?"

"Nope."

"Hmmm." She paused, as if trying to figure out what to say next, then slowly said, "Well, you sent out an e-mail addressed to me and your editor, Andrea, saying—"

"You know what, Delin . . . can I call you back," I cut her off. Something told me I didn't want her to tell me what the e-mail said. It would be better if I read it myself.

I went to the office and turned on the computer. Yeah, she was right, I had written an e-mail—a long, rambling email. It read:

They're all mad at Kitty because they don't know what happened, but I know what happened. And I thought I told but I must not have told good enough because it didn't help her. So now, guess what? I'm telling. That's right, I'm telling. I'm telling everybody that it isn't Kitty's fault. I know I'm supposed to be writing a book for you, but I can't because I'm telling. See, I can tell because I know what happened. I was there. I saw it. I squeezed my eyes real tight but I couldn't get what I had just seen out of my mind. Mr. Leroy's face in between my twin sister's legs. Even with my eyes closed I could still see them. And I could smell them, too. A funny smell. Kind of like sweat and something else. So you see, I gotta tell. I'm very sorry, but I can't write your book because I'll be too busy. Because I'm telling.

What the hell? I rubbed my hands over my eyes, and reread the e-mail. I had just finished when the telephone started ringing again. This time it was my editor, Andrea Mullins. I told her I'd call her back.

Again, I read the e-mail. It was true, I wasn't going to be able to concentrate on writing a book when I was so worried about Kitty. At least not the book they wanted me to write. I pulled up a blank document on the computer and began typing.

I then called both Delin and Andrea and apologized for sending them the rambling e-mail, and told them I was going through a lot of personal stuff at the moment regarding my sister. I then told them that I'd like to request permission to change the title and nature of the second book. It was no longer going to be about a woman who was accused of murdering her former husband; it was about, well . . . I decided to read them the first three paragraphs of what I'd written.

I squeezed my eyes real tight, but I couldn't get what I had just seen out of my mind. My stepfather's face in between my twin sister's legs. Even with my eyes closed I could still see them. And I could smell them, too. A funny smell. Kind of like sweat and something else.

And I could hear them whispering and scrambling around like they were trying to grab up their clothes. I kept my eyes shut and squatted down in the corner of the bathroom, covering my ears and clenching my teeth so hard they hurt.

I wanted to run downstairs and hide under the blanket in my bed, but if I did I would have to run past the bedroom door where I had just seen them doing the nasty.

The title of the book, I told them, was *I'm Telling.*

Later that night I was in the living room watching television when the telephone started ringing again. It was Kitty.

"Hey, Ke-Ke! Whatchoo up to?"

"Man, Kitty . . . where the hell have you been? Everyone's been worried sick about you!" I said, both relieved and exasperated.

"Really? Why? Hey, guess what? I ran into our first-grade teacher, Mrs. Davis. You remember her?"

"What? Huh?" I paused to make sure I'd heard right. Yeah, I decided. I did. "Kitty, did you hear me? I've been going crazy worrying about you, man!"

"I'm sorry. But I don't get it. Why were you so worried?"

"Why was I worried? Kitty, c'mon, no one's heard from you in months! We thought something had happened to you. Me and Puddin' was even checking the morgue."

"Get outta here!" Kitty said excitedly. "You got to look at dead bodies and shit? What was that like?"

I sighed. I just couldn't make her understand.

She never did give me all the details about her disappearance, but from what I could make out, it seems she'd been busy acting as a mule for a couple of drug dealers. You know how that goes, right? When dealers need to have drugs driven from one state to another, they get people whom they don't think the police would normally stop on the road. Let's face it, if a dealer is a young black man driving up Interstate 95 he is ten times more likely to get stopped on the road on some minor traffic violation than a middle-aged black woman. It's profiling. Police feel that if they stop young black men on some pretense or another—like going five miles over the speed limit, or having a broken taillight—that they will likely find some kind of contraband in the car. The middle-aged woman is not likely to be stopped unless she actually does something worth being stopped over. Like going twenty miles over the speed limit.

I was pissed that Kitty would risk going to prison for someone else's contraband in exchange for a little bit of money, but I wasn't even dwelling on that. It was her not checking in with someone to let them know that she was okay that really teed me off.

"I guess if you got into an accident we'd at least be notified since the police or hospital could find your family through your driver's license, but . . . wait a minute." It suddenly hit me. "When did you get a driver's license?"

Kitty laughed. "You know I ain't got no damn license. I wasn't driving. I was just going along with some other guy they hired to make it look like a middle-aged couple."

"Well, do you have any ID on you?" I already knew the answer and was just pissed waiting on her to verify it.

"Um, nope. But I knew nothing was gonna happen, anyway."

"Yeah, alright, Kitty."

I finished writing *I'm Telling* a few months later and turned it in to my editor at Simon & Schuster. She loved it.

I'm Telling is about an eleven-year-old girl who finds her twin sister in bed with her stepfather, and is devastated when she tells their mother and the mother does nothing about it.

The story goes on to detail how the pedophilia contributed to the dysfunction of the twins and the rest of the family. The twin who was the victim turned to drugs as an adult, and sold her body to purchase crack cocaine. It was ultimately brought out, however, that she went down that road because the emotional turmoil that she'd went through as a child had not been dealt with. If she just realized that she was a victim rather than a guilty party, she would not have had to live with guilt and low self-esteem that triggered her self-destructive behavior.

The novel was on the *Essence* Best Seller's List for three months. When Kitty read it she said she enjoyed the book. She made no comment on how it related to us, and when I finally brought it up months later she said she didn't really want to talk about it. That's when I realized that writing the book might have been cathartic for me, but it had done nothing to help Kitty.

★ ★ ★

"Uncle Joe T.! I told you! See, she's doing it again, her eyes are fluttering, and I think she's moving her finger a little."

Oh, good. I am doing it. I've been trying for the longest, and it's taken all my fucking energy, too. I need to rest. No, I can't rest. That bitch is still waiting for me to rest. I know damn well that Death is right around the corner just trying to wait me out.

"Camille, ring for the nurse, or the doctor, or whoever it is that's supposed to be here!"

"I did! I did already. Oh, Uncle Joe, I knew she could do it."

Everyone's so excited. Why is everyone so excited? Me? I'm just real fucking tired.

sixteen

I have a what?"

"A brain tumor, Mrs. Miller," Dr. Clarence Martin repeated.

"A brain tumor. How the hell did I get that?" I asked, crossing my arms over my chest and tapping my foot while I waited for a worthy explanation.

"Yaddah yaddah yaddah. Yaddah yaddah yaddah. Yaddah yaddah yaddah. Yaddah yaddah yaddah. Yaddah yaddah yaddah. Yaddah yaddah yaddah." He was saying something about no one knows how they come about, but luckily my tumor was in a part of the brain that was easily accessible, so while there's always a risk with brain surgery, they do these types of operations all the time. I nodded my head while I waited for him to finish.

It had started out with headaches, then occasional dizziness, then bouts of confusion where all of a sudden I didn't know where I was. Then, about a month before this particular doctor's appointment I started having seizures. Not the kind where you wiggle around on the floor and someone's running to find a spoon to put in your mouth so you won't swallow your tongue. I had what they call "petit mal" seizures . . . I'd be talking and all of a sudden I'd freeze. It would last anywhere from a few seconds to a few minutes. I could hear and see everything that was going on around me, but I couldn't move. That's when Dr. Martin sent me in for a bunch of CAT scans and MRIs.

"Okay, so is it cancerous?"

"We won't know until they actually remove it. Then there will be a biopsy and we'll know."

"And if it is?" I persisted.

"Well, we'll cross that bridge when we come to it."

He gave me a sympathetic look as he referred me to a neurologist. I guess Dr. Martin had already informed his nurse and receptionist of my diagnosis because they also gave me sympathetic clucks and glances as I left the office.

The timing couldn't be worse. My new agent, Liza Dawson (Delin Cormeny had retired), had just landed me a six-figure, two-book contract with a major publisher, and I only had four months to get the first manuscript done. And Camille was getting ready to graduate from Clark Atlanta University in Georgia. My seizures made it impossible for me to drive, but I could either fly or drive down with somebody. No, not a good time for a brain tumor.

"What do you mean you're too busy to have a brain tumor right now?" my girlfriend, Jenice Armstrong, said over the phone. "You're calling me here at work to tell me you have a brain tumor, and before I can even react to that horrible news you're telling me that you're too busy to have it right now? I don't know whether to cry or to laugh."

That was the reaction of most of my friends. My family, however, wouldn't allow me my cavalier attitude. Camille immediately left school—it was her senior year and she'd already completed all of her required classes—and flew up to Philly. Joe T. was already in Nigeria, and I had hell convincing him that I'd be okay and there was no reason for him to come back to the States.

When I saw the neurologist, Dr. Kevin Judy, a few days later he looked at the MRI results and said his secretary would give me a call in about a week and let me know when they'd schedule the surgery. The nurse called me the very next day and said they wanted to operate the following week.

Inconvenient, I told her; I didn't want to miss Camille's graduation. I ignored the sarcasm in her voice when she asked when would be a more opportune time. I figured three weeks was good. I wanted to go to Atlanta for the graduation, and I wanted to get to a good stopping point in my new manuscript before I had to put it aside because of my operation.

When Dr. Martin heard I put the operation off he told me he'd stop speaking to me for life if I didn't change my mind. And all of my friends and family were also up in arms. But I ain't give a shit! There was no way I was going to miss Camille's big day! And when Camille said she wasn't going to attend, I told her I'd never forgive her if she didn't. Just months before she and I were talking excitedly about the occasion. I didn't want her to change her plans because of me. I told her if she didn't walk, I wouldn't get the damn operation. That straightened her out.

But even if no one else got it, it really was true . . . this fucking brain tumor was a pain in my ass. In addition to the inconvenient timing, it was breaking my fucking bank because, yes, you guessed it . . . my health insurance carrier canceled my insurance as soon as they found out I had a brain tumor. I was now paying for this shit out of my pocket! I was so upset. No, I was fucking pissed! No, damn it, I was fucking angry! And I knew there wasn't a damn thing I could do because they were talking about it being a preexisting condition since my medical records showed I complained about headaches before I got their insurance. Headaches, okay? People have headaches every day, that doesn't mean I had a tumor. Motherfuckers!

Most of my friends and family kept asking why I didn't seem more afraid. After all, a person doesn't go around getting brain surgery every day, but even though I got what they were saying, I really couldn't be bothered being afraid. If I was too busy to have a brain tumor, I sure as hell was too busy to actually die. I had too much to do!

Camille's graduation was beautiful! I flew down for the event and took about a hundred pictures. When we flew back to Philadelphia I gave her a graduation party at the Marathon Grill in Chestnut Hill. The whole time, though, Camille kept looking over at me to make sure I was okay, and she refused to go out with her friends. She wanted to be by my side in case I had a seizure. She even started sleeping in my bed. And when I finally checked into the hospital, she was the last person I saw before I was wheeled into the operating room. She was trying to be brave, but I could see the tears in her eyes and the fear on her face.

"It's only going to be a three-hour procedure," I said, giving her hand a squeeze as she walked alongside my gurney.

"I know that," she said flippantly. "I don't know why you feel like you gotta remind me."

Yeah, right.

"And don't worry, I'm going to be okay. I'm too damn mean to die."

Camille looked at me and said, "You got that right."

Then I was wheeled in the room and . . .

★ ★ ★

Oh, hell no! There she is! What the fuck is she doing here?

"Mom? Mom? Doctor, what's going on? Why is my mother moaning like that?"

"Is my sister in pain? Do you need to give her some narcotics or something? Come on, Ke-Ke, it's all right, sis. We got you!"

I thought the only thing I had to deal with was Death bringing her skank ass over here and trying to fuck with me, but this bitch, too? And look at her, grinning. Not saying a word . . . just grinning, now laughing! I know this bitch doesn't think she's gonna pull the shit on me that she did when I was a teenager.

"Doctor, her heartbeat is speeding up and . . ."

"I'm well aware of that, nurse."

I want to yell at her. I want to tell her that she needs to go some fucking place, because she ain't pulling that "I'm going back instead of you" bullshit. I've done a damn good job defending myself. In fact, fuck a defense, most of the time I go straight for the offense. If I even think someone's gonna fuck with me I fuck with them first. And I don't let no motherfucker tell me what I can and can't do! I do what the fuck I want! Oh, look, she finally stopped laughing. I wonder what that means. Let her come closer to me and I'ma kick her funky ass. I hate her! All this is her fault! I didn't ask to be always on the lookout for someone trying to hurt me! I didn't ask to be so suspicious of people trying to help that I turn them away and let so few people get close! Goddamnit! I didn't ask to be An Angry-Ass Black Woman, but now I'm a damn good one.

Yeah, she may have turned me into An Angry-Ass Black Woman, but I learned what it meant to be An Angry-Ass Black Woman. Not to just curse, carry on, fight, bite, and strike whenever someone pissed me off and I wanted revenge, but to curse, carry on, fight, bite, and strike not just on my behalf, but for everyone else who didn't have the capability. For my sister, my daughter, my friends, my community, for everyone. Angry about injustices, and trying to make sure they stopped happening.

Yeah, that bitch still ain't saying nothing, because I'm on to her now, and she knows it. She thought I needed to be angry? Yeah, she

was right. But not a selfish angry. A selfless angry. That's right, bitch.
Now get the fuck outta here.

And I pray that you'll find peace, sis. God bless you for giving me
the help you thought I needed.

★ ★ ★

"Mom! Oh, Mom!"

"Hey, baby. I'm sorry I can only do a loud whisper, because my throat is sore."

"The doctors said it would be, Ke-Ke, from the feeding
tube they just took out."

"Hey, Joe T. I'm glad you and Camille are still here."

"Of course we're here, Mommy. I've been here since they
took you in the operating room, and Uncle Joe's been here
since you lapsed into a coma."

"A coma? Is that what was going on? Oh that's right. Kitty
did say I was in a coma."

"What? How'd you . . . Ke-Ke, you could hear everything
people said? You know who was in here and everything? Oh,
damn! Ha ha! If I'd known that I'da been a little nicer."

"It's okay, Joe T., I know you did the very best you could.
And I appreciate you being so patient with Kitty and David.
Well, I mean, patient for you, anyway."

"Yeah, it was a chore."

"Oh, Mom, you don't even know how worried I was.
Mom . . ."

"Hey, baby, don't cry. I'm okay now, right?"

"Yeah, because death knows better than to mess with a—"

"A very happy woman."

"Huh? Ke-Ke?"

"Mom?"

"What? Look, how about you two just smile and enjoy the new me. Life is too short to be going around angry all the time. Now, don't get worried, but I'm going to go ahead and get some sleep. No coma, just sleep."

"Well, I'll go downstairs and get something to eat while you take your nap, Ke-Ke. I'll be back in about an hour to check on you. Love you!"

"Love you, too, Joe!"

"Mom, I'm staying right here, all right? You don't mind, do you?"

"No, babe, I don't mind at all. Shoot, you're the source of my happiness, don't you know that? You're the one who brought me happiness."

"Um, all right, but I don't get it. How come all of a sudden you're happy? I mean, I've been in your life for twenty-two years now."

"Yeah, but I was . . . how do I explain this? . . . I was medi-tating, or thinking, or something, while I was in the coma. And I can't really explain why, but I know that my anger, you know, it was more an act than anything else. It's how I thought I was supposed to act. But, well, I know that under-neath the anger was a smart, sassy, happy person waiting in the cut. Oh, don't worry, I'll always get angry when need be."

"No, Ma, I'm fine with it."

"Me, too. Now come on and let me get some sleep. Then when I wake up, we'll talk about the rest of our lives."

acknowledgments

I want to start out by thanking the Creator for my life, my talent, and my blessings.

I also want to thank all of the ancestors—literary, familial, and otherwise—who had to endure so much to ensure that I would be able to enjoy the life that I have all these years.

Because of some very severe health issues, it has been a few years since I've had a book published, and so there are so many people I have to thank for this one, that I barely know where to start. And I know already, before I begin, that there will be many whom I will fail to remember. I ask your forgiveness.

The first person whom I would like to thank is Sara Camilli, who read my manuscript as a fluke, and encouraged me to try to get it published when I had already given up on the possibility.

I also want to shout-out the members of the Evening Star Writers Group—Akanke Washington, Carla Morales, Fiona Harewood, Sharai Robin—they are, and have always been, my rock of support.

I thank the medical professionals who have done their best by me: Dr. Akili DeBrady, who has the best attitude in the medical profession, and is the epitome of what a family doctor should be; and Tammy and Samantha from the good doctor's office, who were always so professional but accommodating. Dr. Michael R. Silver, formerly of Thomas Jefferson University Hospital and now at Emory, who went out of his way to help me.

And just as important as the medical professionals are my spiritual rocks—whose prayers, advice, and guidance have done so much for me: Facundo Harris (what an Egun Pot!), Beatrice Adderly (I love you like a mother), Raj James (Hang in there, Raj. We'll both pull through!), Yvonne Stringer Gentle (I'm so glad we've been able to reconnect!), Imani Gross (Nothing better than an Oshun Lade!), Akanke Washington (I've always wanted a younger sister, and to have one as sweet and intelligent as you makes me so happy!), Oyin Harris, Kevin Green, Valorie Flynn, Suzanne (Your Oya astounds me!).

My friends and Prayer Warriors—Nancy Churchville, Fiona Harewood, Victoria Christopher Murray, Jenice Armstrong, Kim Beverly, Johnny Black, Senemeh Burke, Makeela Thomas.

I also have to mention Beverly and Clinton Moore—two of the kindest and most understanding folks I know (I don't know how to ever thank you for having faith in me. I won't let you down.); Beth Gambole, formerly of Liberty Resources, who heard me cry and didn't turn away. Antoria Walker and Dayna Watkins, who were both so helpful to me when I needed help.

I have to shout-out my literary friends: Zane (Thanks for always being available to talk!), Victoria Christopher Murray (So nice I've had to mention you twice! You don't know how much your friendship, prayers, and literary respect mean to me!), Daaimah S. Poole and Miasha (The two of you keep talking to me about how much you owe me . . . you just don't know how much I feel I owe you!), Julia Pressman Simmons (You're crazy as hell, but you're still cool! LOL), Kwan (Thanks for keeping my secrets!), Treasure Blue (I STILL think we should get married. <grin>), and Danielle Santiago (I just LOVE working with you!).

I also want to thank the members of the Brothers and Sisters Book Club of Philadelphia/South Jersey—with a special shout-out to Barbara Wallace and Audrey Johnson. Thank you for welcoming me as a member, and thank you for being my friends.

I owe so much to all my readers who have stood by me during my literary absence, and have continually let me know that they were waiting on my next book. You don't know what it means to know that you're not forgotten. Thank you SO much. Peter Garcia . . . you have to get a special shout-out, because you really lifted my spirits when we met earlier this year and you started talking about being thrilled to actually meet a writer whose books you've read and loved.

What the heck . . . also a big shout-out to Ginene Lewis! Congrats on getting your law degree!!!!!! You go, girl!!!!! I know one day you're going to be mayor!

Very important—I want to remember those who have passed, but who have meant so much to me: David Allen Quinones, Mayme Johnson, Fatima Ali, Willie Mary Gillespie. May you all rest in peace. Ibaiye.

I want to thank everyone in my family who has stood by me in my time of physical strife, Kitty, Tunde, Charnelle, Gloria Truss, Camille Miguel, and especially my brother Joe T. No matter what—no matter how many times we argue and fight—you've always stood by me, Joe . . . and I thank you.

A very special thanks to my daughter, Camille R. Quinones Miller, who means more to me than anyone else in the world.

In closing, I want to once again ask for forgiveness for those whose names I have failed to remember, but without whom my life would not be the same.

Oh wait! I forgot to mention Karen Hunter! My editor, my publisher, and my friend! I've never had an editor get behind a book the way Karen has gotten behind this one. I thank you so much for believing in me and giving me a chance to once again greet my readers. And Brigitte Smith for sharing that belief and shepherding the book in its journey toward publication.

Special Thanks to the Students of Hunter College:

Bibi Ali, Devin Callahan, Rita Calviello, Lucia Cappuccio, Monica Carr, Stefania Consarino, Giselle Diaz, Monika Galik, Ivan Garcia, Radames Garcia, Caroline McKeon, Nina Milnes, Kristina Nocerino, Gabrielle Noel, Peri Rosenweig, Cialina Ngo, and Carlo Rodrigo Rojas.

An Angry-Ass Black Woman

Karen E. Quinones Miller

INTRODUCTION

Best-selling author Karen E. Quinones Miller turns the mirror on herself in *An Angry-Ass Black Woman*—her first autobiographical novel. After a medical crisis leaves her in a coma, Ke-Ke reflects on her childhood and the events that led her to take charge of her own destiny. This part biographical, part fictional account opens on the streets of Harlem, where poverty, abuse, violence, racism, and drugs are a fixture of everyday life. Filled with vibrant anecdotes about growing up in an urban jungle and her journey from dropping out of school to reentering and graduating from college and becoming a successful writer, Miller captures the hardships and the bonds that formed between families and neighbors growing up in Harlem.

QUESTIONS AND TOPICS FOR DISCUSSION

1. Discuss the provocative title of this autobiographical novel—*An Angry-Ass Black Woman*. What were your first reactions to this title? Why were you drawn to read this "true-life" novel? Did your interpretation of the description "an angry-ass black woman" change after you finished this book? If so, how?

2. The setting of *An Angry-Ass Black Woman* plays a very important role in Ke-Ke's story. Discuss the ways in which growing up in Harlem and in an urban environment shaped her childhood. How would you characterize her relationship with the city?

3. Of the four Quinones children, two grew up to lead productive, successful lives, while the other two succumbed to a life of abuse and addiction. Why do you think Ke-Ke and Joe T. were able to overcome the suffering and hardship of their youth and turn their lives around in a way that Kitty and David were not?

4. Both of Karen's parents were knowledgeable and well-read, traits they tried to pass on to their children. Why do you think Ke-Ke's mother eventually allowed her to drop out of school? How might educating herself through books and newspapers have molded Ke-Ke in a way that learning in a classroom couldn't have?

5. While there were many negative influences on the streets of Harlem, there were also a few bright spots in Ke-Ke's childhood. Discuss the people in her life who made a positive influence or set a good example.

6. For the author, it's easy to pinpoint when she became a self-described "angry-ass black woman." It wasn't until a few weeks after her traumatic rape that her anger really set in. Reread and discuss the hallucination she experiences when given gas at the dentist's office. (pages 142–144) How did you react to this passage? Discuss the running theme and prevalence of racism in *An Angry-Ass Black Woman*.

7. When does Ke-Ke come up against racism and how does she deal with it? How does racism affect the people around her? On pages 46–48, Ke-Ke discusses her mother's thoughts on racial integration. Do you agree? Why or why not?

8. After giving birth to Camille, readers witness Ke-Ke's transformation into a mother. In what ways do you think becoming a mother changed Karen's life? How did Camille, specifically, change her life?

9. Family ties and loyalty is paramount to both Ke-Ke and the character in *An Angry-Ass Black Woman*. How do the Quinoneses show their loyalty to each other? How does this loyalty both empower them and cause them pain?

10. *An Angry-Ass Black Woman* is an autobiographical novel. How did the knowledge that this novel was based on true events impact your reading? Have you ever read an autobiographical novel before? Why do you think the author chose to approach her life story from a fictional perspective?

11. At the end of the novel, the author writes: "I know that my anger . . . was an act more than anything else. . . . I know that underneath the anger was a smart, sassy, happy person waiting in the cut. It's time I let the anger go." (page 267) Why do you think she describes her anger as an act? Do you think her near-death experience allowed her to let go of her anger? What other factors in her life do you think led her to find her place of peace?

Enhance Your Book Club

1. Try your hand at autobiographical fiction. Reflect on a pivotal, interesting, or humorous moment in your life and then write a short story about it. What is it like to take a fictional approach to your own life?

2. Take a cue from Ke-Ke and spend some time learning more about a topic that caught your eye in *An Angry-Ass Black Woman*. Maybe you're interested in learning more about the race riots of the 1960s, how the United States' welfare program works, "Bumpy" Johnson, or Harlem in general. Head to the library or do some research online and share your findings at your book club meeting. What was the most interesting or surprising thing that you learned?

3. Karen E. Quinones Miller is the author of several bestselling books, including *Satin Doll* and *I'm Telling*. Consider reading one of her other novels for your next book club discussion. How does the writing, plot structure, and characters compare to those in *An Angry-Ass Black Woman*?

A Conversation with Karen E. Quinones Miller

After having already written a few novels that were, to various extents, based on your life, when and why did you decide to tell your own story more openly and directly in *An Angry-Ass Black Woman*?

It was in 2005, after I came home and was recovering from my brain surgery. I really had time to reflect on my life, and how it affected the way I interact with people and how I view issues. I'm funny about a lot of things. For instance, I don't allow people to use the "n" word in my house. I don't drink orange soda. I hate the date March 21. People have asked me why, and most of the time I didn't bother to try to explain because I didn't think they'd get it. I thought this book would be a good way to explain a lot of the reasons I do what I do, and feel how I feel. But also writing this book has been *quite* therapeutic for me . . . writing about the various events that shaped my life has made me really analyze them and myself. And I actually feel I know myself better because of it.

An Angry-Ass Black Woman is an autobiographical novel. What does that phrase mean to you and what does it mean in terms of the content of this book? Why did you decide to tell your story in this format as opposed to in a straight-up memoir?

An autobiographical novel, in my view, is an autobiography that doesn't change the outcomes of events, but sometimes downplays some things, and changes some of the minor details as to protect identities. Most people don't realize it, but Claude Brown's classic, *Manchild in the Promised Land,* is also an autobiographical novel.

How was the experience of writing this book different from that of your previous books?

It took me longer to write this book because there was a lot of real reflection and self-analyzing going on as I was writing. At times it was hard, like when I was replaying the deaths of loved ones, and the tragedies that happened to others. Several times I was writing a passage, and I had to wonder . . . was there something I could have done that would have made things turn out better. I do think I'm a better person for writing this book. Really having to look back at your life has to have some effect on you.

How did your family members feel about your decision to write an autobiographical novel? How did they react to your portrayal of them?

There were none who specifically said they didn't want me to write it, but I know some were—and are—a little nervous. No more nervous than me, though. <smile>

If you had the power to change the ending for one character in *An Angry-Ass Black Woman,* who would it be?

Kitty. And I'll just leave it at that.

Throughout the book it's clear that you've always been an avid reader. Who are some of the authors that have influenced you as an author?

Langston Hughes, most definitely! That man has gotten me through some very hard times! I love both his poetry and prose, and would go back and read certain works when feeling depressed just so I could start feeling better . . . and it never failed to work. I especially love his short stories featuring Jess Semple, aka Simple.

And I pretty much feel the same way about Mark Twain. I love his novels and his short stories. Like Hughes, the sharp wit that is always displayed by his down-home-sprung characters really appeals to me.

Do you have any advice for aspiring writers who are looking to turn their dreams into a reality?

My advice is if you want to write, just go ahead and write! Worry about getting published, yes . . . but not to the point that you don't even start writing.

Also, you've *got* to read. There are two things that will make you a better writer—reading and writing. You've got to do both!

Lastly, I would suggest that—if possible—you join a writing group. You'll love the support, but also your manuscript will be the better because of it.

Do you still return to Harlem often? If so, how has it changed or how has your vision of it changed since you were young?

I still visit ten–twelve times a year, and yes . . . it has changed drastically. Many of the changes are for the good—I'm glad to see it being built up, and dilapidated buildings being renovated, but I *hate* that the rents are now so high that many African-American people can no longer afford to live there. It's ironic . . . the way things are going, ten years from now people are going to read *Manchild in the Promised Land* and/or *An Angry-Ass Black Woman* and not be able to relate it to the Harlem of their present.

How does your story continue from here? Are you working on any new projects?

My story continues because my life continues . . . and the combination of family and writing is what keeps me going. I'm actually working on a suspense novel at the moment, and I recently wrote a screenplay that I'm thinking of shopping around. But you can count on me sticking around in the literary world, and I hope not to have a four-year disappearance like I had since my last book was published!

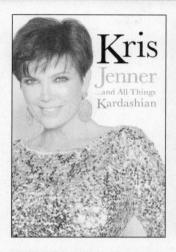

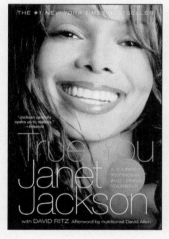
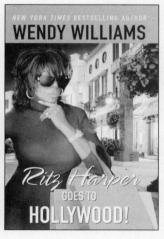